THE COMPLETE STORIES
OF
MORLEY CALLAGHAN

THE COMPLETE STORIES

OF

MORLEY CALLAGHAN

Volume Three

Introduction by
Anne Michaels

Library and Archives Canada Cataloguing in Publication

Callaghan, Morley, 1903-1990
    The complete stories of Morley Callaghan.

(Exile classics series ; no. 22-25)
Introductions by Alistair MacLeod (v. 1), André Alexis (v. 2), Anne
    Michaels (v. 3), and Margaret Atwood (v. 4).
Includes bibliographical references.
ISBN 978-1-55096-305-2 (v. 2).--ISBN 978-1-55096-304-5 (v. 1).--
ISBN 978-1-55096-306-9 (v. 3).--ISBN 978-1-55096-307-6 (v. 4)

    I. Title. II. Series: Exile classics ; no. 22-25

PS8505.A43A15 2012   C813'.54   C2012-906213-8

Design and Composition by Digital ReproSet~mc
Cover Photograph by Nigel Dickson
Printed by Imprimerie Gauvin

Published by Exile Editions Ltd ~ www.ExileEditions.com
144483 Southgate Road 14 – GD, Holstein ON, N0G 2A0
Printed and Bound in Canada; Publication Copyright © Exile Editions, 2012

The publisher would like to acknowledge the financial support of the Canada
Council for the Arts, the Government of Canada through the Canada Book Fund
(CBF), the Ontario Arts Council, and the Ontario Media Development Corpora-
tion, for our publishing activities.

North American and International Distribution:
Independent Publishers Group, 814 North Franklin Street,
Chicago IL 60610   www.ipgbook.com   toll free: 1 800 888 4741

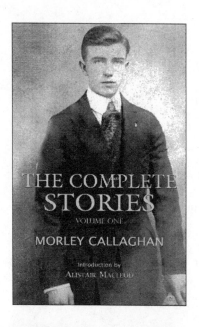

THE COMPLETE
STORIES
VOLUME ONE

MORLEY CALLAGHAN

Introduction by
ALISTAIR MACLEOD

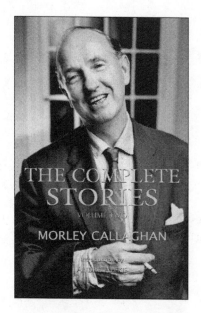

THE COMPLETE
STORIES
VOLUME TWO

MORLEY CALLAGHAN

Introduction by
ANDRÉ ALEXIS

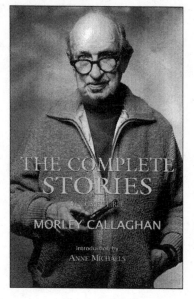

THE COMPLETE
STORIES
VOLUME THREE

MORLEY CALLAGHAN

Introduction by
ANNE MICHAELS

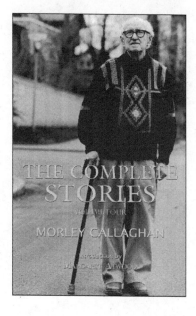

THE COMPLETE
STORIES
VOLUME FOUR

MORLEY CALLAGHAN

Introduction by
MARGARET ATWOOD

INTRODUCTION

by Anne Michaels

It is a privilege to read an author's body of work as a whole. But it is a blessing when this represents not only the work of a lifetime but also the work of a life.

"There are (writers) whose entire body of work represents a rare integrity of compassion . . . The(ir) protagonists are stretched beyond the limits of their comprehension, emotionally and otherwise, (and) are trying to find their way in circumstances that are beyond them; this is a particular struggle, in which all the strength and limitations of love are laid bare. The circumstances may be large or small, yet the consequences for a particular character are profound. These are the moments for which we are most often judged in real life, and are the moments when we most need the compassion of others. It is this compassion . . . that I find most compelling: a depth of respect for the ways we negotiate the complexities of our own psyches; (writers) who are uncompromising in their probing acceptance of human frailty and who understand the abject necessity of opening our hearts precisely when it is most painful to do so." I originally wrote these words regarding the work of filmmakers I respect. I believe this integrity of compassion is extraordinary. Morley Callaghan's short fiction exemplifies this kind of compassion.

There is no attempt to persuade us with moral judgments, yet a moral clarity exists around these stories, a space Callaghan deliberately creates for the reader. By leaving behind the "noise" of time and place, by accumulating only the most telling detail, he creates in the reader an extraordinary quality of attention, allowing us to think through a character's actions even as we feel. He creates in the reader a suspension of judgment and a contemplative empathy, and an opportunity to reach a rare, essential, intimacy with his characters. Callaghan said that he spent much time thinking before he wrote, allowing connections to form in his mind and allowing these connections to form the story. It is this state that he manages also to create in the reader, as events unfold in ways that always seem both surprising and surprisingly inevitable, because of the particular quality of intimacy we have with the characters.

These stories are sunk deeply into human motivation, human frailties, vulnerabilities; into defensiveness, desire, hopes, shame, loneliness. A woman walks from car to house or smoothes the hem of her dressing gown . . . A man lifts a boy on his shoulders . . . In Morley Callaghan's stories, a gesture, a simple action, a single line of dialogue, is all that's needed to stir profound psychological complexity. The prose surface may seem calm, accessible, apparent. But it is only because Callaghan has penetrated to such depths of character that he is able to write with such seemingly casual accuracy, and with such clarity of character and purpose. Through tone and detail the reader comprehends fully the nuance and meaning of seemingly simple actions.

The emotional precision in these stories is remarkable. "The Blue Kimono," for example, is a small masterpiece of psychological acuity, laying bare, in so few words, the complicated nuances of a marriage. We see the husband's frustration with circumstances beyond his control turn to anger at his wife, in an instant. We understand that his longing to hurt her, his cruelty is not only out of his own shame, and not only out of a desire to make her feel complicitous in his misery, but is also a pleading for a potent understanding — "his eagerness to make his wife feel the bad luck he felt within him" — so as not to feel so wretchedly alone. Nuance continues to shift as the husband begins to share his wife's worry over their ill son. The wife's blue kimono is a symbol of newlywed happiness and hopes; now faded and worn, the kimono seems to mock the husband and for this too, he feels the need to wound his wife: "It's terrible to look at you in that thing" he tells her. He speaks "brutally." But Callaghan makes sure that we understand that his cruelty is not simple. When the husband realizes that he no longer finds his wife beautiful, he also realizes that this has "nothing to do with his love for her." The wife, obviously accustomed to this treatment, and terrified for her son, does not rise to her husband's cruel remarks, and makes no attempt to defend herself against them. Instead she ministers to the child and later considers how to mend the kimono. The husband chastises her for fussing over it. If Callaghan left out her remark "I think I can fix it up so it'll look fine . . . " the reader would still have understood what she was thinking and the symbolism of such a thought. But it is a fine example of Callaghan's precision that he makes her speak this aloud. For it is another subtle yet clear measure of the state of their relationship; they have not yet reached the point when she would no longer bother to speak such a thought aloud, even if her husband is incapable of understanding her.

Callaghan brings the same insight into such a diversity of characters; petty criminals, eager young women, older disillusioned women, a public executioner, abandoned wives, betrayed brothers, men seeking their way in the world, men with no hope left in the world . . . Characters from every social class, every degree of innocence and experience and every economic standing. His view is clear-eyed without being cold-hearted. All is precise nuance, mitigating circumstance, family background, economic stresses, the consolation or torment of memory . . .

It is as if part of the redemption for these broken lives, for these lives in transition into hope or out of hope, rests somehow in the telling of these stories, in bringing this intensely private pain a kind of dignity through an accurate witnessing. And because these lives are so familiar in their grief and dreams, it is a dignity we can all share. From the relatively simple "Bachelor's Dilemma" to the complexity of "The Two Brothers" or "The Magic Hat," we feel the poignancy of recognition that is also often partly shrouded in layers of self-rationalization. In "The Lucky Lady": ". . . he knew that something was wrong and while he hesitated uneasily she had a moment of wild hope as, half-ashamed, he struggled against being who he was." And here, of course, is Callaghan's relentless accuracy again — so masterful. Her hope is "wild" and he is only "half" ashamed.

Each of these stories pivot on a moment when a truth is suddenly, sometimes only briefly, illuminated. The moment arises and, more importantly, it passes. How the character makes use of that moment when it is over is the heart of the narrative.

These stories explore the great influences of memory, habit, habit of thought, the daily wearing down of hope, the sudden gleam of hope. How deeply human and humane Callaghan's vision is. Here we find ourselves, in all our pettiness and nobility of intent, in all our distress and longing.

It is very appropriate that these volumes of Callaghan's works are called *The Complete Stories*. Yes, these stories are, in every way — poignantly — complete.

Two
Fishermen

---

*T*he only reporter on the town paper, *The Examiner*, was Michael Foster, a tall, long-legged, eager fellow, who wanted to go to the city some day and work on an important newspaper.

The morning he went to Bagley's Hotel, he wasn't at all sure of himself. He went over to the desk and whispered to the proprietor, "Did he come here, Mr. Bagley?"

Bagley said slowly, "Two men came here from this morning's train. They're registered." He put his spatulate forefinger on the open book and said, "Two men. One of them's a drummer. This one here, T. Woodley. I know because he was through this way last year and just a minute ago he walked across the road to Molson's hardware store. The other one . . . here's his name, K. Smith."

"Who's K. Smith?" Michael asked.

"I don't know. A mild, harmless looking little guy."

"Did he look like the hangman, Mr. Bagley?"

"I couldn't say that, seeing that I never saw one. He was awfully polite and asked where he could get a boat so he could go fishing on the lake this evening, so I said likely down at Smollet's place by the powerhouse."

"Well, thanks. I guess if he was the hangman, he'd go over to the jail first," Michael said.

He went along the street, past the Baptist church to the old jail with the high brick fence around it. Two tall maple trees, with branches drooping low over the sidewalk, shaded one of the walls from the morning sunlight. Last night, behind those walls, three carpenters, working by lamplight, had nailed the timbers for the scaffold. In the morning, young Thomas Delaney, who had grown up in the town, was being hanged: he had killed old Matthew Rhinehart whom he had caught molesting his wife when she had been berry picking in the hills behind the town. There had been a struggle and Thomas Delaney had taken a bad beating before he had killed Rhinehart. Last night a crowd had gathered on the sidewalk by the lamppost, and while moths and smaller insects swarmed around the high blue carbon light, the crowd had thrown sticks and bottles and small stones at the out-of-town workmen in the jail yard. Billy Hilton, the town constable, had stood under the light with his head down, pretending not to notice anything. Thomas Delaney was only three years older than Michael Foster.

Michael went straight to the jail office, where the sheriff, Henry Steadman, a squat, heavy man, was sitting on the desk idly wetting his long moustache with his tongue. "Hello, Michael, what do you want?" he asked.

"Hello, Mr. Steadman, *The Examiner* would like to know if the hangman arrived yet."

"Why ask me?"

"I thought he'd come here to test the gallows. Won't he?"

"My, you're a smart young fellow, Michael, thinking of that."

"Is he in there now, Mr. Steadman?"

"Don't ask me. I'm saying nothing. Say, Michael, do you think there's going to be trouble? You ought to know. Does anybody seem sore at me? I can't do nothing. You can see that."

"I don't think anybody blames you, Mr. Steadman. Look here, can't I see the hangman? Is his name K. Smith?"

"What does it matter to you, Michael? Be a sport, go on away and don't bother us any more."

"All right, Mr. Steadman," Michael said, "just leave it to me."

Early that evening, when the sun was setting, Michael Foster walked south of the town on the dusty road leading to the powerhouse and Smollet's fishing pier. He knew that if Mr. K. Smith wanted to get a boat he would go down to the pier. Fine powdered road dust whitened Michael's shoes. Ahead of him he saw the power plant, square and low, and the smooth lake water. Behind him the sun was hanging over the blue hills beyond the town and shining brilliantly on square patches of farmland. The air around the powerhouse smelt of steam.

Out on the jutting, tumbledown pier of rock and logs, Michael saw a fellow without a hat, sitting down with his knees hunched up to his chin; a very small man who stared steadily far out over the water. In his hand he was holding a stick with a heavy fishing line twined around it and a gleaming copper spoon bait, the hooks brightened with bits of feathers such as they used in the neighborhood when trolling for lake trout. Apprehensively Michael walked out over the rocks toward the stranger and called, "Were you thinking of fishing, mister?" Standing up, the man smiled.

He had a large head, tapering down to a small chin, a bird-like neck and a wistful smile. Puckering his mouth up, he said shyly to Michael, "Did you intend to go fishing?"

"That's what I came down here for. I was going to get a boat back at the boathouse there. How would you like it if we went together?"

"I'd like it first rate," the shy little man said eagerly. "We could take turns rowing. Does that appeal to you?"

"Fine. Fine. You wait here and I'll go back to Smollet's place and ask for a rowboat and I'll row around here and get you."

"Thanks. Thanks very much," the mild little man said, as he began to untie his line. He seemed very enthusiastic.

When Michael brought the boat around to the end of the old pier and invited the stranger to make himself comfortable so he could handle the line, the stranger protested comically that he ought to be allowed to row.

Pulling strongly on the oars, Michael was soon out in the deep water and the little man was letting the line out slowly. In one furtive glance, he had noticed that the man's hair, gray at the temples, was inclined to curl to his ears. The line was out full length. It was twisted around the little man's forefinger, which he let drag in the water. And then Michael looked full at him and smiled because he thought he seemed so meek and quizzical. "He's a nice little guy," Michael assured himself, and he said, "I work on the town paper, *The Examiner.*"

"Is it a good paper? Do you like the work?"

"Yes. But it's nothing like a first-class city paper and I don't expect to be working on it long. I want to get a reporter's job on a city paper. My name's Michael Foster."

"Mine's Smith. Just call me Smitty."

"I was wondering if you'd been over to the jail yet?"

Up to this time the little man had been smiling with the charming ease of a small boy who finds himself free, but now he became furtive and disappointed. Hesitating, he said, "Yes, I was over there first thing this morning."

"Oh, I just knew you'd go there," Michael said. They were a bit afraid of each other. By this time they were far out on the water which had a millpond smoothness. The town seemed to get smaller, with white houses in rows and streets forming geometric patterns, just as the blue hills behind the town seemed to get larger at sundown.

Finally Michael said, "Do you know this Thomas Delaney that's dying in the morning?" He knew his voice was slow and resentful.

"No. I don't know anything about him. I never read about them. Aren't there any fish at all in this old lake? I'd like to catch some," he said. "I told my wife I'd bring her home some fish." Glancing at Michael, he was appealing, without speaking, that they should do nothing to spoil an evening's fishing.

The little man began to talk eagerly about fishing as he pulled out a small flask from his hip pocket. "Scotch," he said, chuckling with delight. "Here, have a swig." Michael drank from the flask and passed it back. Tilting his head back and saying, "Here's to you, Michael," the little man took a long pull at the flask. "The only time I take a drink," he said, still chuckling, "is when I go on a fishing trip by myself. I usually go by myself," he added apologetically, as if he wanted the young fellow to see how much he appreciated his company.

They had gone far out on the water but they had caught nothing. It began to get dark. "No fish tonight, I guess, Smitty," Michael said.

"It's a crying shame," Smitty said. "I looked forward to coming up here when I found out the place was on the lake. I wanted to get some fishing in. I promised my wife I'd bring her back some fish. She'd often like to go fishing with me, but of course she can't because she can't travel around from place to place like I do. Whenever I get a call to go to some place, I always look at the map to see if it's by a lake or on a river, then I take my lines and hooks along."

"If you took another job, you and your wife could probably go fishing together," Michael suggested.

"I don't know about that. We sometimes go fishing together anyway." He looked away, waiting for Michael to be repelled and insist that he ought to give up the job. And he wasn't ashamed as he looked down at the water, but he knew Michael thought he ought to be ashamed. "Somebody's got to do my job. There's got to be a hangman," he said.

"I just meant that if it was such disagreeable work, Smitty."

The little man did not answer for a long time. Michael rowed steadily with sweeping, tireless strokes. Huddled at the end of the boat, Smitty suddenly looked up with a kind of melancholy hopelessness and said mildly, "The job hasn't been so disagreeable."

"Good God, man, you don't mean you like it?"

"Oh, no," he said, to be obliging, as if he knew what Michael expected him to say. "I mean you get used to it, that's all." But he looked down again at the water, knowing he ought to be ashamed of himself.

"Have you got any children?"

"I sure have. Five. The oldest boy is fourteen. It's funny, but they're all a lot bigger and taller than I am. Isn't that funny?"

They started a conversation about fishing rivers that ran into the lake farther north. They felt friendly again. The little man, who had an extraordinary gift for storytelling, made many quaint faces, puckered up his lips, screwed up his eyes and moved around restlessly as if he wanted to get up in the boat and stride around for the sake of more expression. Again he brought out the whiskey flask and Michael stopped rowing. Grinning, they toasted each other and said together, "Happy days." The boat remained motionless on the placid water. Far out, the sun's last rays gleamed on the waterline. And then it got dark and they could only see the town lights. It was time to turn around and pull for the shore. The little man tried to take the oars from Michael, who shook his head resolutely and insisted that he would prefer to have his friend catch a fish on the way back to the shore.

"It's too late now, and we have scared all the fish away," Smitty laughed happily. "But we're having a grand time, aren't we?"

When they reached the old pier by the powerhouse, it was full night and they hadn't caught a single fish. As the boat bumped against the rocks Michael said, "You can get out here, I'll take the boat around to Smollet's."

"Won't you be coming my way?"

"Not just now. I'll probably talk with Smollet a while."

The little man got out of the boat and stood on the pier looking down at Michael. "I was thinking dawn would be the best time to catch some fish," he said. "At about five o'clock.

I'll have an hour and a half to spare anyway. How would you like that?" He was speaking with so much eagerness that Michael found himself saying, "I could try. But if I'm not here at dawn, you go on without me."

"All right. I'll go back to the hotel now."

"Good night, Smitty."

"Good night, Michael. We had a fine neighborly time, didn't we?"

As Michael rowed the boat around to the boathouse, he hoped that Smitty wouldn't realize he didn't want to be seen walking back to town with him. And later, when he was going along the dusty road in the dark and hearing all the crickets chirping in the ditches, he couldn't figure out why he felt so ashamed of himself.

At seven o'clock next morning Thomas Delaney was hanged in the town jail yard. There was hardly a breeze on that leaden gray morning and there were no small whitecaps out over the lake. It would have been a fine morning for fishing. Michael went down to the jail, for he thought it his duty as a newspaperman to have all the facts, but he was afraid he might get sick. He hardly spoke to all the men and women who were crowded under the maple trees by the jail wall. Everybody he knew was staring at the wall and muttering angrily. Two of Thomas Delaney's brothers, big, strapping fellows with bearded faces, were there on the sidewalk. Three automobiles were at the front of the jail.

Michael, the town newspaperman, was admitted into the courtyard by old Willie Matthews, one of the guards, who said that two newspapermen from the city were at the gallows on the other side of the building. "I guess you can go around there too, if you want to," Matthews said, as he sat down on the step. White-faced, and afraid, Michael sat down on the step with Matthews and they waited and said nothing.

At last the old fellow said, "Those people outside there are pretty sore, ain't they?"

"They're pretty sullen, all right. I saw two of Delaney's brothers there."

"I wish they'd go," Matthews said. "I don't want to see anything. I didn't even look at Delaney. I don't want to hear anything. I'm sick." He put his head against the wall and closed his eyes.

The old fellow and Michael sat close together till a small procession came around the corner from the other side of the yard. First came Mr. Steadman, the sheriff, with his head down as though he were crying, then Dr. Parker, the physician, then two hard-looking young newspapermen from the city, walking with their hats on the backs of their heads, and behind them came the little hangman, erect, stepping out with military precision and carrying himself with a strange cocky dignity. He was dressed in a long black cut-away coat with gray striped trousers, a gates-ajar collar and a narrow red tie, as if he alone felt the formal importance of the occasion. He walked with brusque precision until he saw Michael, who was standing up, staring at him with his mouth open.

The little hangman grinned and as soon as the procession reached the doorstep, he shook hands with Michael. They were all looking at Michael. As though his work was over now, the hangman said eagerly to Michael, "I thought I'd see you here. You didn't get down to the pier at dawn?"

"No. I couldn't make it."

"That was tough, Michael. I looked for you," he said. "But never mind. I've got something for you." As they all went into the jail, Dr. Parker glanced angrily at Michael, then turned his back on him. In the office, where the doctor prepared to sign the certificate, Smitty was bending down over his fishing basket, which was in the corner. Then he pulled out two good-sized trout, folded in newspaper, and said, "I was saving these for you, Michael. I got four in an hour's fishing." Then he said, "I'll talk about that later if you'll wait. We'll be busy here, and I've got to change my clothes."

Michael went out to the street with Dr. Parker and the two city newspapermen. Under his arm he was carrying the fish, folded in the newspaper. Outside, at the jail door, Michael thought that the doctor and the two newspapermen were standing a little apart from him. Then the crowd, with their clothes all dust-soiled from the road, surged forward and the doctor said to them, "You might as well go home, boys. It's all over."

"Where's old Steadman?" somebody demanded.

"We'll wait for the hangman," somebody else shouted.

The doctor walked away by himself. For a while Michael stood beside the two city newspapermen, and tried to look as nonchalant as they were looking, but he lost confidence in them when he smelled whiskey. They only talked to each other. Then they mingled with the crowd, and Michael stood alone. At last he could stand there no longer looking at all those people he knew so well, so he, too, moved out and joined the crowd.

When the sheriff came out with the hangman and the guards, they got halfway down to one of the automobile before someone threw an old boot. Steadman ducked into one of the cars, as the boot hit him on the shoulder, and the two guards followed him. The hangman, dismayed, stood alone on the sidewalk. Those in the car must have thought at first that the hangman was with them for the car suddenly shot forward, leaving him alone on the sidewalk. The crowd threw small rocks and sticks, hooting at him as the automobile backed up slowly towards him. One small stone hit him on the head. Blood trickled from the side of his head as he looked around helplessly at all the angry people. He had the same expression on his face, Michael thought, as he had had last night when he had seemed ashamed and had looked down at the water. Only now, he looked around wildly, looking for someone to help him as the crowd kept pelting him. Farther and farther Michael backed into the crowd and all the time he felt dreadfully ashamed as though he were betraying Smitty, who last night had had such a good neighborly time with him. "It's different now, it's different," he kept thinking, as he held the fish in the newspaper tight under his arm. Smitty started to run toward the automobile, but James Mortimer, a big fisherman, shot out his foot and tripped him and sent him sprawling on his face.

Looking for something to throw, the fisherman said to Michael, "Sock him, sock him."

Michael shook his head and felt sick.

"What's the matter with you, Michael?"

"Nothing. I got nothing against him."

The big fisherman started pounding his fists up and down in the air. "He just doesn't mean anything to me at all," Michael said quickly. The fisherman, bending down, kicked a small rock loose from the roadbed and heaved it at the hangman. Then he said, "What are you holding there, Michael, what's under your arm? Fish? Pitch them at him. Here, give them to me." Still in a fury, he snatched the fish, and threw them one at a time at the little man just as he was getting up from the road. The fish fell in the thick dust in front of him, sending up a little cloud. Smitty seemed to stare at the fish with his mouth hanging open, then he didn't even look at the crowd. That expression on Smitty's face as he saw the fish in the road made Michael hot with shame and he tried to get out of the crowd.

Smitty had his hands over his head, to shield his face as the crowd pelted him, yelling, "Sock the little rat! Throw the runt in the lake!" The sheriff pulled him into the automobile. The car shot forward in a cloud of dust.

THE RUNAWAY

I n the lumberyard by the lake there was an old brick building two stories high and all around the foundations were
heaped great piles of soft sawdust, softer than the thick moss
in the woods. There were many of these golden mounds of
dust covering the yard down to the lake. That afternoon all
the fellows followed Michael up the ladder to the roof of
the old building and they sat with their legs hanging over
the edge looking out at the whitecaps on the water. Michael
was younger than some of them but his legs were long, his
huge hands dangled awkwardly at his sides and his thick
black hair curled all over his head. "I'll stump you all to
jump down," he said, and without thinking about it he shoved
himself off the roof and fell on the sawdust where he lay
rolling and laughing.

"You're all stumped," he shouted, "you're all yellow,"
coaxing them to follow him. Still laughing, he watched them,
white-faced and hesitant, and them one by one they jumped
and got up grinning with relief.

In the hot afternoon sunlight they all lay on the sawdust
pile telling jokes till at last one said, "Come on up on the old
roof again and jump down." There wasn't much enthusiasm
amongst them, but they all went up to the roof again and
began to jump off in a determined, desperate way till only

Michael was left and the others were all down below grinning up at him calling, "Come on, Mike. What's the matter with you?" Michael longed to jump down and be with them, but he remained on the edge of the roof, wetting his lips, with a silly grin on his face. It had not seemed such a long drop the first time. For a while they thought he was only kidding them, then they saw him clenching his fists, trying to count to ten and then jump, and when that failed, he tried to take a long breath and close his eyes.

In a while they began to jeer; they were tired of waiting and it was getting on to dinnertime. "Come on, you're yellow, you think we're going to sit here all night?" They began to shout, and when he did not move they began to walk away, still jeering. "Who did this in the first place? What's the matter with you guys?" he shouted.

But for a long time he remained on the edge of the roof, staring unhappily and steadily at the ground. He remained all alone for nearly an hour while the sun, a great orange ball getting bigger and bigger, rolled slowly over the dray line beyond the lake. His clothes were wet from nervous sweating. At last he closed his eyes, slipped off the roof, fell heavily on the pile of sawdust and lay there a long time. There were no sounds in the yard; the workmen had gone home. As he lay there he wondered why he had been unable to move; and then he got up slowly and walked home feeling deeply ashamed and wanting to avoid everybody.

He was so late that his stepmother said to him sarcastically, "You're big enough by this time surely to be able to get home in time for dinner. But if you won't come home, you'd better try staying in tonight." She was a well-built woman with a fair, soft skin and a little touch of gray in her hair and a patient smile. She was speaking now with a restrained, passionless severity, but Michael, with his dark face gloomy and sullen, hardly heard her; he was still seeing the row of grinning faces down below on the sawdust pile, and hearing them jeer at him.

As he ate his cold dinner he was rolling his brown eyes fiercely and sometimes shaking his big black head. His father, who was sitting in the armchair by the window, a huge man with his hair nearly all gone so that his smooth wide forehead rose in a shining dome, kept looking at him steadily. When Michael had finished eating and had gone out to the veranda, his father followed, sat down beside him, lit his pipe and said gently, "What's bothering you, son?"

"Nothing, Dad. There's nothing bothering me," Michael said, but he kept staring out at the gray dust drifting off the road.

His father kept coaxing and whispering in a voice that was amazingly soft for such a big man. As he talked his long fingers played with the heavy gold watch fob on his vest. He was talking about nothing in particular and yet by the tone of his voice he was expressing a marvelous deep friendliness that somehow seemed to become part of the twilight and then of the darkness. Michael began to like the sound of his father's voice, and soon he blurted out, "I guess by this time all the guys around here are saying I'm yellow. I'd like to be a thousand miles away." He told how he could not force himself to jump off the roof the second time. But his father lay back in the armchair laughing in that hearty, easy way that Michael loved to hear; years ago when Michael had been younger and he was walking along the paths in the evening, he used to try and laugh like his father only his voice was not deep enough and he would grin sheepishly and look up at the trees overhanging the paths as if someone hiding up there had heard him. "You'll be alright with the bunch, son," his father was saying. "I'm betting you'll lick any boy in town that says you're yellow."

But there was the sound of the screen door opening, and Michael's stepmother said in her mild, firm way, "If I've rebuked the boy, Henry, as I think he ought to be rebuked, I don't know why you should be humoring him."

"You surely don't object to me talking to Michael."

"I simply want you to be reasonable, Henry."

In his grave, unhurried way, Mr. Lount got up and followed his wife into the house and soon Michael could hear them arguing; he could hear his father's firm, patient voice floating clearly out to the street; then his stepmother's voice, mild at first, rising, becoming hysterical till at last she cried out wildly, "You're setting the boy against me. You don't want him to think of me as his mother. The two of you are against me. I know your nature."

As he looked up and down the street, Michael began to make prayers that no one would pass by who would think, "Mr. and Mrs. Lount are quarreling again." Alert, he listened for faint sounds on the cinder path, but he heard only the frogs croaking under the bridge opposite Stevenson's place and the faraway cry of a freight train passing behind the hills. "Why did Dad have to get married? It used to be swell on the farm," he thought, remembering how he and his father had gone fishing down at the glen. And then while he listened to the sound of her voice, he kept thinking that his stepmother was a fine woman, only she always made him uneasy because she wanted him to like her, and then when she found out that he couldn't think of her as his mother, she had grown resentful. "I like her and I like my father. I don't know why they quarrel. Maybe it's because Dad shouldn't have sold the farm and moved here. There's nothing for him to do." Unable to get interested in the town life, his father loafed all day down at the hotel or in Bailey's flour-and-feed store but he was such a fine-looking, dignified, reticent man that the loafers would not accept him as a crony.

Inside the house now, Mrs. Lount was crying quietly and saying, "Henry, we'll kill each other. We seem to bring out the very worst qualities in each other. I do all I can and yet you both make me feel like an intruder."

"It's just your imagination, Martha. Now stop worrying."

"I'm an unhappy woman. But I try to be patient. I try so hard, don't I, Henry?"

"You're very patient, dear, but you shouldn't be so suspicious of everybody, don't you see?" Mr. Lount was saying the voice of a man trying to pacify an angry, hysterical wife.

Then Michael heard footsteps on the cinder path, and then he saw two long shadows: two women were approaching, and one tall, slender girl. When Michael saw this girl, Helen Murray, he tried to duck behind the veranda post, for he had always wanted her for his girl. He had gone to school with her. At night he used to lie awake planning remarkable feats that would so impress her she would never want to be far away from him. Now the girl's mother was calling, "Hello there, Michael," in a very jolly voice.

"Hello, Mrs. Murray," he said glumly, sure his father's or his mother's voice would rise again.

"Come on and walk home with us, Michael," Helen called. Her voice sounded so soft and her face in the dusk light seemed so round, white and mysteriously far away that Michael began to ache with eagerness. Yet he said hurriedly, "I can't. I can't tonight," speaking almost rudely as if he believed they only wanted to tease him.

As they went along the path and he watched them, he was really longing for that one bright moment when Helen would pass under the high corner light, though he was thinking with bitterness that he could already hear them talking, hear Mrs. Murray saying, "He's a peculiar boy, but it's not to be wondered at since his father and mother don't get along at all." And inside one of the houses someone had stopped playing a piano, maybe to hear one of the fellows who had been in the lumberyard that afternoon laughing and telling that young Lount was scared to jump off the roof.

Watching the corner, Michael felt that the twisting and pulling in the life in the house was twisting and choking him. "I'll get out of here. I'll go away." And he began to think of going to the city. He began to long for freedom in strange places where everything was new and fresh and mysterious. He began to breathe heavily at the thought of freedom. In the city he had an uncle D'Arcy who sailed the lake boats in the summer months and in the winter went all over the south from one racetrack to another following the horses. "I ought to go down to the city tonight and get a job," he thought: but he did not move; he was still waiting for Helen Murray to pass under the light.

For most of the next day, too, Michael kept to himself. He was uptown once on a message, and he felt like running on the way home. With long sweeping strides he ran steadily on the paths past the shipyard, the church, the railway tracks, his face serious with determination.

But in the late afternoon when he was sitting on the veranda reading, Sammy Schwartz and Ike Hershfield came around to see him.

"Hello Mike, what's new with you?" they said, sitting on the steps.

"Sammy, hello, Ike. What's new with you?"

They began to talk to Michael about the colored family that had moved into the old roughcast shack down by the tracks. "The big coon kid thinks he's tough," Sammy said. "He offered to beat up any of us so we said he wouldn't have a snowball's chance with you."

"What did the nigger say?"

"He said he'd pop you one right on the nose if you came over his way."

"Let's go over," Michael said. "I'll tear his guts out for you."

They went out to the street, fell in step very solemnly, and walked over to the field by the tracks without saying a word. When they were about fifty paces away from the shack, Sammy said, "Wait here. I'll go get the coon," and he ran to the unpainted door of the white-washed house calling, "Art, Art, come on out." A big colored boy with closely cropped hair came out and put hand up, shading his eyes from the sun. Then he went back into the house and came out again with a straw hat on his head. He was in his bare feet. The way he came walking across the field with Sammy was always easy to remember because he hung back a little, talking rapidly, shrugging his shoulders. When he came close to Michael he grinned, flashing his teeth, and said, "What's the matter with you white boys? I don't want to do no fighting." He looked scared.

"I'm going to do a nice job on you," Michael said.

The colored boy took off his straw hat and with great care laid it on the ground while all the time he was looking mournfully across the field and at his house, hoping maybe that somebody would come out. Then they started to fight, and Michael knocked him down four times, but he, himself, got a black eye and a cut lip. The colored boy had been so brave and he seemed so alone, licked and lying on the ground, that they sat down around him, praising him and making friends with him. Finding out that Art was a good ball player, a left-handed pitcher who specialized in a curve ball, they agreed they could use him, maybe, on the town team.

Lying there in the field, flat on his back, Michael liked it so much that he almost did not want to go away. Art was telling how he had always wanted to be a jockey but had got too big; he had a brother who could make the weight. Michael began to boast about his Uncle D'Arcy who went around to all the tracks in the winter making and losing money at places like Saratoga, Blue Bonnets and Tia Juana. It was a fine, friendly, eager discussion about faraway places.

It was nearly dinnertime when Michael got home; he went in the house sucking his cut lip and hoping his mother would not notice his black eye. But he heard no movement in the house. In the kitchen he saw his stepmother kneeling down in the middle of the floor with her hands clasped and her lips moving.

"What's the matter, Mother?" he asked.

"I'm praying," she said.

"What for?"

"For your father. Get down and pray with me."

"I don't want to pray."

"You've got to," she said.

"My lip's all cut. It's bleeding. I can't do it," he said.

Late afternoon sunshine coming through the kitchen window shone on his stepmother's graying hair, on her soft smooth skin and on the gentle, patient expression that was on her face. At that moment Michael thought that she was desperately uneasy and terribly alone, and he felt sorry for her even while he was rushing out of the back door.

He saw his father walking toward the woodshed, walking slow and upright with his hands held straight at his side and with the same afternoon sunlight shining so brightly on the high dome of his forehead. He went into the woodshed without looking back. Michael sat down on the steps and waited. He was afraid to follow. Maybe it was because of the way his father was walking with his head held up and his hands straight at his sides. Michael began to make a small desperate prayer that his father should suddenly appear at the woodshed door.

Time dragged slowly. A few doors away Mrs. McCutcheon was feeding her hens who were clucking as she called them. "I can't sit here till it gets dark," Michael was thinking, but he was afraid to go into the woodshed and afraid to think of what he feared.

"What's he doing in here, what's he doing?" Michael said out loud, and he jumped up and rushed to the shed and flung the door wide.

His father was sitting on a pile of wood with his head on his hands and a kind of beaten look on his face. Still scared, Michael called out, "Dad, Dad," and then he felt such relief he sank down on the pile of wood beside his father and looked up at him.

"What's the matter with you, son?"

"Nothing. I guess I just wondered where you were."

"What are you upset about?"

"I've been running. I feel all right."

So they sat there quietly till it seemed time to go into the house. No one said anything. No one noticed Michael's black eye or his cut lip.

Even after they had eaten Michael could not get rid of the fear within him, a fear of something impending. In a way he felt that he ought to do something at once, but he seemed unable to move; it was like sitting on the edge of the roof yesterday, afraid to make the jump. So he went back of the house and sat on the stoop and for a long time looked at the shed till he grew even more uneasy. He heard the angry drilling of a woodpecker and the quiet rippling of the little water flowing under the street bridge and flowing on down over the rocks into the glen. Heavy clouds were sweeping up from the horizon.

He knew now that he wanted to run away, that he could not stay there any longer, only he couldn't make up his mind to go. Within him was the same breathless feeling he had had when he sat on the roof staring down, trying to move. Now he walked around to the front of the house and kept going along the path as far as Helen Murray's house. After going around to the back door, he stood for a long time staring at the lighted window, hoping to see Helen's shadow or her body moving against the light. He was breathing deeply and smelling the rich heavy odors from the flower garden. With his head thrust forward he whistled softly.

"Is that you, Michael?" Helen called from the door. "Come on out."

"What do you want?"

"Come on for a walk?"

For a moment she hesitated at the door, then she came toward him, floating in her white organdie party dress over the grass toward him. She was saying, "I'm dressed to go out. I can't go with you. I'm going down to the dance hall."

"Who with?"

"Charlie Delaney."

"All right," he said. "I just thought you might be doing nothing." As he walked away he called back to her, "So long, Helen."

It was then, on the way back to the house, that he felt he had to go away at once. "I've got to go. I'll die here. I'll write to Dad from the city."

No one paid any attention to him when he returned to the house. His father and stepmother were sitting quietly in the living room reading the paper. In his own room he took a little wooden box from the bottom drawer of his dresser and emptied it of twenty dollars and seventy cents, all that he had saved. He listened solemnly for sounds in the house, then he folded a clean shirt and stuffed a comb and a tooth-brush into his pocket.

Outside he hurried along with his great swinging strides, going past the corner house, on past the long fence and the bridge and the church, and the shipyard, and past the last of the town lights to the highway. He was walking stubbornly, looking solemn and dogged. Then he saw the moonlight shining on the hay stacked in the fields, and when he smelled the oats and the richer smell of sweet clover he suddenly felt alive and free. Headlights from cars kept sweeping by and already he was imagining he could see the haze of bright light hanging over the city. His heart began to thump with eagerness. He put out his hand for a lift, feeling full of hope. He looked across the fields at the dark humps, cows standing motionless in the night. Soon someone would stop and pick him up. They would take him among a million new faces, rumbling sounds and strange smells. He got more excited. His Uncle D'Arcy might get him a job on the boats for the rest of the summer, maybe, too, he might be able to move around with him in the winter. Over and over he kept thinking of places with beautiful names, places like Tia Juana, Woodbine, Saratoga and Blue Bonnets.

SILK STOCKINGS

*D*ave Monroe went into a department store to buy silk stockings as a birthday present for his landlady's daughter, Anne. Many times he hesitated as he walked the length of the hosiery counter, and he smiled shyly at the salesgirl who was trying to help him. He was a rather stout young man, dressed conservatively in a dark overcoat with a plain white scarf, but he had such a round, smiling face that he looked more boyish than he actually was. He blushed and kept on smiling as he tried to look at many pairs of stockings very critically. He wondered whether it would help if he explained to the lady that he was getting the stockings for a girl who was very dainty and stylish, as smart as any girl anyone ever saw hurrying along the street in the evening. But all he said was: "I wonder if these mesh hose would look good with a black seal jacket and a little black muff? She has so many different dresses that you can't go by them. I want something good. I don't care whether they're expensive."

At last he paid for a pair of gun-metal mesh stockings that were so fine he could squeeze them into a ball and conceal them in his hand. When he went out to the lighted streets that were crowded with people who were hurrying home, he began to scrutinize all the well-dressed women to see if one of them had on a pair of stockings as nice as those he had in his pocket for Anne. He was anxious about the way the stockings would look on her because he had been wondering for a week what he could give her that would suggest his intimate interest in her, that would indicate he didn't want to be just a friend. He hurried, wanting to get home to the boarding house before Anne did.

His house was like most of the other boarding houses in the quiet neighborhood except that the woodwork always looked clean and freshly painted. As soon as he opened the door he bumped into Anne's mother, Mrs. Greenleaf, a steady-eyed widow who had always been motherly and patient with Dave. They spoke cheerfully, as if they liked each other. The only time Dave ever saw a harsh, stern expression on Mrs. Greenleaf's face was in the evenings at eleven-thirty when she was walking up and down in the hall waiting for Anne to come home. If Anne happened to be only a few minutes late, her mother argued with her bitterly, as if she alone understood there was a blemish in the girl's nature. The trouble was that Mrs. Greenleaf was a prude and didn't want Anne to go out with men at all, and every time Dave heard her arguing with her daughter in the hall, he thought: "What does she think the girl's doing?"

"Is Anne home yet, Mrs. Greenleaf?"

"Not yet, but she'll be here in a minute. I've got something nice to eat because it's her birthday. Goodness, it must be crisp out; you're just bursting with good health. And here I am driven to bed with my neuralgia all down the side of my face!"

"It's nippy out, but it makes you feel good. It's a shame about that neuralgia," he said. When Mrs. Greenleaf suffered from neuralgia she took many aspirins to try to sleep. As Dave went upstairs he wondered why it was that two people like Anne and her mother, who were so sympathetic in many ways, were never able to understand each other. In his own room he put the stockings carefully under his pillow and sat down on the bed to wait. But he couldn't help thinking of the stockings on Anne's legs; in his head he was making little pictures of her hurrying along the street, a slim, stylish girl with tiny feet wearing expensive fashionable hose that anyone ought to notice, especially when she passed under a streetlight. Then he heard Anne coming upstairs. He could imagine her running with her coat open and billowing back, her toes hardly touching the steps. She seemed to be in a great hurry, as if she wanted to get dressed before dinner so she could go out right after eating. Dave, standing at his open door, said: "Just a minute, Anne, here's something for your birthday. And Anne, would you ever go out with me some night?"

Pulling off her hat, she held it in her left hand. Her black hair was parted in the middle and pulled back tight across her ears. She dangled the silk stockings in one hand, her expression quite serious. Then her face lit up eagerly and she said: "Oh, aren't they lovely! They're just what I wanted. Would I go out with you? I certainly would!"

"They're yours. I hoped you'd like them."

"You're a dear, Dave. I'm crazy about them. I'll wear them tonight. I could kiss you." She almost seemed ready to laugh, but her eyes were soft as she looked away bashfully. Then she crimsoned, hesitated, stood up on her tiptoes, took his head in her hands and kissed him, and then ran along the hall, leaving him standing there with a wide grin on his face.

Before she went out that night she called to him: "How do you like them, Dave?" She was standing under the hall light, holding her dress up a few inches so he could see the stockings. She was wearing her seal jacket and carrying her little black muff in one hand, and she looked so smart he said: "You look like a million dollars, Anne."

"Don't the stockings look great?" she said. "Bye-bye, Dave."

He would have liked to ask her where she was going, but the main thing was that wherever she went that night, she would be wearing silk stockings that were his, and for the first time, as he thought of her, he had a feeling of possession.

That night he went to the armory to see the fights. On his way home he went into the corner store to get a package of cigarettes. When he came out he stood on the sidewalk, lit a cigarette, and as he looked across the street he thought he recognized the girl with the little black muff who was talking to a fellow wearing one of those long, straight dark overcoats with wide padded shoulders. A small light-grey hat was pulled down over one eye. He looked like a tough guy who had made good and bought himself some sharp clothes. "What's Anne doing with a mug like that?" Dave thought. He felt like going across the street and pushing the man away. Anne and the man moved under the light by the newsstand and he could see the man's swarthy, bluish cheek. Anne was holding his arm loosely as they argued with each other. Twice she turned to leave and each time went back and said something to him. Dave didn't actually feel angry till he saw the light shining on her silk stockings, and then he remembered the way she had kissed him and he wanted to shout across the street at her and insult her. But Anne was leaving the man, who was patting her shoulder. Instead of going away himself, the man turned, bought a morning paper at the newsstand, put a cigar in his mouth, and leaned against the post.

Dave, who was following Anne along the street, let her go into the house without catching up to her. In the hall upstairs he heard Anne answering her mother, who was calling sleepily.

"Are you in for the night, Anne?"

"Yes, I'm in, Mother," Anne said.

In his room, Dave sat on the bed, rubbing his face with his hand and trying to figure out what Anne would be doing with a guy who looked like a gangster. "No wonder her mother tries to keep an eye on her!" he thought. He felt both jealous and humiliated, and his only comforting thought was that she had promised to go out with him, too. Then he heard someone moving softly outside in the hall, tiptoeing downstairs. As he pulled his door open, he saw Anne, who still had on her fur jacket, halfway downstairs. With one hand on the banister she looked up at him, blinking, scared. He walked down toward her.

"Where are you going, Anne?" he said.

"Out for a little while," she whispered, putting her finger up to her lips. "Please be quiet, or Mother will hear you."

"You're going back to that guy you left down at the corner, I know," he said stubbornly. "I didn't think you ever sneaked out this late at night."

"Only when Mother's had neuralgia and put herself to sleep."

"Anne, don't go back."

"Dave, please; I'm in a hurry."

He stared at her, shaking his head; all evening while he had been at the armory watching the fights, he had been dreaming of the way she had kissed him. Now he felt that her delight at his birthday gift meant nothing, her kiss was just a casual incident, and that she was hurrying out, wearing the stockings he had given her as a first intimate gesture, to meet the man on the corner. She tried to push him aside. Stuttering with rage, he said: "I know all about that guy without even speaking to him." When she didn't answer, he grabbed hold of her arm and pulled her back from the door. He was so full of jealous rage he tripped her and pushed her back on the stairs and tried to hold her there with a forearm across her chest.

"You're hurting me!" she gasped.

"I'm going to pull those stockings off you," he said, pushing her back roughly. Then she started to cry, as if he had hurt her badly, and all the energy went out of him. She was sitting on the stairs with one hand on her breast as she tried to get her breath.

"You hurt me, you hurt me," she whispered, biting her lip.

"I'm so sorry, Anne."

"You've got to watch it, you can't be that rough with a girl."

"I'm sorry, sorry," he said, helping her up as if she had become so fragile he hardly dared touch her.

"I know you didn't mean to hurt me, Dave," she said, wiping her eyes. "I know you like me."

"I've always liked you, Anne."

"I like you, too," she said, taking a deep breath and looking as if she might cry again.

"Why's a girl like you going out at this hour?"

"He's all right, I've been going out with him for two years. He's been good to me, he loves me. I've got so I love him."

"Is he waiting for you?"

"Yes!"

There was a sudden fear in his heart and he said haltingly: "If you want, I'll leave the latch off the door, Anne!"

"If you want, Dave," she said, looking away. "Don't tell Mother, will you?"

"I won't."

She went out. He waited, then he hurried up the stairs to put on his hat and coat. Mrs. Greenleaf must have wakened, for she called: "Did I hear you talking to somebody, Dave?" He said: "I guess you heard me coming in. It's all right, Mrs. Greenleaf." He tiptoed downstairs and went out to the street.

Anne was quite a way ahead. By the time she reached the corner, he was almost up to her, but on the other side of the street. Seeing her coming, the man who was waiting, leaning against the post, tossed his paper into a refuse can, and without saying a word, took hold of her arm possessively. They went walking along the street. Dave stood watching, increasingly resentful of the man's long, straight, wide-shouldered overcoat. Then he saw the light flash on Anne's stockings. At first he felt glad to think that something of his was going with her. The couple turned a corner. Dave hurried after them, following for three blocks till he saw them turn into a brownstone rooming house. There was only one hall light in the house. Anne was standing behind the man while he bent down and fumbled with a key in the lock. As Dave stood there, clenching his fists and not knowing whether to be angry at Anne or her mother, he was desperately uneasy, for he remembered he had called out: "It's all right, Mrs. Greenleaf." Then he saw the man against the hall light holding the door open, and Anne went in, and the door was shut.

A Girl
with Ambition

---

*A*fter leaving school when she was sixteen, Mary Ross
worked for two weeks with a cheap chorus line at the
old La Plaza, quitting when her stepmother heard the girls
were a lot of toughs. Mary was a neat, clean girl with short,
fair curls and blue eyes, looking more than her age because
she had very long legs, and knew it. She got another job as
cashier in the shoe department of Eaton's, after a row with
her father and a slap on the ear from her stepmother.

She was marking time in the store, of course, but it was
good fun telling the girls about imaginary offers from big
companies. The older salesgirls sniffed and said her hair was
bleached. The salesmen liked fooling around her cage, telling
jokes, but she refused to go out with them: she didn't believe
in running around with fellows working in the same department. Mary paid her mother six dollars a week for board and
always tried to keep fifty cents out. Mrs. Ross managed to get
the fifty cents, insisting every time that Mary would come to
a bad end.

Mary met Harry Brown when he was pushing a wagon
on the second floor of the store, returning goods to the department. Every day he came over from the mail-order building,

stopping longer than necessary in the shoe department, watching Mary in the cash cage out of the corner of his eye. Mary found out that he went to high school and worked in the store for the summer holidays. He hardly spoke to her, but once, when passing, he slipped a note written on wrapping paper under the cage wire. It was such a nice note that she wrote a long one the next morning and dropped it in his wagon when he passed. She liked him because he looked neat and had a serious face and wrote a fine letter with big words that were hard to read.

In the morning and early afternoons they exchanged wise glances that held a secret. She imagined herself talking earnestly, about getting on. It was good having someone to talk to like that because the neighbors on her street were always teasing her about going on the stage. If she went to the butcher to get a pound of round steak cut thin, he saucily asked how was the village queen and actorine. The lady next door, who had a loud voice and was on bad terms with Mrs. Ross, often called her a hussy, saying she should be spanked for staying out so late at night, waking decent people when she came in.

Mary liked to think that Harry Brown knew nothing of her home or street, for she looked up to him because he was going to be a lawyer. Harry admired her ambition but was shy. He thought she knew how to handle herself.

In the letters she said she was his sweetheart but never suggested they meet after work. Her manner implied it was unimportant that she was working at the store. Harry, impressed, liked to tell his friends about her, showing off the letters, wanting them to see that a girl who had a lot of experience was in love with him. "She's got some funny ways but I'll bet no one gets near her," he often said.

They were together the first time the night she asked him to meet her downtown at 10:30. He was waiting at the corner and didn't ask where she had been earlier in the evening. She was ten minutes late. Linking arms, they walked east along Queen Street. He was self-conscious. She was trying to be very practical, though pleased to have on her new blue suit with the short stylish coat.

Opposite the cathedral at the corner of Church Street, she said, "I don't want you to think I'm like the people you sometimes see me with, will you now?"

"I think you are way ahead of the girls you eat with at noon hour."

"And look, I know a lot of boys, but they don't mean nothing. See?"

"Of course, you don't need to fool around with tough guys, Mary. It won't get you anywhere," he said.

"I can't help knowing them, can I?"

"I guess not."

"But I want you to know that they haven't got anything on me," she said, squeezing his arm.

"Why do you bother with them?" he said, as if he knew the fellows she was talking about.

"I go to parties, Harry. You got to do that if you're going to get along. A girl needs a lot of experience."

They walked up Parliament Street and turned east, talking confidently as if many things had to be explained before they could be satisfied with each other. They came to a row of huge sewer pipes along the curb by the Don River bridge. The city was repairing the drainage. Red lights were about fifty feet apart on the pipes. Mary got up on a pipe and walked along, supporting herself with a hand on Harry's shoulder, while they talked in a silly way, laughing. A night watch-man came along and yelled at Mary, asking if she wanted to knock the lights over.

"Oh, have an apple," she yelled back at him.

"You better get down," said Harry, very dignified.

"Let him chase me," she said. "I'll bet he's got a wooden leg." But she jumped down and held onto his arm.

For a long time they stood on the bridge, looking beyond the row of short poplars lining the hill in the good district on the other side of the park. Mary asked Harry if he didn't live over there, wanting to know if they could see his house from the bridge. They watched the lights on a streetcar moving slowly up the hill. She felt that he was going to kiss her. He was looking down at the slow-moving water wondering if she would like it if he quoted some poetry.

"I think you are swell," he said finally.

"I'll let you walk home with me," she said.

They retraced their steps until a few blocks away from her home. They stood near the police station in the shadow of the fire hall. He coaxed so she let him walk just one more block. In the light from the corner butcher store they talked for a few minutes. He started to kiss her. "The butcher will see us," she said, but didn't care, for Harry was respectable-looking and she wanted to be kissed. Harry wondered why she wouldn't let him go to the door with her. She left him and walked ahead, turning to see if he was watching her. It was necessary she walk a hundred yards before Harry went away. She turned and walked home, one of a row of eight dirty frame houses jammed under one long caving roof.

She talked a while with her father, but was really lik-ing the way Harry had kissed her, and talked to her, and the very respectable way he had treated her all evening. She hoped he wouldn't meet any boys who would say bad things about her.

She might have been happy if Harry had worked on in the store. It was the end of August and his summer holidays were over. The last time he pushed his wicker wagon over to her cash cage, she said he was to remember she would always be a sincere friend and would write often. They could have seen each other for he wasn't leaving the city, but they took it for granted they wouldn't.

Every week she wrote to him about offers and rehearsals that would have made a meeting awkward. She liked to think of him not because of being in love but because he seemed so respectable. Thinking of how he liked her made her feel a little better than the girls she knew.

When she quit work to spend a few weeks up at Georgian Bay with a girlfriend, Hilda Heustis, who managed to have a good time without working, she forgot about Harry. Hilda had a party in a cottage on the beach and they came home the night after. It was cold and it rained all night. One of Hilda's friends, a fat man with a limp, had chased her around the house and down to the beach, shouting and swearing, and into the bush, limping and groaning. She got back to the house all right. He was drunk. A man in pajamas from the cottage to the right came and thumped on the door, shouting that they were a pack of strumpets, hussies, and if they didn't clear out he would have to call the police. He was shivering and looked very wet. Hilda, a little scared, said they ought to clear out next day.

Mary returned to Toronto and her stepmother was waiting, very angry because Mary had quit her job. They had a big row. Mary left home, slamming the door. She went two blocks north to live with Hilda in a boarding house.

It was hard to get a job and the landlady was nasty. She tried to get work in a soldiers' company touring the province with a kind of musical comedy called *Mademoiselle from Courcelette*. But the manager, a nice young fellow with tired eyes, said she had the looks but he wanted a dancer. After that, every night Mary and Hilda practiced a step dance, waiting for the show to return.

Mary's father came over to the boarding house one night and coaxed her to come back home because she was really all he had in the world, and he didn't want her to turn out to be a good-for-nothing. He rubbed his face in her hair. She noticed for the first time he was getting old and was afraid he was going to cry. She promised to live at home if her stepmother would mind her own business.

Now and then she wrote to Harry, just to keep him thinking of her. His letters were sincere and free from slang. Often he wrote, "What is the use of trying to get on the stage?" She told herself he would be astonished if she were successful, and would look up to her. She would show him.

Winter came and she had many good times. The gang at the east-end roller rink knew her and she got in free. There she met Wilfred Barnes, the son of a grocer four blocks east of the fire hall, who had a good business. Wilfred had a nice manner but she never thought of him in the way she thought of Harry. He got fresh with little encouragement. Sunday afternoons she used to meet him at the rink in Riverdale Park. Several times she saw Harry and a boyfriend walking through the park, and leaving her crowd, she would talk to him for a few minutes. He was shy and she was a little ashamed of her crowd that whistled and yelled while she was talking. These chance meetings got to mean a good deal, helping her to think about Harry during the week.

In the early spring *Mademoiselle from Courcelette* returned to Toronto. Mary hurried to the man that had been nice to her and demonstrated the dance she had practiced all winter. He said she was a good kid and should do well, offering her a tryout at thirty dollars a week. Even her stepmother was pleased because it was a respectable company that a girl didn't need to be ashamed of. Mary celebrated by going to a party with Wilfred and playing strip poker until four a.m. She was getting to like being with Wilfred.

When it was clear she was going on the road with the company, she phoned Harry and asked her to meet her at the roller rink.

She was late. Harry was trying to roller skate with another fellow, fair-haired, long-legged, wearing large glasses. They had never roller skated before but were trying to appear unconcerned and dignified. They looked very funny because everyone else on the floor was free and easy, willing to start a fight. Mary got her skates on but the old music box stopped and the electric sign under it flashed "Reverse." The music started again. The skaters turned and went the opposite way. Harry and his friend skated off the floor. Mary followed them to a bench near the soft-drink stand.

"What's the hurry, Harry?" she yelled.

He turned quickly, his skates slipping, and would have fallen, but his friend held his arm.

"Look here, Mary, this is the damnedest place," he said.

His friend said roguishly, "Hello, I know you because Harry has told me a lot about you."

"Oh well, it's not much of a place but I know the gang," she said.

"I guess we don't have to stay here," Harry said.

"I'm not fussy, let's go for a walk, the three of us," she said.

Harry was glad his friend was noticing her blue coat with the wide sleeves and the light brown fur.

They left the rink and arm-in-arm the three walked up the street. Mary was eager to tell about *Mademoiselle from Courcelette.* The two boys were impressed and enthusiastic.

"In some ways I don't like to think of you being on the stage, but I'll bet a dollar you get ahead," Harry said.

"Oh, baby, I'll knock them dead in the hick towns."

"How do you think she'll do, Chuck?" said Harry.

The boy with the glasses could hardly say anything, he was so impressed.

Mary talked seriously. She had her hand in Harry's coat pocket and kept tapping her fingers. Harry gaily beat time as they walked. They felt that they should stay together after being away for a long time. When she said it would be foolish to think she would cut up like some girls in the business did, Harry left it to Chuck if a fellow couldn't tell a mile away that she was a real good kid.

The lighted clock in the tower of the fire hall could be seen when they turned the bend in the street. Then they could make out the hands on the clock. Mary, leaving them, said she had had a swell time, she didn't know just why. Harry jerked her into the shadow of the side door of the police station and kissed her, squeezing her tight. Chuck leaned back against the wall, wondering what to do. An automobile horn hooted. Mary, laughing happily, showed the boys her contract and they shook their heads earnestly. They heard footfalls around the corner. "Give Chuck a kiss," Harry said suddenly, generously. The boy with the glasses was so pleased he could hardly kiss her. A policeman appeared at the corner and said, "All right, Mary, your mother wants you. Beat it."

Mary said, "How's your father?" After promising to write Harry, she ran up the street.

The boys, pleased with themselves, walked home. "You want to hang on to her," Chuck said.

"I wonder why she is always nice to me just when she is going away," Harry said.

"Would you want her for your girl?"

"I don't know. Wouldn't she be a knockout at the school dance? The old ladies would throw a fit."

Mary didn't write to Harry and didn't see him for a long time. After two weeks she was fired from the company. She wasn't a good dancer.

Many people had a good laugh and Mary stopped talking about her ambitions for a while. Though usually careful, she slipped into easy careless ways with Wilfred Barnes. She never thought of him as she thought of Harry, but he became important to her. Harry was like something she used to pray for when a little girl and never really expected to get.

It was awkward when Wilfred got into trouble for tampering with the postal boxes that stood on street corners. He had discovered a way of getting all the money people put in the slots for stamps. The police found a big pile of coins hidden in his father's store. The judge sent him to jail for only two months because his parents were very respectable people. He promised to marry Mary when he came out.

One afternoon in the late summer they were married by a Presbyterian minister. Mrs. Barnes made it clear that she didn't think much of the bride. Mr. Barnes said Wilfred would have to go on working in the store. They took three rooms in a big boarding house on Berkley Street.

Mary cried a little when she wrote to tell Harry she was married. She had always been too independent to cry in that way. She would be his sincere friend and still intended to be successful on the stage, she said. Harry wrote that he was surprised that she had married a fellow just out of jail, even though he seemed to come from respectable people.

In the dance pavilion at Scarborough beach a month later, she saw Harry. The meeting was unexpected and she was with three frowsy girls from a circus that was in the east end for a week. Mary had on a long blue-knitted cape that the stores were selling cheaply. Harry turned up his nose at the three girls but talked cheerfully to Mary. They danced together. She said that her husband didn't mind her taking another try at the stage and he wondered if he should say that he had been to the circus. Giggling, and watching him closely, she said she was working for the week in the circus, for the experience. He gave her to understand that always she would do whatever pleased her, and shouldn't try for a thing that wasn't natural to her. He wasn't enthusiastic when she offered to phone him, just curious about what she might do.

Late in the fall a small part in a local company at the La Plaza for a week was offered to her. She took the job because she detested staying around the house. She wanted Harry to see her really on the stage so she phoned and asked if he would come to the La Plaza on Tuesday night. Good-humoredly he offered to take her dancing afterward. It was funny, he said laughing, that she should be starting all over again at the La Plaza.

But Harry, sitting solemnly in the theater, watching the ugly girls in tights on the stage, couldn't pick her out. He wondered what on earth was the matter when he waited at the stage door and she didn't appear. Disgusted, he went home and didn't bother about her because he had a nice girl of his own. She never wrote to tell him what was the matter.

But one warm afternoon in November, Mary took it into her head to sit on the front seat of the rig with Wilfred, delivering groceries. They went east through many streets until they were in the beach district. Wilfred was telling jokes and she was laughing out loud. Once he stopped his wagon, grabbed his basket and went running along a side entrance, yelling, "Grocer!" Mary sat on the wagon seat.

Three young fellows and a woman were sitting up on a veranda opposite the wagon. She saw Harry looking at her and vaguely wondered how he got there. She didn't want him to see that she was going to have a baby. Leaning on the veranda rail, he saw that her slimness had passed into the shapelessness of her pregnancy and he knew why she had been kept off the stage that night at the La Plaza. She sat erect and strangely dignified on the seat of the grocery wagon. They didn't speak. She made up her mind to be hard up for someone to talk to before she bothered him again, as if without going any further she wasn't as good as he was. She smiled sweetly at Wilfred when he came running out of the alley and jumped on the seat, shouting, "Giddup," to the horse. They drove on to a customer farther down the street.

ROCKING CHAIR

All the way home from work that evening Thomas Boult-bee thought of Easter Sunday, which was only two days away, and of his young wife, Elsie, who had died of pneumonia and been buried in the last winter month. As Thomas Boultbee started to climb the stairs to his apartment he felt very lonely. His feet felt heavy. By the time he got to the landing he seemed unreasonably weary and he rested to take a deep breath. He was a tall, thin young man wearing a baggy tweed suit. He had a fair curling moustache, which he sometimes touched with the tip of his tongue, and his blue eyes behind the heavy tortoiseshell glasses were deep-set and wistful. He had been thinking how all the church bells would ring on Easter Sunday while the choirs sang of the Lord who had risen from the dead, and he hoped it would be a crystal-clear, sunlit day. Last Easter, at a time when he and Elsie had been married only a few weeks, they had gone to the church together and he had held her hand tightly even while they knelt down to pray. Her eyes had been closed as she knelt beside him and he had kept on looking at the expression of contentment on her nervous face half-framed in her bobbed dark hair. "I guess there's no use thinking of that," he said, as he started to climb the stairs again, yet he went on thinking stubbornly that all over the country on Sunday there would be a kind of awakening after the winter, in the city the church choirs would chant that the dead had returned to life, and for some reason it stirred him to feel that Elsie was so alive and close to him in his own thoughts.

In the narrow hall below his own apartment he encountered Hilda Adams, a friend of his wife, who was going out, dressed in a smart blue suit and a little blue straw hat. She was an assertive, fair-haired, solidly built girl. Since Elsie had died Hilda Adams had taken it for granted with too much confidence that Boultbee wanted her to look after him. In the dimly lit hall, she waited, smiling, leaning back against the wall.

"Hello, Hilda," he said. "Have you got your new Easter suit on?"

"I sure have. How do you like it, Tom?" she said, turning and pivoting with one foot off the floor.

"It looks good. When I was coming along the street I was thinking that Easter was Elsie's favorite time of the year."

"I know, Tom, but be a little fairer to yourself," she said brusquely, as she pulled on her black gloves. "You oughtn't to go around always with a long face like that. It isn't right." And for no other reason than that she had a malicious disposition and was irritated by his persistent devotion to his dead wife, she said, "Poor little Elsie. I was thinking of her today. She didn't have much of a chance to enjoy anything, did she? There were even little things she missed."

"What little things?" he said.

"Oh, nothing much," she said, smoothing her coat at the hips with her gloved hands. "You know, just a few days before she died the poor soul told me about a rocking chair she saw downtown and had her heart set on. Fancy that."

"You must have got her wrong," he said. "She didn't really want that chair. We were saving to get along. With me studying engineering at nights we needed every nickel. But I had planned to get her the chair for her birthday."

Taking a sly, knowing look at him, Hilda Adams patted him on the shoulder, took a deep, sighing breath and said, "Cheer up. See you later, bye-bye."

Thomas Boultbee was such a serious young man that as soon as he was alone in his own room he sat down, took off his glasses and thought of the last time he had been downtown with Elsie and they had seen the wicker rocking chair in the furniture department. She had hardly mentioned wanting the chair. When passing along the aisle in the department she had felt tired and had sat down in the rocker and smiled up at him. Then she had got up, still smiling, and had patted the chair with her hand. It had never occurred to him that she would come home and tell Miss Adams that she wanted that chair.

That night Boultbee did not sleep well: he had a bad dream, and then he lay awake wondering why Elsie had been afraid to ask him for the chair.

All the next day while at work Boultbee was wishing earnestly that he could find some way to show Elsie that he would not have begrudged her anything in the world. He thought of telling her in a prayer. The more he thought of it the closer she seemed to him, and then he decided at noontime, when he was out in the crowded streets, that he would like to do something more definite than praying. He had just come out of a drugstore after having a sandwich and a cup of coffee and was looking at the noonday crowd passing along the street. A great many of the women were wearing their winter clothes for the last time. On Easter Sunday they would put on their new dresses and if it were a fine clear day they would go for a walk down the avenue. Boultbee and his wife had watched the fashion parade last year. It had been like watching people coming to life in new raiment and getting ready for the new season. As he lit a cigarette, he smiled and thought, "Maybe nothing, or no one, ever dies."

Then he grinned shyly to himself and said, "I'd like an awful lot to go and buy that chair and take it home and have it in the room for Easter Sunday." He wouldn't admit to himself that he was trying to prove he had never begrudged anything to Elsie.

On Saturday afternoon Boultbee went to the store and into the furniture department. At first he had the notion that the one wicker chair might be gone, but as he stood in the aisle, looking around at long rows of chairs, he at once saw eight or nine brown wicker ones just like the one Elsie had wanted, plain wicker rockers with a little padding on the seat and on the arms. But when the salesman approached him he felt uneasy and foolish. "If I want to buy a chair why can't I buy a chair?" he thought stubbornly. His sudden amiable grin startled the salesman who had been too tired to notice him particularly. "I've had this chair picked out for some time," Boultbee said as he put his hand in his pocket for the money. Then he surprised himself by adding confidentially, "I had planned to get this chair for my wife. I don't know why she liked this one particularly."

"If she liked it then, she'll like it now," the salesman said with judicial assurance. "And it will stand up against a lot of wear, too."

"Well, that's what you always want in a chair," Boultbee agreed. "It isn't so much what a chair looks like as what it'll stand up under," he added, wanting the fellow to think him a sage and practical man.

On Easter Sunday when he got up he wouldn't admit that he was eager, but he was quite pleased with himself. He didn't wait to dress. He put on his brown dressing gown and his bathroom slippers and went into the living room to look at the rocking chair. There it was by the table. With a gentle motion he rocked it back and forth a few times, a faint, tender smile at the corners of his mouth because it was so easy to imagine that Elsie was sitting there in her pale-blue printed housedress. He began to walk up and down, his slippers slapping the floor. Then he went over to the window and looked out: it was just the kind of a Sunday he had wanted it to be, with a cloudless blue sky and streaming sunlight. For a long time he listened to the clanging church bells and watched the people moving on the sidewalk. "I ought to let Hilda Adams look at the chair and see if she gets the idea at all," he said.

He got dressed in a hurry. But when he went downstairs and rapped on Miss Adams's door he felt both shy and awkward, for it occurred to him it would be hard to explain why he bought the chair, if he were asked, especially if she didn't get the idea at once. Her blue eyes snapped wide open when she saw him. She held her pink dressing gown across her throat. As she began to show that she was pleased at seeing him there, he said, with a kind of boyish expression on his face, "Say, Hilda, come on upstairs and have a bit of breakfast with me, will you? You know, it's Easter and we'll boil a lot of eggs."

She almost laughed to herself. "The poor fellow's lonely and can't hold out any longer," she thought. As she ran in and out of her bedroom, daubing powder on her face and twisting her yellow hair back into a knot, she smiled brightly and gaily at him. She began to hum. When they went upstairs to his apartment she had a hold of his arm as if they were going off to some quiet place to have tea.

"I bought something yesterday. Maybe it'll surprise you a bit to see it," he said with a certain diffidence.

"What is it?"

"Just something I thought I ought to have around," he said.

In his living room he stood behind her to conceal his embarrassment as she glanced quickly at the chair. She turned and he gave her one wistful smile. She seemed to puff out with good humor. "He's trying to please me by showing me he's not afraid to spend his money now on something he was too tight to give Elsie," she thought. Flustered with pleasure, she began to giggle. Then she sat down slowly in the chair, relaxed, put her heels together and rocked back and forth.

"You're a dear boy, Tom," she said. "You really are a dear boy."

Running his hand through his mop of hair, he waited for her to participate in his own secret feeling. But she was rocking back and forth, her face creased with little fat smiles, with both her hands on the arms of the chair as if she were solidly established in the room and in his life forever. He felt angry. "The stupid woman," he thought. He knew she thought he was trying in some clumsy way to please her. As she rocked back and forth, beaming, she looked so comfortable he felt outraged.

"Please don't sit in that chair," he said in a mild voice.

"What's the matter with me sitting here, Tom?"

He felt that he was going to appear absurd, so he said, coaxing her, "I just want you to come over here by the window, that's all."

"This chair's so comfortable. You come here," she said coyly.

"Why do you want to stay there?" he said impatiently. "You can't have your breakfast there, can you?"

Reluctant, she got up, and as she came towards him, humming, she started to sway her hips. But he went right past her to the chair and sat down himself with a stubborn expression on his face while he blinked his eyes and watched her putting her hands on her hips and her head on one side in exasperation. He watched her embarrassment increase. Her face got red. With sober angry faces they kept on staring at each other. "My, you're rude," she said at last. "Such a stupid way to act."

He took off his glasses and wiped them with his handkerchief because his eyes felt moist. "I suppose I didn't want anybody to sit in this chair," he said, trying to make a decent apology. "It's something I thought Elsie would like, that's all."

"I see, I see," she said sharply as she tried to prevent herself from going into a jealous rage. "Of course I see. But I can't help thinking you're a fool," she said. "You can't blame me for that. Though I suppose it's more likely you went out and bought the chair for yourself." Nodding her head up and down, she said contemptuously, "Imagine you going out and buying that chair after refusing it to your poor wife."

"You don't get the idea at all," he said.

"Maybe I don't," she said. "But I'll be hanged if I stay and have breakfast with anybody as rude as you." She gave him one bitter glance and walked out of the room.

He put his glasses on and adjusted them on his nose. Then he closed his eyes and with his hands on the arms of the chair he rocked back and forth, back and forth. "What did I expect anyway?" he thought. He pondered the matter: in the beginning he had been thinking of the church choirs that would sing "Christ the Lord has risen today." He stopped rocking and leaned forward with his eyes open and his hands gripped between his knees, "But what did I expect the chair to do? Did I actually think it would help bring Elsie closer to me?" Then he started to rock again, and frowning he wondered why he had bought the chair at all. Outside, the last of the church bells were ringing. Closing his eyes, he went rocking, rocking, back and forth.

A WEDDING DRESS

*F*or fifteen years Miss Lena Schwartz had waited for Sam Hilton to get a good job so they could get married. She lived in a quiet boarding house on Wellesley Street, the only woman among seven men boarders. The landlady, Mrs. McNab, did not want women boarders; the house might get a bad reputation in the neighborhood, but Miss Schwartz had been with her a long time. Miss Schwartz was thirty-two, her hair was straight, her nose turned up a little and she was thin.

Sam got a good job in Windsor and she was going there to marry him. She was glad to think that Sam still wanted to marry her, because he was a Catholic and went to church every Sunday. Sam liked her so much he wrote a cramped homely letter four times a week.

When Miss Schwarz knew definitely that she was going to Windsor, she read part of a letter to Mrs. McNab. The men heard about the letter at the table and talked as if Lena were an old maid. "I guess it will really happen to her all right," they said, nudging one another. "The Lord knows she waited long enough."

Miss Schwartz quit work in the millinery shop one afternoon in the middle of February. She was to travel by night, arrive in Windsor early next morning and marry Sam as soon as possible.

That afternoon the downtown streets were slushy and the snow was thick alongside the curb. Miss Schwartz ate a little lunch at a soda fountain, not much because she was excited. She had to do some shopping, buy some flimsy underclothes and a new dress. The dress was important. She wanted it charming enough to be married in and serviceable for wear on Sundays. Sitting on the counter stool she ate slowly and remembered how she had often thought marrying Sam would be a matter of course. His lovemaking had become casual and good-natured; she could grow old with him and be respected by other women. But now she had a funny aching feeling inside. Her arms and legs seemed almost strange to her.

Miss Schwartz crossed the road to one of the department stores and was glad she had on her heavy coat with the wide sleeves that made a warm muff. The snow was melting and the sidewalk steaming near the main entrance. She went lightheartedly through the store, buying a little material for a dress on the third floor, a chemise on the fourth floor and curling-tongs in the basement. She decided to take a look at the dresses.

She rode an elevator to the main floor and got on an escalator because she liked gliding up and looking over the squares of counters, the people in the aisles, and over the rows of white electric globes hanging from the ceiling. She intended to pay about twenty-five dollars for a dress. To the left of the escalators the dresses were displayed on circular racks in orderly rows. She walked on the carpeted floor to one of the racks and a salesgirl lagged on her heels. The girl was young and fair-headed and saucy looking; she made Miss Schwartz uncomfortable.

"I want a nice dress, blue or brown," she said, "about twenty-five dollars."

The salesgirl mechanically lifted a brown dress from the rack. "This is the right shade for you," she said. "Will you try it on?"

Miss Schwartz was disappointed. She had no idea such a plain dress would cost twenty-five dollars. She wanted something to startle Sam. She never paid so much for a dress, but Sam liked something fancy. "I don't think I like these," she said. "I wanted something special."

The salesgirl said sarcastically, "Maybe you were thinking of a French dress. Some on the rack in the French Room are marked down."

Miss Schwartz moved away, a tall commonplace woman in a dark coat and an oddly shaped purple hat. She went into the gray French Room. She stood on a blue pattern on the gray carpet and guardedly fingered a dress on the rack, a black canton crepe dress with a high collar that folded back, forming petals of burnt orange. From the hem to the collar was a row of buttons, the sleeves were long with a narrow orange trimming at the cuffs, and there was a wide corded silk girdle. It was marked seventy-five dollars. She liked the feeling it left in the tips of her fingers. She stood alone at the rack, toying with the material, her mind playing with thoughts she guiltily enjoyed. She imagined herself wantonly attractive in the dress, slyly watched by men with bold thoughts as she walked down the street with Sam, who would be nervously excited when he drew her into some corner and put his hands on her shoulders. Her heart began to beat heavily. She wanted to walk out of the room and over to the escalator but could not think clearly. Her fingers were carelessly drawing the dress into her wide coat sleeve, the dress disappearing steadily and finally slipping easily from the hanger, drawn into her wide sleeve.

She left the French Room with a guilty feeling of satisfied exhaustion. The escalator carried her down slowly to the main floor. She hugged the parcels and the sleeve containing the dress tight to her breast. On the streetcar she started to cry because Sam seemed to have become something remote, drifting away from her. She would have gone back with the dress but did not know how to go about it.

When she got to the boarding house she went straight upstairs and put on the dress as fast as she could, to feel that it belonged to her. The black dress with the burnt orange petals on the high collar was short and loose on her thin figure.

Then the landlady knocked at the door and said that a tall man downstairs wanted to see her about something important. Mrs. McNab waited for Miss Schwartz to come out of her room.

Miss Schwartz sat on the bed. She felt that if she did not move at once she would not be able to walk downstairs. She walked downstairs in the French dress, Mrs. McNab watching her closely. Miss Schwartz saw a man with a wide heavy face and his coat collar buttoned high on his neck complacently watching her. She felt that she might just as well be walking downstairs in her underclothes; the dress was like something wicked clinging to her legs and her body. "How do you do," she said.

"Put on your hat and coat," he said steadily.

Miss Schwartz, slightly bewildered, turned stupidly and went upstairs. She came down a minute later in her coat and hat and went out with the tall man. Mrs. McNab got red in the face when Miss Schwartz offered no word of explanation.

On the street he took her arm and said, "You got the dress on and it won't do any good to talk about it. We'll go over to the station."

"But I have to go to Windsor," she said, "I really have to. It will be all right. You see, I am to be married tomorrow. It's important to Sam."

He would not take her seriously. The streetlights made the slippery sidewalks glassy. It was hard to walk evenly.

At the station the sergeant said to the detective, "She might be a bad egg. She's an old maid and they get very foxy."

She tried to explain it clearly and was almost garrulous. The sergeant shrugged his shoulders and said the cells would not hurt her for a night. She started to cry. A policeman led her to a small cell with a plain cot.

Miss Schwartz could not think about being in the cell. Her head, heavy at first, got light and she could not consider the matter. The detective who had arrested her gruffly offered to send a wire to Sam.

The policeman on duty during the night thought she was a stupid silly woman because she kept saying over and over, "We were going to be married. Sam liked a body to look real nice. He always said so." The unsatisfied expression in her eyes puzzled the policeman, who said to the sergeant, "She's a bit of a fool, but I guess she was going to get married all right."

At half past nine in the morning they took her from the cell to the police car along with a small wiry man who had been quite drunk the night before, a colored woman who had been keeping a bawdy house, a dispirited fat man arrested for bigamy, and a Chinese man who had been keeping a betting house. She sat stiffly, primly, in a corner of the car and could not cry. Snow was falling heavily when the car turned into the city hall courtyard.

Miss Schwartz appeared in the Women's Court before a little olive-skinned magistrate. Her legs seemed to stiffen and fall away when she saw Sam's closely cropped head and his big lazy body at a long table before the magistrate. A young man was talking rapidly and confidently to him. The magistrate and the Crown attorney were trying to make a joke at each other's expense. The magistrate found the attorney amusing. A court clerk yelled a name, the policeman at the door repeated it and then loudly yelled the name along the hall. The colored woman who had been keeping the bawdy house appeared with her lawyer.

Sam moved over to Miss Schwartz. She found it hard not to cry. She knew that a Salvation Army man was talking to a slightly hard-looking woman about her, and she felt strong and resentful. Sam held her hand but said nothing.

The colored woman went to jail for two months rather than pay a fine of $200.

"Lena Schwartz," said the clerk. The policeman at the door shouted the name along the hall. The young lawyer who had been talking to Sam told her to stand up while the clerk read the charge. She was scared and her knees were stiff.

"Where is the dress?" asked the magistrate.

A store detective with a heavy moustache explained that she had it on and told how she had been followed and later on arrested. Everybody looked at her, the dress too short and hanging loosely on her thin body, the burnt orange petals creased and twisted.

"She was to be married today," began the young lawyer affably. "She was to be married in this dress," he said and good humoredly explained that yesterday when she stole it she had become temporarily a kleptomaniac. Mr. Hilton had come up from Windsor and was willing to pay for the dress. It was a case for clemency. "She waited a long time to be married and was not quite sure of herself," he said seriously.

He told Sam to stand up. Sam haltingly explained that she was a good woman, a very good woman. The Crown attorney seemed to find Miss Schwartz amusing.

The magistrate scratched away with his pen and then said he would remand Miss Schwartz for sentence if Sam still wanted to marry her and would pay for the dress. Sam could hardly say anything. "She will leave the city with you," said the magistrate, "and keep out of department stores for a year." He saw Miss Schwartz wrinkling her nose and blinking her eyes and added, "Now go out and have a quiet wedding." The magistrate was satisfied with himself.

Miss Schwartz, looking a little older than Sam, stood up in her dress that was to make men slyly watch her and straightened the corded silk girdle. It was to be her wedding dress. Sam gravely took her arm and they went out to be quietly married.

THREE LOVERS

---

*T*he first to see him coming down the road was Al Stevens. He was sitting on the veranda with his Uncle Andrew. Thin misty rain had been falling for hours on green grass and meadowland sloping down to the river. No one else was on the road. A mist was hanging over the river between the trees, and there was the hollow clanging of a cowbell by Burnam's pasture, sounding loud and clear on the moist air.

Stepping down suddenly from the veranda and standing in the rain in his shirtsleeves, Al Stevens said to his uncle, "Dick Bennet's coming up the road and looking as if he's going somewhere in a hurry." But old Uncle Andrew, who had been deaf and dumb all his life, went on reading his paper. Al tried to sign, slapping his fingers on his palms, got impatient, and went into the house, calling, "Mollie, come here a minute, take a squint down the road and see what you see." The rich, sweet odor of baking tea biscuits came from the kitchen.

"Leave me in peace in my kitchen," Mollie called.

"It's a sight that'll burn you up, woman." His wife came from the kitchen, wiping her hands on her apron, her plump cheeks rosy from the heat of the stove. They hurried out to the veranda and looked down the road at the tall young man with the wide shoulders, who was swinging toward them with his big stride. His thick hair was shining in the soft rain. "He's coming up here," Mollie said. Dick Bennet was almost up to the veranda. They could see his solemn young face, his dark eyes, and his massive, loose-jointed body.

"Hello, Mrs. Stevens. Hello, Al. How's everybody?" he said.

"Hello, Dick," Al said, shaking hands heartily. "Where have you been? We'd like to ask you in Dick, but as it is we've got no room."

"It's a great pity that we can't ask you in," Mollie said firmly. "I dare say you'll be going on up to the hotel."

"It's very likely," Dick said. For such a big man it was odd to see him go suddenly shy. He turned and called back, "I'm sorry to have disturbed you, Mrs. Stevens. So long, Alfred." He went down the path, and on up the road.

Joe Tobin, the hotelkeeper, was cleaning glasses at the counter when Dick came in and said, "Hello, Joe. Have you got a room to spare?"

"Man alive, is it you, Dick? You've got no sense in your head to come back here."

"Don't I come back every year?" Dick asked, laughing.

"Not with the way people have been talking about you now."

While Dick's face was reddening, Joe Tobin said, "Look, there's the Tudhope car. Stand here at the window." They saw a man about forty getting down from beside the girl on the front seat. Edward Tudhope had on a large gray raincoat. As he walked around the car, walking with a slight limp, he took off his hat to a long row of elderly loafers on the veranda. All his life he had had a physical shyness because of his limp but in this place, at least, he was at home. Here nearly everybody owed him money, farmers unable to sell their crops had borrowed from him, and they came along with the storekeeper and the villagers, to the old colonial house overlooking the glen to pay the interest on their notes.

Tudhope was looking up at the girl in the car while filling the tank with gasoline. You could see only her shoulders and face and thick auburn hair, but she seemed full of composure, as if for a long time she had been looking dreamily along the road. The old men watching and the boys on the step, too, knew of the love big Tudhope had always had for Cretia Tolmie, waiting patiently for her to grow up; and now these men staring at her were puzzled that Tudhope and his mother had so gladly taken her into their home after young Bennet had loved and then abandoned her. So they were staring, trying to see more of her, feeling the soft beauty of her face, remembering how just a few months ago even the little kids had looked after her and whistled as she went along the road. Her face now glowing in the mist.

Joe Tobin said, "She's as pretty as a peach in sunlight, ain't she now? I'm surprised at a man like you passing her up."

"What's Cretia doing with Tudhope, Joe?"

"She's marrying him in a week or so."

"Where's Cretia staying?"

"She's staying with Tudhope and his old mother. Her father died, you know," Tobin said, and he began to whistle thinly as he watched Dick's big dark face.

But Cretia Tolmie, herself, did not hear that Dick Bennet was back till the next morning. Cretia came out of the house and began to putter around the flowerbeds on the wide lawn.

It was the warmest of spring days with no breeze, and brilliant sunshine all over the hilly country. Dark plowed land was streaked with rich furrows and oat fields were a heavy green. Cretia bent down, poking with a light stick at the earth. The late spring flowers were opening.

Then she saw Joe Tobin's dilapidated car passing by the road and she called out, "Hello, Joe." He stopped the car, watching her for a long time as though waiting for her to come down to him. And when she did come striding toward him he muttered, "She's the prettiest thing I ever set my eyes on in these parts. There's something rosy about her."

As Cretia smiled up at him, he said, "Are you going my way?"

"No, why do you ask, Joe?" she said.

"Cretia, Dick is back. You ought to know."

They looked at each other, but could not speak for a moment, and then she said fearfully, "Where is he Joe?"

He said, "I had no room. He's in the old stone cottage opposite the hotel. People are getting to hear about it."

Along the highway and in the village at the foot of the glen people were hearing that young Bennet had returned, but no one had dared to go up to the house and tell Tudhope. Once more Joe Tobin looked into Cretia's face; then he shook his head and started the car.

Cretia could not understand why she was suddenly afraid to go back and into the house. She sat on the veranda in the rocking chair with her skirt billowing out around her, sitting in the shade and listening to an oriole over on the edge of the orchard, while all the time she seemed to be really knowing that Dick would come. She was startled, feeling full of guilt, when old Mrs. Tudhope opened the door and said, "We're going into town. Are you all right, Cretia? Is there anything you need?" There was something fierce and yet tender about the woman's pinched little face. She had begun to like Cretia. She wanted to be as devoted to her as she was to her son. "There's nothing you want, eh?" she said, peering at Cretia and wondering at the hushed expectant look she saw.

"No, there's nothing I need at all," Cretia said.

When Edward Tudhope and his mother got into the car, Cretia saw the shy smile lighting his solemn eyes as he threw a kiss to her. She felt there would always be peace and gentleness in a life with him, and she wondered if her love for him might now grow steadily from year to year. And yet almost at once she found herself thinking, "If I could just see Dick for a moment. If I could just see his big awkward body, so I could tell him to go away." She was also saying, "He had better not come around here. I wouldn't even let him set eyes on me." There was a stillness of waiting in her, even deeper than the dreadful uneasiness she felt, which seemed a part of the blue sky and the seeds growing in the rich earth.

Not much later Cretia heard a car coming up the road and she thought the Tudhopes must have turned back. But this car was swerving from side to side. It stopped in front of the house and she saw that Dick Bennet was driving. He came running toward her with his hand reaching up. "Hey, Cretia," he called.

"What are you doing here, Dick?"

"Cretia, put on your coat and get some things. I've come to get you."

"Go away, Dick," she said. "You're not coming near me. You've neither shame nor pride."

"I got the car from the garage in the village," he said. Out of breath, he stood a few feet away, wanting to edge closer, yet knowing, if he moved, she would run into the house.

"You must never come up here again," she said vehemently, but he looked so bold and sure of himself that she was bewildered. "You ought to know how I'd hate the sight of you," she said.

"I know I've been a fool, Cretia. I had a crazy notion I ought to be free and not tied down, so I could see a lot of places. I've been all over. I've been to Detroit, Montreal, and New York, but I couldn't sleep at night for seeing you always there in my dreams."

"I've made up my mind, Dick. It doesn't matter. You didn't care what happened to me. What would I have done without Edward Tudhope? Whatever happiness I'm going to have in this world I want to have here with the Tudhopes."

"I thought you'd be saying something like this," he said in a reasonable, confidential voice. "You think you've got to say it, so I'm coming up there to get you and pick you up and put you down in the car. Don't get scared. I'm not going to hurt you."

"You must be crazy as a cricket," she said, putting her hand out, feeling for the door. He came toward her almost sidelong in his slow step because there was a soft reverence in him for her body that made him afraid to grab hold of her, and she quickly stepped back into the house and slammed the door and locked it. She got so weak she thought she might faint, and she knelt down leaning heavily against the door, listening. She heard him step off the veranda and run around to the back of the house and start shaking the locked back door. When she was calmer she got up and looked out the window, and there he was walking up and down, looking up at all the windows. "He'd never leave me now," she thought.

Still hoping she might come out, he kept looking at the house, and then he took a few steps in an aimless, puzzled way. He began to walk, slow and dejected, down to the car, and he got in without looking back.

As she watched him passing out of sight Cretia felt she had hurt herself so deeply nothing now could matter. "Why can't I stop loving him? I don't want to love him. He never brought me anything but misery," she thought. But she felt the hurt she had given herself sinking deep into her.

She went up to the big, sunlit room with the fine, old furniture, but she felt that she had become more of a stranger in this room than she had ever been. Lying on the bed, she longed for the Tudhopes to return. She waited, with her breath held, with her fists clenched hard. At first she heard every slight noise outside, then faint and farther away she heard the water falling over the rocks in the glen, the same water she had heard running the last night she had walked with Dick before he went away, when he had walked beside her, swinging his big body, trying to pull away from her on the night road while she cried a little and there had been no sound except the noise of the freight train passing by Clover Hill and the water falling in the glen. Standing by the fence he had kissed her clumsily. "I'll be here next week," he kept saying. Then he was gone, without looking back, as if it had become a new night.

The sun was almost down in the late afternoon when the Tudhope car came back up the drive and was backed into the garage. From the window Cretia watched Tudhope help his mother out of the car. His little white fox terrier yelped joyfully and scampered forward to welcome them. Tudhope stopped to smell the blossoms from the apple orchard. "It always made him happy to know I loved the orchard," Cretia thought. "Maybe he's thinking we'll walk down the road like we did two nights ago with him holding my arm so gently. When I told him I loved the smell of the apple blossoms and the white glory of them in the moonlight ever since I was a child, he seemed so happy, as if now he understood the orchard had been growing all the time for the purpose, growing for me." She began to make a little prayer that she might have a fuller love for Edward Tudhope. He came into the house like a quiet man who is glad to be home with his books and his tobacco.

"Cretia, where are you?" he called. When she came he looked at her for a long time, as if ashamed of something he dared not define, but when he saw that she was smiling with more tenderness than she had ever shown to him, he smiled broadly.

"I'm glad you've come back," she said. "I don't like being alone."

"Who around here would harm you, Cretia?"

"Nobody here. I know every sound that comes from the glen, and yet when it gets dark now I don't want to be alone."

"I brought the city papers. I'll get them and read to you while dinner is being prepared," he said. "I left them out on the veranda." He was fond of reading aloud, for when he read slowly there was a sonorous rolling to his words, and a dignity that was not there at other times.

He went out, and when he came in he was carrying the papers loosely, as if he had forgotten about them. He said softly, with the words sliding out easily as if they had been in his mind a long time, "I saw Dick Bennet down at the hotel."

"He will not come here," she said, feeling at once that she should not alarm him.

"As soon as I saw him I felt sure he had been here, Cretia."

"It's terrible that you should feel sure of it. Don't you see what that means?"

"On the way to town my mother kept saying there was a queer look on your face, an expectant look that made her uneasy," he said. Then he called out suddenly to his mother who had gone upstairs, "Light the light, mother. It's dark down here."

"It's not dark yet," Cretia said, "The light's streaming in the window."

"You can't see in that light. It'll be dark in a minute," he said irritably. Then he began again, "It's odd the way I felt sure he had been here as soon as I saw him. Maybe it was the way he and the hotelkeeper looked at me." His voice sounded guttural. After pausing, his words gained fresh strength, his big body was thrust forward, "Cretia, you saw Dick Bennet this afternoon, didn't you?"

"Yes," she said simply. "He came up here and I did not expect to see him. I ran from him and stayed in the house."

"Why didn't you tell me? I waited for you to tell me. You were with him while we were away."

"I did not want him to come here," she said.

"He came while we were away."

"Can't you see I did not want him to come?"

His face was red as he shouted, "You'll not have him coming around here badgering us. You've never stopped loving him. You've never stopped hoping. Day after day you've hoped." But his own words were hurting him so much he could hardly breathe. Then they heard the old woman, who had heard them talking, come hobbling down the stairs as fast as her weak old legs would carry her. At the door she stopped and peered angrily at Cretia though as yet she did not know what the quarrel was about. She only knew that her son was looking like a sick man, and she saw Cretia standing straight with her breasts rising and falling and her whole face full of resentment.

"There's no reason why you should shout at me," Cretia was saying. "What do you want me to do? You've always been so good to me that I'd rather do anything than hurt you. If you don't trust me . . ."

"What's the matter with her?" the old woman interrupted.

"Dick Bennet's come back. I saw him at the hotel. He was here with her while we were away and she lied about it."

The old woman, with her hands up to her head, rocked from side to side and then she stopped and whispered coaxingly to her son, "Be easy, Edward. It does not matter. Don't look so miserable, son." All that passionate part of her life since her marriage, and even more so after the death of her husband, had been devoted to shielding her son from disappointment. The more he had endured, the more she wanted to suffer for him. She seemed to live on, without a life of her own, as if there would be no purpose in dying before her son died. Paying no attention to Cretia, she continued to stare at her son, full of anxiety and compassion, but the hurt eagerness in her old eyes only made him more angry. He seemed to have been seeing it in her eyes all his life, since he was a boy, slow and awkward, when the kids used to tease him on the way home from school. There had been a little girl he had liked once named Susie, who had asked him to pick her a flower from a hedge on a private lawn, and he had said, "All right, Susie," and the other kids who were there had shouted their laughter and started calling him "Susie." They teased him for years and made him full of rage and yet impotent because he was so much bigger. His mother used to wait at the window of their house, watching for him to come home, watching him for a long time while he turned, throwing stones at kids who were following him, and when he went into the house she was waiting with this passionate look in her eyes, this same expression that he saw now and had seen for so many years. "Cretia," he said harshly, "God knows, everybody in the whole countryside knows I've been a fool about you."

"What do you mean, Edward?" she said.

"Never mind what I mean. But I'll not have you here with him seeing you and you loving him."

"Your mother asked me to come here, and you asked me to marry you and I said I would."

"If young Bennet came once, he'll come again. I know how you feel about him and how you'll watch for him."

"You don't trust me at all, Edward."

"Let her go," the old woman said bitterly. She had never wanted him to marry her, feeling there was a stigma attached to her that could never be forgotten. "Let her go where she wants to go," she said.

Cretia was looking up at Tudhope, half pleading, with her hands straight down at her sides, the three of them knowing that he couldn't help loving her. "Where do you think you will go?" he asked, as she turned away, walking slowly across the room in her loose print dress. For a while she stood by the window, unanswering, with her face pressed against the pane. "I told Dick to go," she said. Her voice was so low they could hardly hear her. "I told him that whatever happiness I could have in the world I wanted to try and have it here."

"I don't believe you," he said. Except for the people who were in debt to him, or people to whom he gave work, he did not believe that anyone was really grateful to him, or could love him. He longed to believe Cretia; in all his life there had been no experience to justify such a belief. "It's so very quiet out," she was saying. "You can't hear a bit of sound in the trees." Her voice was soft, as if she had forgotten where she was and was dreaming.

"What are you thinking of?" he asked irritably. "Aren't you listening to me at all?"

"No. I don't care if I never hear your voice again," she said.

"You were thinking of Bennet and wondering where he was waiting."

"Mrs. Tudhope," she said suddenly, "why should he talk to me like that? You shouldn't want to hear him talk like that. What's the matter with both of you? Why are you staring at me? You're both waiting for me to go? All right."

Tudhope looked away uneasily, and then he said, "There's no hurry."

"I'll go down to the village," Cretia said.

Tudhope tried to say something gentle and considerate, but his fierce resentment would not permit him to speak.

The old woman, watching him, knew how he was groping for the tender remark that always came after his anger had gone, so she said, "Let her do what she wants to do, son."

But when Cretia passed by him with her light, loose coat now covering her body, he bent forward anxiously so that she would see how humble he had become. She did not turn. She went to the door and opened it and said quietly, "Good-bye," and she stepped out.

His bitterness became so great that he shouted, "Go ahead. I'll see that you go. Go faster, faster, hurry." He was standing with his heavy body framed in the door, his strong hands clutching the posts, watching her go down the path with her open coat ballooning back. Then he shouted in alarm, "Cretia, wait a minute," and he went out and started to follow her. His fox terrier came out of the shadow and circled around him. He was watching Cretia so intently as he followed that he stumbled off the path.

The night was so absolutely still that every rustle could be heard from the fields, and the night bird circling around the great elm by the road leading down to the highway screeched and swung in a wide circle against the clear sky. Cretia looked up, startled.

By one side of the bridge on the highway there was a low flat rock. Cretia sat down on this rock and her body became a part of it in the shadow. Tudhope stopped about twenty yards from her, and he watched, hesitating. The lower part of her body was hidden, but her head was turned toward the hill, looking up the road. The water was running smoothly under the old bridge, and Cretia thought, "Next month the yellow pond-lilies will nearly cover the surface of the water." Steadily she kept on staring up the stone cottage opposite the hotel. "I won't go near that cottage. Dick must not see me," she was thinking. "In a moment, when I have rested, I'll go on." Yet without moving she continued to stare at the lighted windows of the cottage. "Why wouldn't Edward Tudhope trust me. He seemed so sure, I wonder why?"

While she watched the lighted window, all those days that had passed since Dick had gone away seemed to become full of purpose. She could hear her father speaking to her as he had spoken that night when he had found her leaning against the picket fence, watching the automobiles passing on the road. Her father pretended to be bending down examining roots in the ground, then he suddenly touched her shoulder and said, "Dick's gone for good, girl. Make up your mind to that." But she had said calmly, "He'll be back, Dad, I can feel it in my bones." Then her heart began to thump so loudly she pressed her hand against the spot, for all the time of her waiting seemed triumphantly fulfilled in her now.

Someone was calling softly, "Cretia, Cretia." Aroused she looked back and saw Edward Tudhope standing on the road. Then his big body began to lurch toward her. She was scared. She had never had a fear of Edward Tudhope like she had now, hearing the sound of his foot scraping on the gravel road and seeing him raise one arm slowly. "Don't you dare come near me," she called. "You go back."

"Cretia. I was stupid. Cretia, you'll catch a cold. Come back to the house."

"Keep away," she said, jumping up. "Don't you come up here."

He hesitated, half turned as if afraid of offending her, and then came on steadily. She started to run, and when she turned, he was far back on the road, she was opposite the stone cottage. Light from the window was thrown across the road. There was a big patch of darkness and then another stream of light from the hotel. Her heart began to beat so heavily she wondered what she might be planning to do. "If I just rest here a minute, maybe Dick will come out. Maybe he will know I'm out here because it's so still you could almost hear a person breathing," she thought, but, suddenly she grew bold and walked up the little path through the wild flowers, and rapped on the cottage door.

Dick opened the door, his thick hair rumpled and his shirt open at the throat. "Cretia," he said. "What's the matter? What happened? You've been running."

"Let me come in, Dick," she said.

When she sat down in a chair in the small room he stood a few feet away, so upset at seeing her that he could not speak, but could only wait for her to look up again, her face full of fright and wild surprise. In between deep breaths, she told him why she had come up the road. "It got that I just had to come," she said. "I don't understand it. I just had to come." They sat looking at each other. "Dick," she cried. "We must not stay here. I want to go away."

"We'll go to the city, we'll have to get someone to take us."

"We'll walk along the road," she said, standing up.

"You couldn't do that," he said.

"We'll walk along the road and someone driving will pick us up," she said.

They went out to the road, but they had not taken many steps before they heard someone running. "Cretia, Cretia, come back," they heard Tudhope calling.

With his terrier prancing behind him Tudhope put his hand on Cretia's arm and tried to hold her. His face was wild in the twilight. But he said nothing more.

"Let go her arm," Dick said.

"You left her once, Bennet. Go away," he said. The three of them were on the road, only now Tudhope was pulling at Dick's arm. Then he stopped, and he held Dick by the shoulder. "You can't do this, Bennet," he said. Even when Dick shoved him and began to strike at him blindly he would not let go, and his dog was barking madly and snapping at Dick's legs.

Then Tudhope sank to his knees on the grass beside the road, and he did not try to get up. His head was bowed. His dog circled around him, rushed back toward the house, then turned again and came hurling back to him where it suddenly stood howling in the first bit of moonlight.

"We can't leave him there," Cretia said. "I won't leave him like that. Edward, please get up. I won't leave him. He was so good to me," she cried.

"No, go on, go on, Cretia," Tudhope said. "I shouldn't try and stop you."

"He's all right," Dick said.

They went walking down the road, speaking no words but full of rising eagerness. An old car with dim lights came toward them and Dick stepped out and waved his arm. "Give us a lift," he called.

"Where are you going?" the farmer asked, stopping.

"As far as you're going toward the city," Dick said.

"Then get in with your missus," the farmer said, glancing shrewdly at Cretia and grinning. He had a heavy rough moustache and a battered hat.

They were sitting in the back seat of the car, silent and wondering. When they came to the top of the hill Cretia leaned out, looking over the whole country in the gathering darkness. As she watched the country sloping away in that light she felt she would never see it again, the soft rolling farm hills, the mesh of tiny lakes, the solitary elms; away to the right was Clearwater, farther on ahead was the great beach by the bay and a blur of many soft lights that was Orangeville — the whole country rolling and rising till it was lost in the one thin line of light toward the bay.

THE CHEAT'S REMORSE

*P*hil was sipping a cup of coffee in Stewart's one night, sitting at the table near the radiator so that the snow would melt off his shoes and dry, when he saw a prosperous-looking, blue-jowled man at the next table slowly pushing a corned beef sandwich on rye bread away from him as if the sight of it made him sick. By the way the man sighed as he concentrated on the untouched sandwich anyone could see that he was pretty drunk. He was clutching his food check firmly in his left hand as he used the other to tug and fumble at a roll of bills in his pocket. He was trying to get hold of himself, he was trying to get ready to walk over to the cashier in a straight line without stumbling, pay his check with dignity, and get into a taxi and home before he fell asleep.

The roll of bills in the man's hand under the table, as he leaned his weight forward staring at the cashier, started Phil thinking how much he needed a dollar. He had been across the country and back on a bus. He was broke, his shirts were in a hand laundry on Twenty-sixth Street, and a man he had phoned, a man he had gone to school with, and who worked in a publisher's office now, had told him to come around and see him and he might be able to get him a few weeks' work in the shipping-room. But they wouldn't let him have the shirts at the laundry unless he paid for them. He couldn't bear to meet a man he had grown up with who was making a lot of money unless he had a clean shirt on.

As he leaned forward eagerly watching the man's thick fingers thumbing the roll of bills, trying to detach one while he concentrated on the cashier's desk, the thing that Phil had hardly been daring to hope for happened: a bill was thumbed loose from the roll, the fat fingers clutched at it, missed it, and it fluttered in a little curve under the table and fell in the black smudge on the floor from the man's wet rubbers.

With a dreamy grin Phil kept looking beyond the man's head, beyond all the tables as if he were sniffing the rich odors from the food counter. But his heart gave a couple of jerks. And he had such a marvelously bright picture of himself going into the laundry in the morning and getting the shirts and putting on the light-blue one with the fine white stripe that he had paid seven dollars for a year ago in Philadelphia.

But the drunk, having noticed him, was shaking his head at him. He was staring at Phil's battered felt hat and his old coat and his mussy shirt. He didn't like what he saw. It didn't help to make him feel secure and in full possession of himself. The dreamy look on Phil's face disgusted him.

"Hey, dreamy," he said, "what's eating you?"

"Me?"

"Yeah, you, dreamy."

"I wasn't looking at you. I'm making up my mind what I want."

"Excuse me, dreamy. Maybe you're right. I've been making mistakes all evening and I don't want to make any more," he said.

While he smiled at Phil a girl in a beige-colored coat spotted with raindrops and snow, a girl with untidy hair and with good legs and a pale face, came over and sat down at his table. An unpunched food check was in her hand. She put her elbows on the table and looked around as if she was waiting for someone. The dollar bill on the floor was about two feet away from her foot.

The drunk rose from the table with considerable dignity and began to glide across the floor toward the cashier, his check held out with dreadful earnestness, his roll of bills tight in the other hand now. When he had gone about twenty feet Phil glanced at the girl, their eyes met in a wary appraisal of each other. They looked steadily at each other, neither one moving. Her eyes were blue and unwavering, and then, in spite of herself, her glance shifted to the floor before she had time to move.

Phil lurched at the bill, one knee on the floor as he grabbed it, but she knew just where the bill was and her toe held it down with all her weight, unyielding as he tugged at it. While holding the bill he stared helplessly at her worn shoe that was wet, and then he looked at her ankle and the run in her stocking that went halfway up the calf of her leg. He knew she was bending down. Her face was close to his.

"I guess it's a saw-off," he said, looking up.

"Looks like it," she said. She smiled a little in a hard, unyielding way.

If she had taken her toe off the bill while they talked he mightn't have done the thing he did, but she made him feel she was only waiting for him to straighten up and be friendly to draw the bill closer to her; and the expectation of having the dollar and getting the shirt had given him quite a lift too, so he said, shrugging good-humoredly, "What do you think we should do?"

"What do you think yourself?"

"Tell you what I'll do," he said. "Figuring maybe we both saw it at the same time and that we both need it, how about if I toss you for it?"

She hesitated and said, "Seems fair enough, go ahead."

They both smiled as he took a nickel out from his vest pocket, and when she smiled like that he saw that she was quite young. There was a faint little bruise under her eye as though someone had hit her, but her face seemed to open out to him in spite of the pallor, the bruise and her untidy hair, and it was full of a sudden, wild breathless eagerness. "Heads I win, tails you win," he said, getting ready to toss the coin.

"Let it land on the table and don't touch it and let it roll," she said, nodding her head and leaning forward.

"Watch me, lady," he said, and he spun the coin beautifully and it rolled in a wide arc on the table around the little stand that held the sugar, mustard, vinegar, and horseradish. When it stopped spinning they leaned forward so quickly their heads almost bumped.

"Heads, eh? Heads," she said, but kept looking down at it as if she couldn't see it. She was contemplating something, something in her head that was dreadful, a question maybe that found an answer in the coin on the table. Her face was close to his, and there were tears in her eyes, but she turned away and said faintly, "Okay, pal. It's all yours."

She raised her foot and smiled a little while he bent down and picked up the bill.

"Thanks," he said. "Maybe you're lucky in love."

"Very likely. More power to you," she said, and she walked away and over to the cashier, where she handed in her unpunched food check.

He watched her raising the collar of her beige coat that was spotted from the rain and snow. A little bit of hair was caught and held outside the collar. While she was speaking to the cashier he was looking at the coin flat in the palm of his hand, looking at it and feeling dreadfully ashamed. He turned it over slowly and it was heads on both sides, the lucky phony coin he had found a few years ago. And then he could hardly see the coin in his hand: he could see nothing but the expression on her face as she watched it spinning on the table; he heard her sigh, as if all the hope she had ever had in her life was put on the coin; he remembered how she had stiffened and then smiled: he felt that somehow her whole fate had depended on her having the bill. She had been close to it, just close enough to be tantalized, and then he had cheated her.

She was going out, and he rushed after her, and saw her standing twenty feet away in the doorway of a cigar store. It was snowing again. She had walked through the snow; her bare shoes were carrying the snow as she stood there in the wet muddy entrance looking up and down the street. Before he could get near her she put her hands deep in her pockets and started to walk away rapidly with her head down.

"Just a minute, lady. Hey, what's the hurry?" he called.

Unsmiling and wondering she turned and waited. "What's the matter with you?" she said.

"Do me a good turn, will you?"

"Why should I?"

"Why not if it don't hurt?"

"That depends on what it is," she said.

"Take the buck, will you, that's all," he said.

She tried to figure him out a moment, then she said, "What is this, mister? You won it fair and square enough. Okay. Let it go at that." Her face looked much harder, suddenly much older than it had in the restaurant.

"No, I didn't win it on the level," he said. "Here, Miss, take it, please," and he reached out and held her arm, but she pulled away from him frowning. He grew flustered. "That was a phony coin I tossed, don't you see? I'll show it to you if you want to. You didn't have a chance."

"Then why with the big heart now?" she said.

"I don't know. I was watching you go out and I got a hunch it was worse for you than it was for me. You had a bigger stake in it . . . " He went on pleading with her earnestly.

Mystified, she said, "Look here, if you cheated me you cheated me and I might have known it would be phony anyway, but —"

"I thought I needed the buck badly, but I felt lousy watching you go out. I needed to get my laundry tomorrow. I need a clean shirt. That's what I was thinking watching the guy fingering the roll. And it was tough to see you come in on it. I didn't stop to think. I just went after it."

She was listening earnestly as if his remorse truly puzzled her, and then she put out her hand and gave him a pat on the arm that made him feel like they knew each other well and had been together all evening, and that she was very old and he a green kid.

"Listen, you figure a clean shirt will help you?" she said.

"I figured it would give me a head start that's all."

"Maybe it will. Go ahead. Get the shirt."

"No, please, you take it."

"A clean shirt won't help me, not the price of one," she said harshly. "So long," she said, with that bright, unyielding smile.

She walked away resolutely this time, as if she had made some final destructive decision, a decision she had dreaded and that she mightn't have made if he hadn't cheated her and she had got the dollar.

Worried, he went to run after her, but he stopped, startled and shaken, perceiving the truth as she had seen it, that the dollar in the long run was no good to her, that it would need some vast upheaval that shook the earth to really change the structure of her life. Yet she had been willing to stop and help him.

But the clean shirt became an absurd and trivial thing and the dollar felt unclean in his hand. He looked down the street at the tavern light. He had to get rid of the dollar or feel that he'd always see her walking away resolutely with her hands deep in her pockets.

It Must
Be Different

*S*ylvia Weeks and Max Porter had known each other five months, but she'd never taken him home to her place till that autumn evening when they had walked in the streets after the show, and the rain had begun to fall.

It had started when Max began suddenly to tell her that there was a real chance for him to get along in the radio business, and then her heart had begun to beat unevenly, for she became aware that he was getting ready to talk about wanting to marry her. He was so simple and honest about it that she became humble and shy, and they walked along silently, both anxious about what was to be said; and then the rain began to fall in large heavy drops. Ducking their heads, they ran along the street hand in hand and stood breathless on the stoop outside her place, watching the wet pavement shining under the street light.

Sylvia could not bear to let him go as he had gone on other nights; it was as though they had looked for each other for months, and had now met suddenly face to face. That magical feeling was still flowing between them, and she couldn't bear to let him go until all the necessary words had been said, or the things done that would hold them together forever.

"Come on in for a little while, Max," she said.

"Are you sure it'll be all right?"

"I think they'll be in bed," she said.

They laughed a little while she fumbled in her purse for her latchkey; then they tried to go in quietly. When they were in the hall, they heard someone coughing in the living room. Sylvia whispered uneasily: "I thought they'd be in bed."

"Maybe I'd better not come in," he said.

"Come on anyway," she said.

In the living room Sylvia's mother, a large woman with a face that had been quite pretty once, but which was now soft and heavy, was standing with an alarm clock in her hand. She was on her way to bed and she had been urging her husband, who still sat in the armchair in his shirtsleeves and suspenders reading the paper, to go along with her, so he would not disturb her later on. When Sylvia came in with Max following shyly, the mother was flustered and began to tidy her gray hair with her hand. "We were on our way to bed. We were just waiting for you, Sylvia," she said reproachfully.

"We wanted to walk after the show, Mother; but it rained. This is Max, Mother," Sylvia said.

"Oh, hello, Max. We've heard about you."

"If it's too late, I won't stay, Mrs. Weeks."

"So you're Max, eh?" the father said, getting up. He was a furniture maker who worked hard all day and who usually hurried out of the room when a visitor came in the evening; but now he stood staring at Max as if he had been wondering about him a long time.

Mrs. Weeks, looking at Sylvia, said: "You must have been having a good time, dear. You look happy and kind of excited."

"I'm not excited. I was just hurrying in the rain," Sylvia said.

"I guess it's just the rain and the hurrying that makes your eyes shine," the mother said; but the free ecstatic eagerness she saw in her daughter's face worried her, and her glance was troubled as she tried to make her husband notice that Sylvia's face glowed with some secret delight that had come out of being with this boy, who was a stranger and might not be trustworthy. Sylvia and Max were standing underneath the light, and Sylvia with her flushed cheeks and her dark head seemed more marvelously eager than ever before. It was easy for them to feel the restlessness and the flowing warmth in her, and the love she had been giving; and then the mother and father, looking at Max, who seemed very boyish with his rain-wet hair shining under the light, smiled a little, not wanting to be hostile, yet feeling sure that Sylvia and this boy had touched some new intimacy that night.

In a coaxing, worried voice Mrs. Weeks said: "Now don't stay up late, Sylvia darling, will you?" Again her husband's eyes met hers in that thoughtful, uneasy way; then they said pleasantly: "Good night, Max. We're glad to meet you. Good night, Sylvia." And then they went to bed.

When they had gone, Max said: "They certainly made that pretty clear, didn't they?"

"Made what clear?"

"That they wouldn't trust me alone with my grandmother."

"They didn't say anything at all, Max."

"Didn't you see how they stared at me? I'll bet they're listening now."

"Is that why you're whispering?"

"Sure. They expect us to whisper, don't they?"

They sat down on the couch, but they both felt that if they caressed each other, or became gentle and tender, they were only making a beginning at something that was expected of them by the mother and father going to bed in the next room. So they were awkward and uneasy with each other. They felt like strangers. When he put his arm on her shoulder, it lay there heavy, and they were silent, listening to the rain falling outside.

Then there was a sound in the hall, the sound of shuffling slippers, and when they looked up quickly, they saw a bit of her mother's dressing gown sweeping past the door. Then the slippers were still. In a little while there was a worried, hesitant shuffling; then they came back again past the door.

"Did you want something, Mother?" Sylvia asked.

"No, nothing," the mother said, looking in. She tried to smile, but she was a little ashamed, and she would not look directly at Sylvia.

"I couldn't get to sleep," she said.

"Aren't you feeling well?"

"I lie awake, you know. I hear every sound in here. I might just as well be in the room with you, I guess." Then, with a half-ashamed droop of her head, she shuffled away.

"Is she policing us?" Max asked irritably.

"I think she's just not feeling well." Sylvia said.

They both sat stiffly, listening, though she wanted to put her cheek down on Max's shoulder. In a little while they heard the murmur of voices in the bedroom; and Sylvia knew that her father and mother were lying awake worrying about her. Out of their own memories, out of everything that had happened to them, they felt sure they knew what would be happening to her. The murmuring voices rose a little; the sounds were short and sharp as the mother and father wrangled and worried and felt helpless. Sylvia, trying hard to recover those moments she had thought so beautiful, hurrying along the street with Max, knew that it was no use, and that they were gone, and she felt miserable.

"I think I'll get out," Max whispered.

"Please don't go now," she coaxed. "It's the first night we've felt like this. Please stay."

She wanted to soothe the anger and contempt out of him by rubbing her fingers through his hair; yet she only sat beside him stiffly, waiting, while the house grew silent, for warmth and eagerness to come again. It was so silent she thought she could hear the beating of his heart. She was ashamed to whisper. Max kept stirring uneasily, wanting to go.

Then they were startled by the father's voice calling roughly: "Sylvia!"

"What is it?" she said.

"What's keeping you there? Why are you so quiet? What are you doing?"

"Nothing."

"It's getting late," he called.

She knew her father must have tried hard to stop himself calling out like that; yet she felt so humiliated she could not look at Max.

"I'm getting out quick," Max said.

"All right. But it's nothing; he's just worrying," she pleaded.

"They've been lying in bed all the time listening."

"They're very fond of me," she said. "They'd do it, no matter what it was."

But hating the house and her people, he snapped at her, "Why don't they put a padlock on you?"

Then she felt that the feeling that had been so good between them, that she had tried to bring into the house and bring into her own life, could not last here, that his voice would never grow shy and hesitant as he fumbled for a few words here, that this was really what she was accustomed to and it was not good. She began to cry softly. "Don't be sore, Max," she said.

"I'm not sore at you."

"They felt pretty sure they know how it goes; that's all," she pleaded with him. "They think it'll have to go with me the way it went with them."

"That's pretty plain."

"I don't think either one of them want to see me get married. Nothing ever happened the right way for them. I can remember ever since I was a kid."

"Remember what?"

"They parted once, and even now when they get mad, they're suspicious of each other and wouldn't trust each other around the block. But that was years ago, really," she said, holding him tightly by the arm, and pleading that he understand the life in her home was not unhappy. "They're both very fond of me," she said apologetically. "They've had a tough time all their lives. We've been pretty poor, and — well — they worry about me, that's all."

Her eyes looked so scared that Max was afraid to question her, and they stood together thinking of the mother and father lying awake in the bedroom.

"I guess they feel that way about people, out of what's happened to them, eh?" he said.

"That's it."

"Their life doesn't have to be your life, does it?"

"It certainly doesn't," she said, and she was full of relief, for she knew by his face that the things she had blurted out hadn't disturbed him at all.

"I wrote my people about you," he said. "They want to see you. I sent them a snapshot."

"That was a very bad one; I look terrible in it."

"Can you get your holidays in August, Sylvia?"

"I think so. I'll ask a long time ahead."

"We'll go to the country and see my folks. I swear you'll like them," he said.

That moment at the door was the one fine free moment they had had since coming in, and it did not seem to belong to anything that had happened in the house that night. While they held each other whispering, "Good-bye, good-bye," they were sure they would always be gentle and faithful, and their life together would be good. Then they laughed softly, knowing they were sharing a secret contempt for the wisdom of her people.

Without waiting to hear the sound of his footfalls outside, she rushed resolutely to her parents' bedroom and turned on the light, and called sharply: "Mother."

But her mother and father, who were lying with their heads together on the pillow, did not stir, and Sylvia said savagely: "Wake up — do you hear? I was never so ashamed in my life."

One of her father's thin arms hung loose over the side of the bed, the wrinkled hand drooping from the wrist, and his shoulders were half uncovered. Her mother was breathing irregularly with her mouth open a little, as though her dreams too were troubled. They looked very tired, and Sylvia wavered.

Then her father stirred, and his blue eyes opened and blinked, and he mumbled sleepily: "Is that you, Sylvia?"

"Yes," she said.

"All right. Turn out the light," he said and he closed his eyes.

Yet she stood there, muttering to herself: "It's just that I don't want to get to feel the way you do about people."

Then she grew frightened, for the two faces on the pillow now seemed like the faces of two tired people who had worked hard all their lives, and had grown old together; and her own life had been simply a part of theirs, a part of whatever had happened to them. Still watching the two faces, she began to long with all her soul that her own love and her hope would be strong enough to resist the things that had happened to them. "It'll be different with me and Max. It must be different," she muttered.

But as she heard only their irregular breathing, her fright grew. The whole of her life ahead seemed to become uncertain, and her happiness with Max so terribly insecure.

POOLROOM

*H*ardly anyone was on the street, the afternoon sunlight was shining so steadily on the pavement and the air was heavy, sticky, and hot. Steve, carrying his coat in one hand and fanning himself with his hat, was going to the rooming house where Shorty Horne lived, to take a lesson on the banjo. He was going along slowly and lazily, feeling the hot sun burning his neck.

The front porch of the rooming house was badly in need of paint, and on such a dry afternoon it looked even worse with the blistering flakes of paint curling in the heat. Mrs. Scott, who had many roomers, was very clean and tidy inside the house, though she did not seem to care what her place looked like from the street. Shorty Horne had the small attic room, two flights up, with the small window over the front porch and another window looking out over a flat, graveled roof.

Steve, who had known Shorty three or four months, had met him one afternoon in Hudson's poolroom over the cafeteria downtown. Shorty was a small, old fellow, about fifty-five, with very heavy veins on his temples and thin hair he hardly ever bothered combing. His straggly moustache was the same color of his hair, only it was much thicker and stiffer, curling down over his lips, and when he had his hat on, the moustache made him look more vigorous and determined than he was. He always wore a hat with a wide brim. He used to come into the poolroom in the afternoon, look carefully at the men around the tables, and then sit down on one of the long benches by the wall, watching the fellows play while he slowly ate a bag of peanuts. Gradually a small space on the floor at his feet was covered with peanut shells, the sole of his shoe crunching the shells. Yet he was not really untidy, for when he had finished eating he bent down and laboriously scraped the shells into a small pile, got them all into the bag that had been in his pocket and threw it into the wastepaper basket. He used to do that nearly every day. If he hadn't known J.S. Hudson, the proprietor of the poolroom, a large-framed, casual yet formidable man, who stood around snapping his suspenders, he might not have been so clean, though he did seem to enjoy getting the shells into such a neat little pile on the floor. For years he had known Hudson, not intimately, but just as one man knows another from seeing him often and getting used to him. At times he had done a little work for Hudson at Hudson's home, and if the poolroom janitor needed temporary assistance they hired Shorty for a few hours.

Once, after playing a game of billiards, Steve had sat down on the bench beside Shorty, who had begun to make friendly conversation, offering polite criticism of certain shots. Though Shorty rarely played billiards he watched all the interesting shots very critically.

Steve found out that Shorty Horne had no money and no prospect of ever getting steady work. There seemed to be nothing for him to do but pass in and out of the poolroom very quietly without speaking to anyone. He acted like a man who was hiding from the police in a strange city. There was so little to know about him you couldn't help thinking he was deliberately withholding something. He couldn't work steadily because he suffered from some terrible kidney trouble. For two or three hours at a time he would be all right and very genial and happy, and then his insides would seem to get into knots as he bent down holding his sides with his elbows and gripping his hands tightly over his body. Around the poolroom they thought most of his time was spent enduring pain. There seemed to be nothing he could do for it. Steve wondered why he did not die, or why he did not long for death. Yet whenever it rained hard in the afternoons and Shorty couldn't walk from his rooming house to the poolroom where he could sit and talk cheerfully, he was miserable, for this routine seemed to give him happiness; he knew that a few of the steady customers at the poolroom, on the bad days when he did not appear, took it for granted that he had died or had killed himself. They liked him, but felt sorry when they saw him holding his sides. They knew he couldn't sleep at night.

He had casually asked Steve once if he could play the banjo and when Steve replied that he would like to be able to, Shorty had offered to teach him. Steve was surprised; no one thought of Shorty spending much time playing a banjo, and yet, as Steve found out when he went to visit him, that was the way he spent an hour of the early afternoon. He got up late, for it usually was hard for him to get to sleep, and when he had had some bran flakes, a little orange juice and a piece of dry toast, he sat for an hour by the window slowly strumming the banjo and looking out over the roof covered with gravel. He looked forward eagerly to having someone there with him and was delighted when Steve began to learn rapidly. The two of them took turns playing the banjo. Whatever pleasure they got out of each other's company had to be immediate and spontaneous, for Shorty would not talk about himself.

So, on this afternoon when Steve was going down the street to Shorty's rooming house, he was looking forward to a drowsy hour or two, sitting with his shirt off, feeling the faint breeze coming over the roof, cooling his bare shoulder while he strummed at the banjo.

Usually he rapped on the front door and spoke to Mrs. Scott, asking if Shorty were in, before he climbed the long flight of stairs, but today no one answered the door. Mrs. Scott had gone out. Steve went up the carpeted stairs, darkened, for there was no window, dark all the way up to the attic to the door of Shorty's room at the end of the hall. Usually Steve pushed open the door and stood there in the light from the window till Shorty told him to enter. But today, when he tried to open the door, it was locked. Irritated, he rapped and called, "Shorty!"

"Who's there?" Shorty answered.

"Steve."

He heard Shorty getting up and fumbling with the lock, then the door opened onto a kind of a twilight, for the blind, a green one, slit in many places and cracked, was down over the window, with the strong sunlight filtering in to the floor. Shorty, after letting Steve in, went back to the chair by the window. The banjo was leaning against the chair. Shorty was crouching down, his arms wrapped around his waist. Steve, glancing at him, thought he was having pains and wanted to rest.

"Do you mind if I pull up the blind, Shorty?"

"No, go ahead."

"Are you going out this afternoon, Shorty?"

"No."

"What's the matter?"

"Nothing, I just been thinking a bit, I guess. I been thinking. I mean I was downtown last night and saw a fellow. I think I'm going to get bumped off."

"Who'd bump a guy like you off?" Steve said, laughing out loud.

"A couple of hoods," Shorty answered.

"What for?"

"Squealing on them."

"When?"

"Oh, quite a while ago."

His lower lip was trembling. "It isn't that I'm afraid," he said apologetically. "Only I just can't stand the thought of really dying."

"If you don't mind me saying, Shorty, I don't think a guy who puts up with as much as you put up with ought to be much afraid of dying, even if you're not kidding me."

"No, I'm not kidding. I just mean that I'd like to go on living for a long time. I'd like to think about it that way." He spoke so casually and honestly, Steve felt ashamed of himself.

"Well, who are the guys you're afraid of?"

"I'm really not afraid of them, only I know what's going to happen. I guess it's coming to me."

"Who are they, unless you don't want to say?"

"I don't mind. You didn't use to hang around Hudson's poolroom in the old days about five years ago, did you? I don't remember you, anyway."

"No, didn't know the place at all."

"I used to hang around there then. I knew most everybody of a certain kind. It was just about the time I got real sick. If you don't mind me telling you, Steve, I used to pick a pocket now and then, and had a little more money. Hudson was slugged one night when he had a lot of money there, a couple of thousand, I think. I had a hunch who did it. And they were going to get caught for sure, and they came to me."

Steve pulled up the shade on the window. The strong light flooded the room, shining on the rug on the bare floor, on the banjo by the chair, on the iron bedstead painted white and chipping, on some dishes, a can and pail on an upturned box covered with a piece of tin used for a table; and it shone on Shorty, crouched down on the chair, his knees curled up a little, the heels caught on a rung. The toes of the shoes were turned far up. One of the shoes was laced with a piece of brown string.

"Maybe you don't want to fool around with the banjo today, Shorty."

"Oh, I'm feeling all right, Steve."

"Aren't the pains getting you?"

"No."

"Well, what's the matter with you, all hunched up?"

"I'll sit up," he said.

He sat up straight and asked Steve to hand him the banjo. Though he smiled a lot, he was obviously trying to be friendly while his thoughts were far away. The banjo did not interest him, though he strummed it idly, looking out over the graveled roof. At the end of the roof was a short wall of concrete on a brick foundation and behind that a higher wall of brick. The sun shining on the white surface of the concrete made it a heavy white streak against the pinkish light on the brick. In some places on the roof the light gravel had been worn away and the black tar could be seen melting in the heat. Steve, waiting for Shorty to speak, went on looking out the window till he noticed Shorty's eyes blinking. He saw his head perspiring, beads of moisture at the temples and on the heavy blue veins.

"Did your guts bother you as much then?"

"Sure, only it had just started. I couldn't work. That's why these guys came to me. They said they'd arranged to fix it so it would look as if I'd done the job. They knew they were going to get it. They offered me a thousand to go down, to take the rap, and said to a guy like me it would be just the same, and maybe better because they'd look after me in prison, and I said all right. A little later I squealed on them."

"Why did you do that, Shorty?"

"I got to thinking about Hudson. He was always kind of nice to me and I couldn't stand to have him thinking I had done it. I just hated to have him think I had slugged him. But it was mainly because I was sick and couldn't stand the thought of being shut away. So I told the two guys it was all off and I gave them back their money. They wouldn't take it. I tried to tell them money wasn't much good to me, and I wanted to keep on going down to the poolroom. Well, they slapped me a bit and said they had pinned it on me and I had to take the rap after taking the money. The trouble was, when I took the money, I didn't realize how much I liked the poolroom. But I knew all the time that they'd get me in the long run for squealing. I ought to have got out of the city, but what would I do if I left, the way I am? The poolroom was all I wanted. Where could I go?"

"But what's got into you now?"

"Those guys are out. I saw one downtown last night. He had been asking for me in the poolroom. He just smiled at me."

"If I felt like you do, Shorty, I'd tell the cops, and then get on my horse and beat it."

"I got no more chance than a rabbit. I haven't got much use for a squealer myself, I just seem to fit in around the poolroom. See?"

"Sure."

"Well, I figured the way he smiled at me they'd be around sometime today. I know they'll come."

"Is that why you had the door locked?"

"I suppose so. I was sitting here playing the banjo a bit, but it got so I just couldn't stand the notion of someone bumping me off, and I couldn't stop thinking about dying. I hate thinking about dying and I can't help it, it kinda fascinates me."

He picked up the banjo again and looked out the window. His head was sweating. Shorty twanged the strings slowly, three times. "Don't do that," Steve said suddenly, getting up and feeling scared. "I'll stay here with you, Shorty," he said.

"If you don't mind, I'm not gonna give you a lesson today," Shorty said. His blue eyes were wide open.

"Don't you want me to stay?"

"I'd rather be alone."

"I'll come and see you later, then."

"All right."

"There's nothing you want me to do?"

"No, thanks. Nothing."

"I'll get going, then."

Steve went out, leaving Shorty sitting on the chair, the banjo on his knees, his face turned to the window and his teeth biting into his lower lip. The sun was shining full on his small, round wrinkled face. As Steve went downstairs he heard faintly the twanging of the banjo. He walked along the street as far as the corner, then turned and walked back to the house, looking up at the front window. The blind was down. Then, because he was uneasy in his own mind, he went up to the house and sat down on the veranda. Shorty was upstairs waiting, and Steve, wondering how such a sick man could be so eager to go on living, felt young and a little ashamed. Alert, he looked at every passerby, expecting always to see men coming down the street to the house and hear them ask for Shorty Horne. The men, he thought would be well dressed, only they would wear gold bracelets. Steve was trying to think of something very comforting he could say to Shorty. Across the road, down about half a block, was a schoolyard, half the yard cinders and cement, and only a small stretch of green lawn. A bell sounded in the school. Within a few seconds kids came out the wide doors, little girls in light dresses, who did not remain long on the hot cement but ran yelling to the green lawn to play a while before going out the gate.

An automobile stopped opposite the house. A woman was driving the car. Sitting beside her was a young man who talked intimately, leaning toward her, holding her by the arm and refusing to let her get out of the car. Suddenly they both began to laugh out loud, leaning back in the seat.

Though it was late afternoon, hardly anyone came down the street, for the sky was still cloudless and the pavement was hot. Steve sat on the veranda for over an hour. He would not go home and leave Shorty alone in the house.

Then he saw Mrs. Scott coming down the street, a large, ample woman wearing a light blouse and a blue skirt, and carrying a heavy shopping bag. She was leaning forward. From some distance away she began to smile at Steve. He said to her: "I'm going up to see Mr. Horne. He was lying down a while ago resting. I'll go up and see him soon now."

"The poor man!" she said, wiping the moisture off her large red face. "I don't see how he can go on living in weather like this."

"It's rotten weather for anybody," Steve said.

"I don't know how he can stand it at all," she said, shaking her head and drawing in a deep breath before going into the house. "It just burns me to a frazzle."

Steve remained on the veranda twenty minutes longer. Before going he intended to speak to Shorty and then speak to Mrs. Scott, but the woman herself came to the door, breathing heavily after coming downstairs, and said to him: "Steve, would you do something for me? I rapped on Mr. Horne's door and couldn't get an answer. The door's locked."

"What do you want me to do?"

"Please open the door for me," she said nervously.

Steve went ahead of her up the stairs. As they got closer to the attic the air seemed to be mustier, as it was in all the old rooming houses. He tried the door and called out, but Shorty did not answer. Mrs. Scott was standing behind him, her hands up to her face. Finally Steve swung his shoulder against the door, which opened easily. The room was darkened with the blinds down again. The odor of escaping gas made Steve cough and cover his nose with his handkerchief as he hurried to throw up the window and turn off the gas jet.

Shorty was lying on the floor, his knees curled up, his elbows in at his sides, his head toward the window. He had fallen off the bed. A strip of toweling had blocked the open space between the door and the floor. Shorty's hands were cold. The tin can that had been on his table had fallen to the floor beside him. The banjo was at the foot of the bed.

Mrs. Scott, who had run downstairs when she smelled the gas, came into the room slowly, still holding her hands up to her face. "I knew something like this would happen sometime," she said. "The poor fellow, he was so sick, I knew he'd do it."

Steve looked at her and shook his head.

"What'll I do?" Mrs. Scott said.

"You'd better call the police," Steve answered. He was going downstairs. He wanted to get out to the sunlight. He didn't want to be mixed up in the affair at all.

THE BACHELOR'S DILEMMA

*T*he night before Christmas Harry Holmes, the plump young executive with the bow tie, came home to his bachelor apartment near the university and found the janitor had put a turkey on the kitchen table. It was a fine big bird weighing twenty-two pounds, far too big for his small refrigerator and tied to the leg was a note from the manager of his favorite restaurant congratulating him on winning their turkey raffle. Wondering when he had taken the ticket, he thought, "Well. The devil must look after his own," and he telephoned his brother's wife who had invited him for dinner on Christmas Day. "This year, for a change, I'll provide the turkey," he said, feeling exuberant. "I've got it right here."

"Oh, Harry, that's a shame," she said. "We've got a turkey big enough for three days. It's in the fridge." There was no room for his turkey and so she had to disappoint him.

Soon he was smiling and indulging himself, anticipating the pleasure he would get giving the turkey to Tom Hill, his underpaid assistant who had just got married. Then he talked on the telephone to Tom, who had to explain his wife had bought a turkey that afternoon, and he was so apologetic and embarrassed Harry thought, "You'd think I was trying to get him to do something for me," and he felt amused.

He called three old friends. Two were out of town for the holiday; the other had won a turkey in a bowling alley. Then he remembered that two other friends whom he admired, sports columnists on the local newspapers, were accustomed to foregathering at this hour in a café on Bloor Street. With the turkey in his arms he took a taxi to the café, grinned jovially at the hatcheck girl who asked him to check the turkey, strode past her to the familiar corner table, laid the turkey before his astonished friends and invited them to toss for it. One telephoned his wife, the other his sister. Both had turkeys and crowded refrigerators. The hostile waiter glared at the turkey lying on the table. And Harry's friends began to make jokes. "I'm afraid," one said, teasing Harry and pretending to be in the theatrical business, "we have a turkey on our hands." It was all very jolly, and he laughed too, but the fact was they didn't appreciate that he had thought of them, and he had to pick up his turkey and go home.

In his kitchen, standing beside the turkey, he felt irritated; it was as if his brother's wife and Tom and all his friends had joined together to deny him the satisfaction of pleasing them with a gift. And as he looked out the window at the lighted houses of his city of a million souls he suddenly felt discontented with his life which had been going so smoothly until he had to get a turkey cooked. "There's something the matter with the world when you can't give a turkey to anyone who knows you," he thought. "To the devil with it."

Then he tried to sell the turkey to the restaurant but the manager refused to buy back a turkey he had given away. "Why don't you try the butcher?" he asked.

A butcher store a few blocks away on Harbord was still open, but the bald-headed butcher, pointing to his turkey-filled window, said, "Look what I have left, mister! I'll sell *you* one at half price." On the way home the big turkey seemed to take on weight, Harry's arms ached, and he was glad when he dumped it on the kitchen table. Exhausted, he lay down and fell asleep.

At the Christmas dinner at his brother's place, they were surprised to hear his turkey was still on his kitchen table, and he wondered why he felt ashamed. When he got home in the evening he stared uneasily at the naked bird. "It'll go bad," he thought and he sniffed. Picking it up he went out and began to cross Queen's Park. It had begun to snow. Wet dead leaves in the melting snow glistened under the park lights. Shifting the turkey from one arm to the other, he headed for a church along a side street. There he asked the white-haired man who answered the door, "Do you know anyone who would like a Christmas turkey?" He added apologetically, "It's late, I know."

"It's never too late my son," the old man said. "I know a hundred poor families in the neighborhood who'll appreciate a turkey. Won't you give me your name?"

"It doesn't matter," Harry said awkwardly. And as soon as he felt the weight of the turkey being lifted off his arms he understood why he had felt ashamed at his brother's place. He hadn't been looking for someone who would appreciate a turkey. He had been looking for someone who would appreciate him.

GETTING ON IN THE WORLD

———◁◇▷———

T hat night in the tavern of the Clairmont Hotel, Henry Forbes was working at his piano and there was the usual good crowd of brokers and politicians and sporting men sitting drinking with their well-dressed women. A tall, good-natured man in the bond business, and his girl had just come up to the little green piano, and Henry let them amuse themselves playing a few tunes, and then he sat down again and ran his hand the length of the keyboard. When he looked up a girl was leaning on the piano and beaming at him.

She was about eighteen and tall and wearing a black dress and a little black hat with a veil, and when she moved around to speak to him he saw that she had swell legs and an eager, straightforward manner.

"I'm Tommy Gorman's sister."

"Why say . . . you're . . . "

"Sure, I'm Jean," she said.

"Where did you come from?"

"Back home in Buffalo," she said. "Tommy told me to be sure and look you up first thing."

Tommy Gorman used to come into the tavern almost every night to see him before he got consumption and had

· 105 ·

to go home. So it did not seem so surprising to see his sister standing there instead. He got her a chair and let her sit beside him. In no time he saw that Tommy must have made him out to be a glamorous figure. She understood that he knew everybody in town, that big sporting men like Jake Solloway often gave him tips on the horses, and that a man like Eddie Convey, who ran city hall and was one of the hotel owners, too, called him by his first name. In fact, Tommy had told her that playing the piano wasn't much, but that bumping into big people every night, he was apt to make a connection at any time and get a political job, or something in a stockbroker's office.

She seemed to join herself to him at once; her eyes were glowing, and as she swung her head looking at important clients, he couldn't bear to tell her that the management had decided the piano wouldn't be necessary any more, he might not be there more than two weeks.

He sat pointing out people she might have read about in the newspapers. It all came out as if each was an old friend, yet he actually felt lonely each time he named somebody. "That's Thompson over there with the horn-rimmed glasses. He's the mayor's secretary," he said. "That's Bill. Bill Henry over there. You know, the producer. Swell guy, Bill." Then he rose up in his chair. "Say, look, there's Eddie Convey," he said. As he pointed he got excited, for the big, fresh-faced, hawk-nosed Irishman with the protruding blue eyes and the big belly had seen him pointing. He was grinning. Then he raised his right hand a little.

"Is he a friend of yours?" Jean asked.

"Sure he is. Didn't you see for yourself?" he said. But it was the first time Eddie Convey had ever gone out of his way to notice him. He started chattering breathlessly about Convey, thinking all the time, beneath his chatter, that if he could go to Convey and get one little word from him, and if something bigger couldn't be found for him he at least could keep his job.

He became so voluble and excited that he didn't notice how delighted she was with him till it was time to take her home. She was living uptown in a rooming house where there were a lot of theatrical people. When they were sitting on the stone step a minute before she went in she told him that she had enough money saved up to last her about a month. She wanted to get a job modeling in a department store. Then he put his arm around her and there was a soft glowing wonder in her face.

"It seems like I've known you for years," she said.

"I guess that's because we both know Tommy."

"Oh, no," she said. Then she let him kiss her hard. And as she ran into the house she called that she'd be around to the tavern again.

It was as if she had been dreaming about him without ever having seen him. She had come running to him with her arms wide open. "I guess she's about the softest touch that's come my way," he thought, going down the street. But it looked too easy. It didn't require any ambition, and he was a little ashamed of the sudden, weakening tenderness he felt for her.

She kept coming around every night after that and sat there while he played the piano and sometimes sang a song. When he was through for the night, it didn't matter to her whether they went any place in particular, so he would take her home. Then they got into the habit of going to his room for a while. As he watched her fussing around, straightening the room up or maybe making a cup of coffee, he often felt like asking her what made her think she could come bouncing into town and fit into his life. But when she was listening eagerly, and kept sucking in her lower lip and smiling slowly, he felt indulgent with her. He felt she wanted to hang around because she was impressed with him.

It was the same when she was sitting in the tavern. She used to show such enthusiasm that it became embarrassing. Henry liked a girl to look like some of the smart blondes who had a lazy, half-mocking aloofness. With Jean talking and showing all her straightforward warm eagerness, people turned and looked at her as if they'd like to reach out their hands and touch her. It made Henry feel that they looked like a couple of kids on a merry-go-round.

A crowd from the theater came in, and Henry was feeling blue. Then he saw Eddie Convey and two middle-aged men who looked like brokers sitting at a table in the corner. When Convey seemed to smile at him, he thought bitterly that when he lost his job people like Convey wouldn't even know him on the street. Convey was still smiling, and then he actually beckoned.

"Gees, is he calling me?" he whispered.

"Who?" Jean asked.

"The big guy, Convey." He waited till Convey called a second time. Then he got up nervously and went over to him. "Yes, Mr. Convey," he said.

"Sit down, son," Convey said. His face was full of expansive indulgence as he looked at Henry and asked, "How are you doing around here?"

"Things don't exactly look good," he said. "Maybe I won't be around here much longer."

"Oh, stop worrying, son. Maybe we'll be able to fix you up."

"Thanks, Mr. Convey." It was all so sudden and exciting that Henry kept on bobbing his head, "Yes, Mr. Convey."

"How about the kid over there," Convey said, nodding toward Jean. "Isn't it a little lonely for her sitting around?"

"Well, she seems to like it, Mr. Convey."

"She's a nice-looking kid. Sort of fresh and — well . . . huh, fresh, that's it." They both turned and looked over at Jean, who was watching them, her face excited and wondering.

"Maybe she'd like to go to a party at my place," Convey said.

"I'll ask her, Mr. Convey."

"Why don't you tell her to come along, see. You know, the Plaza, in about an hour. I'll be looking for her."

"Sure, Mr. Convey," he said. He was astonished that Convey wanted him to do something for him. "It's a pleasure," he wanted to say. But for some reason it didn't come out.

"Okay," Convey said, and turned away, and Henry went back to his chair at the piano.

"What are you so excited about?" Jean asked him.

His eyes were shining as he looked at her little black hat and the way she held her head to one side as if she had just heard something exhilarating. He was trying to see what it was in her that had suddenly made Convey notice her. "Can you beat it!" he blurted out. "He wants you to go up to a party at his place."

"Me?"

"Yeah, you."

"What about you?"

"He knows I've got to stick around, and, besides, there may be a lot of important people there, and there's always room at Convey's parties for a couple of more girls."

"I'd rather stay here with you," she said.

Then they stop whispering because Convey was going out, the light catching his bald spot.

"You got to do things like that," Henry coaxed her.

She let him go on telling her how important Convey was and when he had finished, she asked, "Why do I have to? Why can't we just go over to your place?"

"I didn't want you to know, but it look's like I'm through around here. Unless Convey or somebody like that steps in, I'm washed up," he said. He took another ten minutes telling her all the things Convey could do for people.

"All right," she said. "If you think we have to." But she seemed to be deeply troubled. She waited while he went over to the headwaiter and told him he'd be gone for about an hour, and then they went out and got a cab. On the way up to Convey's place she kept quiet, with the same troubled look on her face. When they got to the apartment house and they were standing on the pavement, she turned to him. "Henry, I don't want to go up there."

"It's just a little thing. It's just a party," he said.

"All right. If you say so, okay," she said. Then she suddenly threw her arms around him. He found himself hugging her tight too. "I love you," she said. "I knew I was going to love you when I came." Her cheek, brushing against his, felt wet. Then she broke away.

As he watched her running in past the doorman that embarrassing tenderness he had felt on other nights touched him again, only it didn't flow softly by him this time. It came like a swift stab.

In the tavern he sat looking at the piano, and his heart began to ache, and he turned around and looked at the well-fed men and their women and he heard their deep-toned voices and their lazy laughter and he suddenly felt corrupt. Never in his life had he had such a feeling. He kept listening and looking into familiar faces and he began to hate them as if they were to blame for blinding him to what was so beautiful and willing in Jean. He got his hat and went out and started to walk up to Convey's.

Over and over he told himself he would go right to Convey's door and ask for her. But when he got to the apartment house and was looking up at the patches of light, he felt timid. He didn't even know which window, which room was Convey's. She seemed lost to him. So he walked up and down past the doorman, telling himself she would soon come running out and throw her arms around him when she found him waiting.

It got very late. Hardly anyone came from the entrance. The doorman quit for the night. Henry ran out of cigarettes, but he was scared to leave the entrance. Then the two broker friends of Convey's came out, with two loud-talking girls, and they called a cab and all got in and went away. "She's staying. She's letting him keep her up there." He was so sore at her that he exhausted himself, and then felt weak and wanted to sit down.

When he saw her coming out, it was nearly four o'clock in the morning. He had walked about ten paces away, and turned, and there she was on the pavement, looking back at the building.

"Jean," he called, and he rushed at her. When she turned, and he saw that she didn't look a bit worried, but blooming, lazy, and proud, he wanted to grab her and shake her.

"I've been here for hours," he said. "What were you doing up there? Everybody else has gone home."

"Have they?" she said.

"So you stayed up there with him!" he shouted. "Like a tramp."

She swung her hand and smacked him on the face. Then she took a step back, appraising him contemptuously. She suddenly laughed. "Back to your piano," she said.

"All right, all right, you wait, I'll show you," he muttered. He stood watching her go down the street with a slow, self-satisfied sway of her body.

THE NOVICE

The novices used to walk by the high brick wall dividing Dr. Stanton's property from the convent garden and whisper that soon the Mother Superior's prayers would be answered and the doctor would sell his house to her. For five years the Mother Superior had been trying to buy it from the bigoted old man, to use it as a residence.

The Mistress of novices had asked them to pray that the doctor, who had declared his old home would never be part of such an institution, might be persuaded to change his mind. The Mistress pointed out that God was often more willing to grant favors when the prayers came from fresh eager young souls. Sister Mary Rose, who had been a novice for four weeks, and who was determined to endure all the hardships till she one day became a nun, listened to the Mistress telling how she might help the convent. Sister Mary Rose was a well-built slender girl with a round smooth face who looked charming in the habit with the little black cape. She was suffering none of the pains and troubles of some of the novices; the plain food was almost tasteless at first but she ate hungrily; she got to like immensely the well-buttered slice of bread they had at collation hour in the morning; her body ached at first from the hard bed but, to herself, she insisted she did not feel the pains, enduring this small discomfort much more readily than Sister Perpetua, who secretly stretched her pillow out lengthwise every night so her shoulder blades and hips would be well protected. Already two or three of the novices who had sharp pains in the back, or who had lost all appetite, were taking it as a sign that they really did not have a vocation and were wondering how much longer they would stay at the convent. Because she had such very good health, Sister Mary Rose hoped she might be an instrument of great blessing to the convent.

In her nightly prayers she made it a secret between herself and God that she was the one novice who was most anxious that Doctor Stanton might sell his fine house to the convent. She prayed for almost an hour, kneeling on the floor in her long nightgown, her bare heels just touching, her eyes turned toward the long narrow window looking out over the brick wall into Doctor Stanton's garden while the moonlight slanted down over her shoulders. At this time, she was convinced that her prayers would be heeded more readily if she followed the precepts of St. Theresa and tried to live the life the Little Flower lived when she had been a novice. But she didn't ask that a shower of roses fall from heaven; she asked only that Doctor Stanton might sell his house to the convent.

For many days, she prayed and fasted and was as much as possible like a little child and nearly always in a state of grace. When one of her relatives sent her a box of candies she at once gave it to the Mistress of the novices and would not take one for herself. But she got a little thinner. She was pale and her eyes were too big for her face, which was hardly round now. Then at midnight, when she was sitting in her stall in the choir, she fell forward on the floor, fainting.

The Mistress, an elderly, severely kind, practical woman with a finely wrinkled face said, as she rubbed her wrists, "Sister Mary Rose, you haven't been eating."

"I'm sorry," she said, still feeling dizzy, "I've been fasting to receive a favor." She sat awkwardly in her straight-backed stall.

The Mistress praised her admirable sincerity but explained it was not good for a novice to be too severe with herself. Sister Mary Rose, still weak and trembling, almost told her why she was fasting, but then, shaking her head twice, she determined to keep it a secret between herself and God.

As soon as she was alone, she wondered if she might possibly be more effective following some other precept. After all, she was concerning herself with a very material affair, a transaction in property, and she wondered if the Spanish St. Teresa, a more worldly and practical woman, who, too, had been a nun, wouldn't be more likely to assist her than little Theresa of Lisieux. So she began to think of talking, herself, to Doctor Stanton and had a kind of a vision of herself easily persuading the old man to be sensible about a business matter, and then modestly and shyly explaining to the joyful Mother Superior that she had only been an instrument because she so dearly loved the convent. But she heard that the doctor was sick, and anyway, he was supposed to be a harsh, domineering man.

At the recreation hour one day she was walking by the high brick wall, past the statue of the Virgin. Some of the novices were playing catch with a tennis ball. Sister Magdalene of the Cross was tossing the ball to Sister Dolorosa, who turned and tossed it to Sister Mary Rose. It was in the forenoon before the sun began to shine too strongly and the three novices kept on tossing the ball to each other, laughing gleefully whenever one of them missed it, finding extraordinary delight whenever one had to assume a quaint or awkward posture. The Mistress encouraged them to do that; laugh readily and joyfully, for they had their long periods of silence which often left some of them moody and depressed. They were tossing the ball wildly and Sister Magdalene of the Cross, the plump girl, tossed it far over Sister Mary Rose's head, over the brick wall into Doctor Stanton's garden.

The three young novices remained absolutely silent, looking at each other. Then, the ball came in an arc back over the wall again. Sister Mary Rose knew that the gardener, a man with a long brown moustache, who limped, and whom she had often seen from the window, bending down over Dr. Stanton's flower beds, had returned it. At that moment, she got the idea she afterwards attributed to the goodness of her Spanish St. Teresa. She walked off by herself and would not catch the ball when it was thrown to her. It bounced away into the flowerbeds and Sister Dolorosa had to go and get it.

Alone in her bedroom, she looked out the window at the doctor's garden and saw the gardener bending over a flower bed, holding a rake upright with one hand, the other patting the earth at the base of a flower stem. The sun was shining brilliantly through the narrow window. The gardener was close to the iron fence between the street and the garden. Sister Mary Rose detached slowly from her neck a sacred medal and holding it in both hands closed her eyes, telling herself that if she carried out her plan she would be both deceitful and disobedient, but her excitement and determination only got stronger. So she assured herself earnestly, while holding the medal tightly, that her notion might be the cause of so much goodness the extent of her disobedience would be trifling compared with it. Then she said a long prayer, asking for St. Teresa's help, and urging her to be an advocate for her, in case her trifling disobedience should be misunderstood.

She asked permission to visit an aunt who lived in the city. Since she rarely asked for any kind of a favor, she readily received permission. She was told that Sister Magdalene of the Cross would go with her, for neither a novice nor a nun ever went any place alone outside the convent.

The afternoon she was to go out she first of all looked nervously from the window into Dr. Stanton's garden and sighed thankfully when she saw the gardener picking weeds by the fence. It was entirely necessary, if she was to be successful at all, that the gardener should be somewhere close to the street fence.

Trembling and pale, but filled with an exhilarating excitement, Sister Mary Rose walked out sedately with Sister Magdalene of the Cross who was prattling gaily, glad of the opportunity to be walking in the city streets. They had come out the main entrance, down the steps, and were past the convent, almost to the iron fence, walking demurely, their hands folded under their little black capes, their eyes turned down to the sidewalk.

The gardener did not even glance up at them as they passed. He was bending down, his back to the fence. He had on blue overalls and suspenders over a gray shirt. They were ten feet past him when Sister Mary Rose said suddenly to Sister Magdalene of the Cross, "Please, just a second, I want to ask the gardener if he found a tennis ball I lost the other day."

"Oh, you shouldn't do that."

"Please, just a minute."

"But somebody will see you from the window."

Sister Mary Rose turned and before the startled girl could detain her, left her abruptly and walked over to the fence. The gardener, hearing her, straightened up, surprised, and said, "Good afternoon, Sister."

"Good afternoon," she said timidly, hardly above a whisper, "How is the doctor?"

"Poorly, Sister, very poorly."

"Would you do something for me," she said shyly, smiling nervously. "I mean . . . Are you a Catholic?"

"No, Miss. I'm sorry though." She looked sweetly pretty with her round smooth face and her blue eyes and little black cape.

"But just the same you're a Christian, I'm sure of that," she said.

"Oh, I guess I can say that all right," he said, smiling apologetically.

"Will you take this?" she said cautiously, handing him her sacred medal, her back hiding it from Sister Magdalene of the Cross.

"What'll I do with it, Sister?"

"Please bury it in the garden there. Please promise me." Her cheeks began to flush a little.

"It'll be a pleasure to do it for you if it'll amuse you," he said, smiling.

"Oh, thank you very much," she said, smiling and flustered, turning away quickly. "I'll say a prayer for you."

Sister Magdalene of the Cross, who had become impatient and a little offended, said, "What on earth were you talking about?"

"He was saying he'd look especially for the ball, that's all. To be polite I asked him about the doctor."

"The doctor isn't a good man, and anyway, you know I'll have to tell Mistress."

"Please, please promise me you won't tell Mistress."

"But I ought to. That's what I'm here for."

"Please promise, little sister."

"All right," the good natured girl said reluctantly. "I'll promise."

They went on talking seriously as they walked along the sidewalk, their heads held at the same angle, their hands hidden, their long black skirts swinging easily.

A week and a half later, Doctor Stanton died. He was an old man and it was inevitable. The executors of his estate wished to dispose of his property quickly and the convent made much the most attractive offer. So they were assured of getting the property.

Sister Mary Rose was ecstatically happy when she heard the convent would get the fine old house, and she was not bothered by the doctor's death. At first she prayed fervently, thanking St. Teresa for interceding and obtaining her favor. She could hardly resist telling the other novices about her special prayers and how she had persuaded the gardener to bury the sacred medal in the doctor's yard. She suffered the ecstasy of feeling she had been an instrument, but dared not tell the Mistress about it because she had been both sly and disobedient.

It occurred to her at collation hour, when eating a thickly buttered slice of bread, that she might, in a way, have been responsible for the doctor's death by wishing for it. Though she hadn't actually wished the death, it amounted to the same thing. When she first had this thought she said, as she was sure her strong St. Teresa would have, that the good of the whole convent was more important than the life of one man. But suddenly she felt weak and left the other novices, and went up to the bedroom, depressed and disturbed, wondering about her guilt or innocence.

All night she lay awake, tossing on her hard bed, rubbing her shoulders and elbows on the board till they were scraped and sore. She was wondering whether this feeling of depression and sorrow wasn't an intimation that she really had no vocation and ought to leave the convent, as two of the novices were doing at the end of the week. It was plainly her duty in this first period of her novitiate to be watchful of every circumstance indicating that she really did not have a vocation. First, she thought miserably she ought to leave the convent at the end of the week because she was a deceitful worldly woman interested only in material affairs. Then she thought uneasily just before she went to sleep that perhaps, if she waited a week, she might become reconciled to her own conscience, and then no one need ever know.

THE TWO BROTHERS

As she came along the lane in the dusk the little wind from the lake blew her thin dress against her body, and there was still enough light to show the eagerness that was in her face. She came up to the fence where he was leaning so dejectedly, and never before had he felt so sure that she wanted to be with him.

"You're early tonight, Peg," he said.

"I knew you'd be waiting here, Tom. I tried to finish the work early. I was restless. I thought we might walk." Her voice was very soft in her eagerness to soothe him. Tonight she had made herself look more lovely than ever so that when he saw her he would think only of how much he liked her thick, light hair, her full mouth and the curve of her breast. Walking along in the dusk on the dirt road running up from the lake they had never felt so close together. They liked this new warmth of feeling between them. They were quiet, listening to the crickets in the grass. They watched the darker shapes of cows moving lazily in the pasture land, and they knew they were having the same thoughts: they were thinking of yesterday in town, and of the courthouse and of his brother Frank: they were thinking of the last thing

Frank did after the white-haired judge, talking in a measured monotone, had sentenced him to a year and a half in jail for a drunken murderous assault on an officer. Frank had turned, smiling reassuredly at the crowd; and standing there in front of the big window that looked out over the lake he was young, dark and very splendid. Through the window behind him they could see the sweep of the blue lake with the sun on it and the thick bank of clouds overhead. When Tom and Peg went up to shake hands sorrowfully, Frank had said, teasing them, "You'd better marry Peg in a hurry, Tom, because I'll be seeing you both shortly." He was absolutely without shame, and was led away laughing.

As they walked along silently Peg wanted to show Tom all the sympathy she felt for him. She knew that young Frank had always spent most of his time in town with the girls while Tom worked hard on the farm and worried about what his brother might do, with his wild way; Tom had carried around year after year a knowledge in his heart of something fearful impending. Peg could not bear to have Tom walking beside her with such dark, sad thoughts of his brother, and she said, "I know you'll miss him. But a year and a half goes quickly, Tom."

"It's what it may do to him I'm thinking of," he said. "We were always together. You get used to being together no matter what happens." He was ashamed of the way his words were breaking. "I mean it doesn't matter really what he did. We've been a long time together, that's all."

"I've been wondering all the time what he meant when he said, 'I'll be seeing you both shortly.' What did he mean?"

"I don't know," he said uneasily.

"You don't think he'd try to get away?"

"Maybe he'd be just that crazy. It's bad enough now and it would be worse for everybody then with everybody chasing him. Please Peg, let's stop talking about him all my life. I want to stop." His words came from him in such an agitated manner that she was afraid, and she was silent for a while, pondering, and then she brushed close against him, patting his arm, stirring him so he would think only of her.

His troubled thoughts made his thin face haggard and she longed to comfort him and show him plainly that there was a depth of love in her for him that he had never known. She said simply, "Let's go over there by the old elm and sit down."

Leaving the road he helped her over the wire fence, and when they sat in the thick grass by the tree the moon shone out on the fields and there were hardly any sounds. Tom began to think that the silence and the peace between them was beautiful. Peg, who was lying full length on the grass, was looking up at the sky with an expression of tender sadness on her face, content to be there with him. As he stared down at her so solemnly he marveled that she could have such a simple peace. After a long time he touched her thick hair timidly with his hand, brushing it back from her temple, and then he looked away over the field. "Look at the moonlight on the buckwheat, Peg," he said. They both looked over there at the buckwheat, which in daytime in July was like a field of separate white flowers; now with the moonlight flooding it, it glistened like a field of bright snow in the sunlight, but so much softer, more like a bank of light just on the other side of the road. They were both full of wonder and in Tom there was an unexpected elation. "Isn't it beautiful," he heard her saying, and then her head was sinking back and she lay with the same light shining on her face, only there was a marvelous softness and willingness in it that he had never seen before. For two years he had been wanting her for his girl, but he had always been afraid that she would never in any way show that she completely accepted him: it had been hard for him to believe that she would ever want to marry him. Yet now she was smiling up at his sober face, glad of what was so surely in him. With his heart beating heavily he bent down and kissed her, feeling her hands holding his head tenderly as she drew his face close to her. Never in his life, which had been full of hard work and laconic ways, had he felt such happiness. But he did not know what to do, he was so afraid that she might move, or that something would happen to spoil it. There was such a little shadow on her eyelids. Then her eyes were open, watching him, and she waited. After a time the clouds, which were getting thicker, obscured the light.

The fields were stirred by a strengthening wind from the lake. There was no longer a bank of light on the field of buckwheat.

"It's going to rain," she said.

"I don't think it's going to rain."

"Yes, it is. We'd better go," she said, and she got up reluctantly. As they walked along the road she was swinging her body a bit and humming. She had picked up a blade of grass and kept holding the stem to her lip.

"Would you love me, Peg? Would you love me always?" he asked.

"It's never seemed like this before, has it, Tom?"

"What does it make you feel like?"

"Just glad."

He didn't know how to answer he was so excited, and they walked along the lane under the great elms with the leaves rustling loudly to the gate, hanging on one hinge, and there she said, "Good night, Tom. It was lovely." She was very quiet, almost grave now.

As he went away he felt like a happy excited child, he was so lucky. "She would have loved me very much tonight," he thought.

At the orchard he climbed the fence, and when he was passing under the apple trees and hearing the horses moving in the stalls in the barn, he began to think, "Her father'll be in bed. She wanted more love than she got from me tonight. She'll still be wanting, maybe."

For half an hour as he did whatever chores he had to do before going to bed he kept thinking of her being really alone in the house, unsatisfied with the little love he had offered. The eagerness to go back to her became too strong to resist.

Hurrying along the lane he saw that there was no light upstairs where her father slept, just the one light downstairs where he was sure she waited. Tiptoeing to the door, he whistled softly, a signal, though he had never whistled for her before. The wind was blowing strongly from the lake now, blowing his hair back from his head, and he felt weak thinking what he might do. He tapped lightly on the door. When there was no answer he pushed the door open and looked in the big room. Near the window was a black leather couch and she was lying on the couch with her face pressed down against the leather. "Peg," he whispered. "Peg." She raised her head slowly and he saw that her face was sad and troubled, and though she was trying to smile, her eyes were wet.

"What's the matter, Peg?"

"Nothing."

"Why are you crying?"

"I wasn't really crying," she said. She saw how disappointed he was, she felt that he had expected to find her still full of gladness, and she tried to explain. "I was sitting here thinking of the two of us and how everything might be. Then I was thinking just of you because I knew how bad you were feeling over Frank. I felt blue because it all seems to go against you. I was feeling sorry for Frank too."

"Why were you thinking of him now?" he asked irritably. "Why do we always have to think of him?"

"It just seemed a shame. He looked like a fine fellow standing there yesterday."

"You often think of Frank?"

"No I don't, but I've always liked him."

"You've been feeling pretty bad about him, haven't you?"

"It's you that's been feeling bad and giving me the blues."

He couldn't feel her compassion because of his own sharp, unreasonable jealousy. For nights he had hardly slept worrying about Frank, and now he wanted to be alone and free of him; he had been so sure he would find Peg full of gladness for her love of him. It was hard now to believe in that love that he had felt an hour ago in the field; it was so much more than he had ever expected from her. It was so much easier to remember how Frank had always laughed and teased her just as he did the town girls he was sure of. He felt crazy with worry and weariness, wanting to shout, "Frank spoiled everything in my life," but he blurted out,

"Maybe with Frank being away you've found out tonight how you really feel about him."

"It was you I was thinking of," she whispered. "You were so fond of him and I could watch the pain growing in you. If they were hurting you they were hurting me. Please, Tom, don't get crazy thoughts in your head."

"Tonight it was fine," he said quietly, talking almost to himself. "It was all good tonight. But look how it's spoiled now. It didn't last in you at all. Everybody around here talks and worries about Frank and I'm tired, you hear, awfully tired of it. Peg, listen, he always seemed to me to have the inside track with you if he wanted it."

"Sh, sh, you'll wake my father up."

"You know what I'm thinking, Peg? You wouldn't bother with me if you could have him. I've often felt it."

He seemed to be going all to pieces there at the door, jerking his hand up and down. Then he turned quickly, hurrying away from her. "Tom, don't go. Come back, just a minute." She ran after him begging desperately, "You know I loved you more tonight than I ever did before," but he was hurrying away, not hearing.

He went to bed with the wind blowing much stronger, thinking, "It took her a long time to show much love for me. Frank always laughed at me because I was slow and fumbling with her. What got into her in the field, what made her show so much love?" He lay there holding on to his bitterness. His loneliness, the darkness and the sound of the wind began to distort all his thoughts and though he tried to be reasonable and said, "Maybe I was foolish with Peg," he knew he would be afraid of Frank even if he married her. Gusts of wind sometimes hit the house and there was the sound of shingles torn from the roof spinning in the wind. He tortured himself thinking of Frank and the trouble that always pursued him. For a while he listened to the waves breaking on the shore, and then he began to torture himself deliberately with a picture of Peg and Frank living together: he saw them in a room by themselves loving each other and maybe laughing at him. Then he fell asleep.

He woke up thinking he could hear someone moving outside on the veranda, and he sat up, listening, but he could not be sure because of the wind. There again was the sound of footsteps, and then, quite clearly, a firm tapping on the door. Opening the bedroom window he called out, "Who's there?"

"Let me in, Tom."

He could just see the side of his face in the darkness, leaning out from the veranda. "All right, Frank. I'm coming down," Tom said, and he hurried downstairs and opened the door. Frank was waiting in his shirt and trousers. He was very wet, for now it was raining hard, and he was breathing so heavily he could hardly speak.

"What happened, Frank? What did you do?"

"Don't light the light, Tom. It was easy. They were driving me in the car to jail. Old Chief Fowlis was sitting with me and he always liked me so it was pretty easy and I jumped out and went off across the fields."

"What are you going to do?"

"Cross the lake."

"It's too rough. It'll take you all night."

"You take an oar, Tom."

When Frank came in and closed the door it was so fine at first to see him there, free, but that gladness went quickly, and Tom said uneasily, "Maybe you're making a mistake, Frank. If you get away you'll never be able to come back here and you'll always be on the run, and anyway, if they catch you, they'll double your sentence. It isn't worth it. Three years would be a long time."

Frank began to laugh, and shooting out his hand, he slapped Tom on the shoulder. "Dear old Tom, always so cautious. What would a guy like me be doing in a jail for a year and a half?" he said. They were standing close together in the dark room with no light coming from the window and Frank's laughter sounded arrogant. When Tom didn't answer, Frank said anxiously, "What's the matter, Tom?" as if Tom was the one person in the world he was sure of.

"All right, Frank," Tom said. "I'd go with you anyway. You know that. It doesn't matter what I think. I'll put something on. What are you going to do on the other side?"

"Hide in the woods in the daytime and be off when night comes. Bring me some clothes. I'll look around too. Have you got any money?"

When they were ready they went down to the farm's end, carrying a bundle of clothes, and at the water's edge, though it was not so windy now, the lake looked like a restless heaving part of the immeasurable blackness overhead. They carried the rowboat down from its place at the clump of trees, and at the water, when it was tossed back by the first wave, Tom yelled, "It'll take hours, Frank. Maybe you'd better wait," but his words were blown away and Frank didn't answer.

Though they each pulled strongly at an oar it was very difficult getting past the point of land at the end of the farm. The wind swept around the point lashing the rain at their faces. It always seemed to blow harder at the point. Whenever they looked at the tip of land, the black shadow, measuring how far they had gone, it seemed that they had only been bobbing back to the shore, and if they rested a moment they quickly lost whatever they had gained. But they had expected this and they kept on pulling together with all their strength, their backs bending together till they were out on the channel where it suddenly was easier. As they turned and looked back at the shore, Frank yelled, "Good boy, Tom," and they settled down to row steadily. They rowed perfectly together; they had been rowing on the lake in this way ever since they had been children. All their lives they might have been training for this one trip across the eight-mile lake.

During those hours of hard and silent rowing the sound of the oarlocks and the water against the boat became so regular that Tom began to repeat to himself mechanically, "If he gets away he'll never be back around her. The people who used to like him will never see him again. I'll be alone. I'll be alone. I'll be alone." It was such an easy thought to accept. Already he was used to never seeing Frank again, and he was contented; instead of feeling the desolation that such a notion might have brought to him, he was contented. He began to feel, too, that he was carrying Peg deep in his thoughts but that was very secret. An immense willingness came to him to help Frank; he offered to take both oars; there was a vast gentleness within him urging him to do even more than Frank expected.

Then the hard work and the wind began to tire him, driving all the distorted night thoughts of hours ago out of his head, and soon everything that had happened earlier in the evening seemed far away, as if it happened to someone else.

"Frank's never mentioned Peg," he thought. "I've been thinking of nothing but myself for hours." The dark blotch of the
land was just ahead and they were in the shallow water, the
long stretch of it, in the inlet where there was a beach, and
now it was easy rowing with their oars sometimes pulling out
the weeds. "We're there," Tom said. "I'll stay on the beach
with you for a while and then you can get going. Maybe you
better take some of the food and eat it now. It's stopped raining."

"I'll eat something on the beach," Frank said. He was
resting his oars wearily as the boat pushed through the shallow water.

As soon as they pulled the boat high up on the beach
they did not even wait to take out the bundle, they were so
very tired; they lay down on the sand listening anxiously
for any noises that might come from the trees or from out
over the water. They lay close together, their bodies heavy
and tired, listening to each other breathing, too, somehow
being glad that they could hear each other like this. To Tom
it began to seem that he had always heard it like this, years
ago when he had awakened in the night and had heard
Frank sleeping beside him, or maybe after he and Frank had
been fighting and they had rolled over and over together:
there was that time too, years ago, when they had rowed
across the lake for the first time, each at an oar and had lain
maybe on this very spot to rest before going back. A bit
wearily he raised himself on his arm and said, "Frank,
you're making a big mistake."

"Mistake? What do you mean?"

"You ought to go back. You'll be on the run God knows
how long, you'll never be really free and in the long run

they may catch you. A year and a half now would be a little time compared with that. It would soon be over and everybody likes you around here."

"You're talking like a fool, Tom. I got too many thoughts to bother me without listening to stuff like that."

"You ought to go back. You'll never feel free this way. It'll spoil your whole life."

"Shut up, Tom. If you want to talk like that, get into the boat and go back."

Staring out across the dark water, with his wet clothes hanging on him, Tom repeated with a kind of wretched doggedness, "Please, Frank, come back; you know I wouldn't say it if I didn't think it was best. You know how it makes me feel to have you cooped up in a rotten little jail, but I'm telling you to go back. I've always been willing to do almost anything for you . . ." He put out his hand and touched his brother's shoulder, and at that moment with the wind blowing and the water lapping on the beach, his voice faltered, for he felt a great tenderness for his brother that he could not express. He felt helpless as he said, "Come on, Frank?"

Sitting up quick, Frank said, "Do you really think I'd be such a damned fool as that . . . after coming this far? What's on your mind?"

"It's just as I say, Frank."

"You're getting yellow about it, that's probably it," Frank said. He was full of contempt. They were really shouting at each other because of the sound of the breaking waves. "I never thought you'd be so yellow, Tom. You're scared of getting caught with your finger in it; you always were such a nice respectable guy. You'd take me back now because of what the neighbors might think, wouldn't you? You're a fool. Sit here and hold your head. I'm going." He got up slowly and started along the beach, cutting in gradually to the trees.

"Come back, Frank. Please come back," Tom called. Frank's light shirt was moving against the dark line of the trees, going farther and farther away. Tom was frightened, he felt desperate as he used to feel years ago when Frank was in a fight with a bigger boy and getting beaten, so he started to run after him, shouting, "Wait a minute." He caught up and started pulling at Frank's arm. Frank shook his arm free and they both kept walking along the beach in the darkness. "You're not going, that's settled. You've got to come back with me," Tom said.

"Who says so?"

"I said so."

Without even turning his head Frank said, "Try and make me."

Pulling again at his arm Tom pleaded, "If it's the last thing you ever do for me, do this, Frank. I won't ever ask you to do another thing, and if you go back everything'll straighten itself out."

Jerking his arm free, Frank started to run, running slowly and heavily with a lurching stride because his boots sank into the wet sand, and Tom lunged after him, and the two figures were bobbing up and down against the dark background of the trees, with Tom gaining steadily because he was not so tired nor had he run so far. Once Frank looked back, then he cut in sharply towards the trees. There was a little embankment with grass on the top between the line of trees and the sandy beach, and here Frank slipped in the mud, and Tom caught up to him, only Frank lashed out with his foot and caught Tom on the shoulder. Holding tight, though, and pulling, Tom dragged him by the leg back down the embankment, but there he could not hold him. Frank jumped up, ducked and swung both hands, hitting Tom heavily on the head. Then they clenched desperately and rolled over and over on the wet sand and closer to the line of the water till Frank's hands came loose and he flailed away frantically at Tom's head; he kept beating him wildly and when Tom would not move or let go, he suddenly quit, with Tom lying heavily on him and them both gasping for air. They lay there in this way sucking in the air. Then Frank's breathing became a kind of sob. He couldn't help it, he had run far earlier in the evening and he was weak, and without knowing why, he was crying with his face pressed in the sand.

As he lay there, waiting, Tom was so miserable he wanted to die. He began to pray, "Oh, God, please don't let him cry like that. Don't let him make that noise," because he, himself, couldn't stand it there on the beach with the water lapping on the shore.

When Frank's strength began to come back he still kept quiet. There was no use moving; it was ended for him, there, with his face in the sand. Almost timidly, Tom said, "Come on back now, Frank."

"All right. I got to, I guess."

They went back along the beach with Frank lurching with Tom longing to put his arm around him and steady him, but after the way Frank had sobbed on the sand there was a shyness between them that was hard to break.

At the boat Tom said, "You sit there. I'll do the rowing. It's not blowing hard now," so Frank got into the boat and huddled there with his head thrown back on one arm, his mouth still open as if he would never get enough air.

Tom began to row steadily. The wind was still strong but the water was much calmer now. Soon they were far out on the water. When he was tired Tom rested on his oars, his shoulders drooping over them, and he was looking over the water at one little path of light. The wind, scudding the clouds across the sky, had finally parted them. As the bright moonlight shone more fully on the dark water he remembered all the joy he had felt when the same light had shone on the field of buckwheat and Peg had belonged so surely to him. He could hear Peg calling, "Come back, I loved you more tonight than ever before," but that was just a part of his and Peg's world; it didn't touch Frank.

The oars were very heavy as he rowed, and they got heavier with each stroke, for it seemed that something was breaking inside him. "Frank, you're not sore at me, are you? I wouldn't want to do it if it weren't for you. Can't you see that? Why don't you answer? Listen, Frank. You're not sore, are you? If you really want to I'll go back, I mean if you're sore." Huddled there, silent and unanswering, Frank's eyes were wide open, staring up at the darkness of the night above. While he watched, Tom could still hear that desperate sob for freedom that had come from Frank back on the beach, and it brought such an ache in him that he looked around wildly. But he kept on going, one long slow stroke after another, always trying to talk softly to his brother.

THEIR MOTHER'S PURSE

*H*al went around to see his mother and father, and while he was talking with them and wondering if he could ask for a loan, his sister Mary, who was dressed to go out for the evening, came into the room and said, "Can you let me have a little something tonight, Mother?"

She was borrowing money all the time now, and there was no excuse for her, because she was a stenographer. It was not the same for her as it was with their older brother, Stephen, who had three children, and could hardly live on his salary.

"If you could possibly spare it . . ." Mary was saying in her low and pleasant voice as she pulled on her gloves. Her easy smile, her assurance that she would not be refused, made Hal feel resentful. He knew that if he asked for money he would appear uneasy and a little ashamed, and his father would put down his paper and stare at him and his mother would sigh and look dreadfully worried, as though he were the worst kind of spendthrift.

Getting up to find her purse, their mother said, "I don't mind lending it to you, Mary, though I can't figure out what you do with your money."

"I don't seem to be doing anything with it I didn't use to do," Mary said.

"And I seem to do nothing these days but hand out money to the lot of you. I can't think how you'll get along when I'm dead."

"I don't know what you'd all do if it weren't for your mother's purse," their father said, but when he spoke he nodded his head at Hal, because he would rather make it appear that he was angry with Hal than risk offending Mary by speaking directly to her.

"If anybody wants money, they'll have to find my purse for me," their mother said. "Try and find it, Mary, and bring it to me."

Hal had always thought of Mary as his young sister, but the inscrutable expression he saw on her face as she moved round the room picking up newspapers and looking on chairs made him realize how much more self-reliant, how much apart from them she had grown in the last few years. He saw that she had become a handsome woman. In her tailored suit and hat, she looked almost beautiful, and he was suddenly glad she was his sister.

By this time his mother had got up and was trying to remember where she had put the purse when she'd come in from the store. In the way of a big woman, she moved around slowly, with a faraway expression in her eyes. The purse was large, black and flat leather, but there was never a time when his mother had been able to get up and know exactly where her purse was, though she always pretended she was going directly to where she had placed it.

Now she was at the point where her eyes were anxious as she tried to remember. Her husband, making loud clucking noises with his tongue, took off his glasses and said solemnly, "I warn you, Mrs. McArthur, you'll lose that purse some day, and then there'll be trouble and you'll be satisfied."

She looked at him impatiently. "See if you can find my purse, will you, son?" she begged Hal, and he got up to help, as he had done since he was a little boy.

Because he remembered that his mother sometimes put her purse under the pillow on her bed, he went to look in the bedroom. When he got to the door, which was half-closed, and looked in, he saw Mary standing in front of the dresser with her mother's purse in her hands. He saw at once that she had just taken out a bill and was slipping it into her own purse — he saw that it was several bills. He ducked back into the hall before she could catch sight of him. He felt helpless; he couldn't bear that she should see him.

Mary, coming out of the bedroom, called, "I found it. Here it is. Mother!"

"Where did you find it, darling?"

"Under your pillow."

"Ah, that's right. Now I remember," she said, and looked at her husband triumphantly, for she never failed to enjoy finding the purse just when it seemed to be lost forever.

As Mary handed the purse to her mother, she was smiling, cool, and unperturbed, yet Hal knew she had put several dollars into her own purse. It seemed terrible that she was able to smile and hide her thoughts like that when they had all been so close together for so many years.

"I never have the slightest fear that it's really lost," the mother said, beaming. Then they watched her, as they had watched her for years after she had found her purse; she was counting the little roll of bills. Her hand went up to her mouth. She looked thoughtful, she looked down into the depths of the purse again, and they waited, as if expecting her to cry out suddenly that the money was not all there. Then, sighing, she took out a bill, handed it to Mary, and it was over, and they never knew what she thought.

"Good night, Mother. Good night, Dad," Mary said.

"Good night, and don't be late. I worry when you're late!"

"So long, Hal."

"Just a minute," Hal called, and he followed Mary out to the hall. The groping, wondering expression on his mother's face as she counted her money had made him feel savage.

He grabbed Mary by the arm just as she was opening the door. "Wait a minute," he whispered.

"What's the matter, Hal? You're hurting my arm."

"Give that money back to them. I saw you take it."

"Hal, I needed it." She grew terribly ashamed and could not look at him. "I wouldn't take it if I didn't need it pretty bad," she whispered.

They could hear their father making some provoking remark, and they could hear the easy, triumphant answer of their mother. Without looking up, Mary began to cry, then she raised her head and begged in a frightened whisper, "Don't tell them, Hal. Please don't tell them."

"If you need the money, why didn't you ask them for it?"

"I've been asking for a little nearly every day."

"You only look after yourself, and you get plenty for that."

"Hal, let me keep it. Don't tell them."

Her hand tightened on his arm as she pleaded with him. Her face was now close against his, but he was so disgusted with her he tried to push her away. When she saw that he was treating her as though she were a cheap thief, she looked helpless and whispered, "I've got to do something. I've been sending money to Paul Farrell."

"Where is he?"

"He's gone to a sanitarium, and he had no money," she said.

In the moment while they stared at each other, he was thinking of the few times she had brought Paul Farrell to their place, and of the one night when her parents had found out that his lung was bad. They had made her promise not to see him any more, thinking it was a good thing to do before she went any further with him.

"You promised them you'd forget about him," he said.

"I married him before he went away," she said. "It takes a lot to look after him. I try to keep enough out of my pay every week to pay for my lunches and my board here, but I never seem to have enough left for Paul, and then I don't know what to do."

"You're crazy. He'll die on your hands," he whispered. "Or you'll have to go on keeping him."

"He'll get better," she said. "He'll be back in maybe a year."

There was such fierceness in her words, and her eyes shone with such ardor that he didn't know what to say to her. With a shy smile, she said, "Don't tell them, Hal."

"Okay," he said, and watched her open the door and go out. He went back to the living room, where his mother was saying grandly to his father, "Now you'll have to wait till next year to cry blue ruin." His father grinned and ducked his head behind his paper.

"Don't worry. There'll soon be a next time," he said.

"What did you want to say to Mary?" his mother asked.

"I just wanted to know if she was going my way, and she wasn't," Hal said.

And when Hal remembered Mary's frightened, imploring eyes, he knew he would keep his promise and say nothing to them. He was thinking how far apart he had grown from them; they knew very little about Mary, but these days he never told them anything about himself, either. Only his father and mother, they alone, were still close together.

MAGIC HAT

It was not true that Jeannie Warkle had been too easy for Joe Stanin. No truer than saying Joe had been too easy for her. It had worked both ways, and that was how they wanted it. She knew she belonged to him the first time they met, at the end of the summer when she had been modeling sports clothes for Wentmore, who had given a party for visiting professional golfers. Joe was a commercial artist with the agency that handled the Wentmore account and he had wanted to meet some of the big-name golfers, but instead, he had met her modeling a gray flannel ski suit with a ridiculous plunging neckline. The first thing she had said to him was that she, herself, wouldn't dream of wearing it skiing without a heavy scarf around her neck.

He, too, had known that in some way they were committed to each other, but he had said frankly, "I don't want to settle down. Not for years. I know it's a crazy independence in me, but at least I like a girl to feel the same way. We must never feel we have any strings on each other, Jeannie. And anyway, they're moving me to New York in the winter. I'm a bad lot, Jeannie, and I can't do you any good."

Knowing there could be nothing in it for her but the happiness they got out of being together made her love for him seem like a gift more precious than if she had demanded some security, and anyway, no promise he could have given her would have been as good as his free and happy gentle lovemaking.

When January came and it was time for Joe to go away, she knew she was expected to act like a good sport with no regrets and no complaints, but it was very difficult. She felt she belonged completely to him. To have wailed that he was abandoning her would have cheapened her. His last week in Montreal was very hard on her, because she had to hide her dread of the loneliness she would feel when he had gone. What made it worse was that in that week he couldn't spend much time with her; he was having conferences with his advertising colleagues that lasted until late in the evening, and she had to sit around at home under the eyes of her father and mother and sister Alma, looking pale and distracted.

Her father, putting down his newspaper, would look at her and say, "Why wait around for that fellow to call you, Jeannie? I'll be glad when you've seen the last of him." Her mother, looking up quickly, her plump face indignant, would chime in, "I should say so. He took up all your time, and there was never anything in it for you."

They didn't know she felt she belonged to Joe and could not go out with anybody else. It was humiliating. She knew she would have to find an excuse for keeping in her own room until Joe went away. In a fashion magazine she had seen a picture of a Chinese coolie hat, a gay foolish hat with a pink and black silk sectional crown. At the time she had seen it she had no intention of making it, but she had to appear to be busy, and she decided to copy the hat.

The night she came home with the materials, she had a purposeful air that impressed her family. After dinner she went to her room and began to shape the buckram for the crown. Again and again she put it on her head. Then she cut a paper pattern for the silk sections that were to cover the crown completely. There was to be a corded silk tassel hanging from the point of the crown. As soon as she sat down and started sewing, she felt much happier. She felt she was absorbed in her work, although she was hoping, of course, that the telephone would ring and sometimes imagined she heard it, but now it was a more peaceful kind of waiting.

She found consolation in the work she was putting on the hat; she found that the pattern she was making with the pink and black silk segments took on the pattern of the happy months she spent with Joe. While she cut the silk segments according to the pattern she had made and smoothed them on her knee, she would pause and ponder and believe that Joe needed her without knowing it, and even when he went away sooner or later he would realize he needed her. She could tell this to herself over and over again while she sewed, and as the hat took the colorful shape she had planned, so her desperate hope took a real shape, too, and she couldn't bear to stop working. She worked at the hat until her eyes ached, and she knew she was making it for Joe.

But there were only three evenings left, evenings she had counted on having with him, and he had telephoned to tell her that work in the office had to be cleared up. He was in on the planning of the layouts for an account. The conference would go on into the night, he said. And she was left at home again working on the hat in her room, wondering if she would have even one date with him.

Then Alma came into the room. "I thought you were to go out with Joe," she said.

"He's tied up. It's those silly conferences."

"Tied up? You know, Jeannie, the trouble with you, when Joe whistled you always ran."

"I could whistle when I wanted to. I did my share of whistling."

"You don't fool me, Jeannie," Alma said. Then she looked at the hat. "Why are you in such a hurry to finish that hat? Here — let's see it."

Taking the hat from Jeannie's knee, she put it on her own head and looked at herself in the mirror. She had a round, plump face like her mother's. The hat made her look like a peasant. "I don't like it at all," she said, adjusting it at another angle.

"Take it off, then," Jeannie said quickly, for she couldn't bear to see the hat on anyone else. By this time it seemed to her to belong to all that had been good for her and Joe. She took the hat from Alma.

"Let's see it on you, then," Alma said.

It looked like a different hat on Jeannie, for she had a narrow, oval face, and she knew how good it looked on her and she smiled brightly at Alma.

"Just the same, I don't think you'll wear it much. It's too gaudy. You'll throw it away. When does Joe go?"

"In a couple of days, why?"

"A smooth operator, isn't he?"

"How so, Alma?"

"I know the type," Alma said, and she looked wise. She was buxom and sure of herself. "They tell you from the beginning you can't have them, and then they're in the clear."

When Alma had gone, Jeannie had to put down the hat. Her hands were trembling and she couldn't sew. She got up and walked around the room restlessly, asking herself if it could possibly be true that she had only been a cheap soft touch for Joe, and if he were deliberately keeping away from her now to make it easy for himself at the end. It was an unbearable thought, and her head ached and she felt sick. She began to loathe herself. She picked up the hat again. She sewed at it blindly. It was too late now for Joe to phone, but she knew where he was, and while she sewed she seemed to see him sitting in the LaSalle bar with his colleagues. A few months ago she would have felt as free and independent as he did. Breaking the thread with her teeth, she put down the needle, looked at the hat, and suddenly realized it was finished. It was there on her knees, and as she stared at it, all the hope she had felt while working on it returned. "How do I know he isn't cornered by his colleagues and can't get away, no matter how much he's longing to see me?" she asked herself.

If she put on the hat and went down to the LaSalle and met Joe, mightn't she look so new and strange to him that he would be unable to leave her, she asked herself, and the thought enchanted her. She tried to hold back and feel ashamed of herself for running after him possessively and seeking humiliation. "No, he's there, and he'll be glad," she thought. "As soon as he sees me he'll be glad." She got dressed quickly and put on the hat.

It was cold and snowing a little, with a wind from the mountain, and when she got out of the taxi her cheeks were glowing. She sauntered into the bar, tall and elegant, with her well-cut muskrat coat that looked like mink wrapped around her, and though her thumping heart cut off her breath, her manner was what she wanted it to be — easy and untroubled.

Joe was sitting at the corner table with three red-faced advertising men. He looked thinner and younger than the others. "Hi, Joe," she called brightly. He was surprised, of course, but then he grinned and stood up, and she felt weak with relief. "See, I really must—" he said to the others. Joining her, he whispered, "I'm going to miss you, baby. Where am I going to find a girl who'll know when to come along and rescue me?"

"You won't have much trouble, Joe," she said lightly. "Not when you can grin like that."

"But I've got in a rut with you, Jeannie," he teased her.

"You'll do all right, Joe."

"Just the same, I had a good girl in Montreal, Jeannie."

"You'll have a good one in New York," she said gaily. "You always get the girl who's good for you." But she was waiting for him to say something about her hat.

"Let's go down to Charlie's bar and see what's doing," he said. The hat wasn't going to do her any good. It didn't matter what she wore or how she looked — he had made the separation from her in his mind and by this time had accepted it, she thought miserably. She was bewildered, then bitter. All she could think of was: "I don't even look any different to him in this hat. No! He's deliberately refusing to notice it."

They went along St. Catherine to Charlie's bar, and Joe talked about his big plans for New York. He wasn't aware that she was too bright, too gay, and too sympathetic. Afterward, just as if it were any other night, they went to his little apartment on Bishop Street. She took a long time taking off her hat. She put it on the bookcase. But he flopped down in the chair, loosened his collar, and talked and talked. "Please, please stop talking!" she wanted to cry out. But her cry would have been a wail of protest at being left behind and a cheapening of what was left to her of her self-respect. She was simply there, and he was at home with her; he was used to her, and foolishly at ease with her. Her hat, on the bookcase caught her eye. It reminded her of her blind hopefulness. She kept staring at it with a blank concentration even when his arms were around her, so she would not cry out, "How can you be so completely self-centered?"

"I should go home. It's awfully late," she said finally.

"No, let's go somewhere on the way," he said. "It's the last chance we'll have." So they stopped somewhere else and found his friend Lou. He got very sentimental with Lou, talking about how happy he had been in Montreal. There were only three cities on the continent with any real color of their own, Lou said, and they agreed enthusiastically that Montreal was one of them. But Joe did not see that he was breaking Jeannie's heart, telling how happy he had been in Montreal. It was almost dawn when they left Lou, and it was snowing hard.

"Let's walk," he said, taking her arm. "I feel like walking for hours."

"It's pretty wet," she said, looking at the snow streaming across the streetlight. She was going to say, "What about my hat?" but she no longer cared about it.

The snow was wet and three inches thick, but she had on her galoshes, and he walked her west on Dorchester and they both had their heads down against the snow. He talked about writing letters to her. Whenever he thought of Montreal he would think of her, he said; in fact, when he thought of home she would be there, and he wanted her to promise to write him.

Her hat caught the snow but he walked her along, talking eloquently, and they turned up the hill to her street. At the corner under the light he stopped as he turned to speak, and he started to laugh. The heavy, wet snow crown had melted through the silk and the buckram, and the water, in two little rivulets, beginning at her ears, was trickling down her cheeks.

"What's the matter?" she asked.

"Your hat's leaking," he said solemnly.

"What does it matter?" she asked indignantly. "It's ruined anyway, isn't it?"

"Here. Let me shake the snow off it," he said.

Lifting the hat from her head, he shook off the snow, and while she watched him with blank resentment, he held the hat by the tassel and spun the brim like a wheel, and the spraying drops of water made a circle in the light. While the hat was still spinning, he held it high and let it settle at a crazy angle on her head. He started to laugh; then he stopped, looking at her with wonder. "You know something, Jeannie?" he said earnestly. "At that angle on you it looks like a circus hat — sort of crazy and black and pink and shining in the snow."

"Yeah — like a clown's hat," she whispered. "And why not?"

"I'm sorry, Jeannie," he said. "I should have noticed."

"Should you?" she blurted out. "Why would you notice?"

"Why shouldn't I?" he asked innocently.

"Because you don't notice anything that's happening."

"I don't get it," he said. "You don't want to quarrel about a hat. Not tonight, Jeannie. Not about a hat."

"I took a lot of time with that hat," she said fiercely.

"All right. It was a fine hat," he said impatiently. "So, it's ruined and it's my fault. I'll get you a new one."

"A new one," she said bitterly. "Sure. Go ahead. Get everything new."

"I can do that, too," he said quickly.

"And I can get myself a new hat," she said, her voice breaking. She tried to stop herself; she didn't want to make the wild protest that would humiliate her, and she told herself desperately it would be all right and unnoticed if she protested fiercely only about the hat. "I sit up at night," she said angrily. "I sew till my eyes ache—" But he grabbed at her arm, and she jerked away and went running up the street.

Her galoshes sloshed through the snow, and she ran as fast as she could. "Jeannie!" she heard him call, but she knew he still stood there, because there was only the sound of her own footsteps and it was a terrible sound. Yet when she heard his longer, heavier step and the sound of his curse, as he slipped and fell, she wanted frantically to go faster, to fly far beyond his reach and hear him thudding after her and never be able to catch up to her; she wanted the wild happiness of being beyond him.

She stumbled up the steps to her door just as his big hand grasped at her shoulder. Whirling around, exhausted, she gasped fiercely, "Leave me alone. You don't own me."

"All right, you little fool," he said angrily. "And you don't own me."

"That's the way we've played it. Now go away."

The melting snow from his hat dripped on her face as he held her hard against his wet coat.

Struggling with him, she repeated, "Go away. Just go away."

"How can I go away?" he asked angrily. Then he softened and got mixed up. "All evening I've known I didn't want to go away and I didn't know why. I didn't know I couldn't go without you. But when we stopped under the streetlight and I happened to look at you — that hat stuck on your head at that crazy angle—"

"Happened to look," she repeated.

"Yeah, like I said."

"Just a whim." She protested, "Oh, it's unfair."

"What's unfair?" he asked growing bewildered.

"It couldn't be like that with me."

"Sure it could," he insisted, but he sounded surprised, himself. Then she knew that in the silence he was sharing her apprehension that the course of their lives could change as a result of a little thing like an unpremeditated glance at a hat. "Maybe that's the way it goes," he said awkwardly. "Maybe there's always one moment — everything can look different at one moment. Yeah," he said, confused now himself. "Maybe that's always how it happens, maybe that's how a guy knows he wants to marry," he asked helplessly.

But she was sobbing softly, and he couldn't console her. All she said was: "It's just that you're like you are and I'm like I am, and it gets so hard waiting for — for the right moment — with nothing to fall back on but a homemade hat."

"Well, now that we know, Jeannie—" From then on she wasn't sure what they said except that she was agreeing to go away with him and saying how soon she could be ready; but she wanted to close her eyes and hear again the sound of his footsteps thudding after her.

When he had kissed her and gone, she took off her shoes and went in quietly. But her mother, hearing her, called out anxiously, "Is that you, Jeannie? It's nearly dawn."

In her own room she stood in a trance, her shoes in her hand, thinking, "I'm really going to marry him." Then she took off the wet hat and put it carefully on the radiator. While it dried, she undressed. The pink and black silk on the hat wrinkled up in the heat. The crown, as it dried, was twisted out of shape. She would never wear the hat again, but it didn't matter. Picking it up carefully, she smoothed it and put it on the bureau, and she sat down on the bed and looked at it for a long time with profound surprise.

YOUNGER BROTHER

*J*ust after dark on Sunday evening five fellows from the neighborhood stood on the corner under the light opposite the cigar store. They were dressed in dark overcoats, fedoras, and white scarves, except Jimmie Stevens, the smallest, who was without a hat and the only one without an overcoat. Jimmie was eager to please the big fellows, who did not take him seriously because he was a few years younger. They rarely talked directly to him. So he wanted to show off. He got a laugh out of them, whirling and twisting out to the middle of the road, his body hunched down at the knees, his left arm held out and his right arm moving as though he were playing a violin, like a dancer he had seen on the stage. He sang hoarsely till one of the fellows, Bill Spiers, shouted, "What a voice, put the skids under him!" and he ran out in the road and tackled Jimmie around the waist, though not hard enough to make them both fall. He kept pushing Jimmie across the street.

Then somebody yelled, "Lay off the kid!" just as Jimmie's sister, Millie, passed the cigar store, going out for the evening. She was an unusually tall, slim blond girl, graceful and stylish in her short beige-colored jacket, who walked with a free, firm stride, fully aware that she was admired by the fellows at the corner, and at the same time faintly amused as though she knew she was far beyond them. She didn't speak to Jimmie as she passed, for she knew he was always there on a Sunday evening. He was glad she passed so jauntily and was proud and warm with satisfaction because his sister had such fine clean lines to her body and was so smartly independent and utterly beyond any of the corner gang. Sometimes he felt that the big fellows let him hang around because they had so much admiration for his sister, who never spoke to them, though she knew them.

"She's smart," Buck Thompson, a thin fellow, said, looking after her. "If I get some dough one of these days, I'll take her out and give her a chance."

"Fat chance for a little guy like you, just up to her shoulder," Bill Spiers said.

"That so?"

"She got too much class for you, Buck."

"I dunno. I've known her since she was a kid. I saw her uptown a few months ago with Muddy Maguire."

Muddy Maguire, a roughneck, had grown up around the corner and had moved uptown. Jimmie started to snicker: "If my old lady ever heard you say that she'd rip out your tongue." They all knew Mrs. Stevens, a competent, practical woman, who had left her husband fourteen years ago and she had never let her daughter bring one of the fellows near the house. Jimmie grinned, pleased that they had given Buck the horse laugh for thinking he could get anywhere with his sister.

Millie passed out of sight by the newsstand and one of the fellows started to sing a love song softly and the others tried to croon with him, harmonizing as much as possible, wishing they had enough money to take Millie Stevens out.

For almost an hour they talked intimately about girls, cursing each other.

It was nearly eleven o'clock when Jimmie went home. The Stevenses lived in a house with freshly painted shutters, third from the corner in a long row of old three-storey brick houses with high steps. They lived on the ground floor and had the basement also. Jimmie was whistling, a thin tuneless whistle, as he went up the steps. A light was in the big front room, shining through the shutters, and Jimmie wondered if his mother, who had been out for the evening, had brought one of the neighbors home with her. He was going along the hall to the kitchen when he thought he heard Millie's voice, then a man's voice. He knew at once that his mother had not come home. "Millie's crazy bringing a guy home here," he thought. He went through to the kitchen, but he wanted to see who was talking to his sister, so he went back along the hall and quietly opened one of the big folding doors.

Millie was sitting on the sofa with Muddy Maguire. Her fur jacket and a bright scarf were tossed carelessly over the back of the sofa. "She must have come home the other way around the block," Jimmie thought. Maguire was stout with small eyes, his shiny black hair parted in the middle, self-reliant and domineering, his chest too big for his tight vest. As Jimmie saw him sitting there with his sister he felt his whole body become inert with disappointment. "What can Millie see in a guy like that?"

Millie, leaning toward Muddy, talked earnestly, her face pale, her eyes red as though she had been crying, and Muddy was leaning away from her, looking sour as though there was no mystery in her for him and he didn't want to be there, at all. Jimmie heard her say "Ma" and then suddenly she must have said something insulting to him, for he slapped her lightly across the face.

Jimmie expected Millie to tear Maguire's face with her nails; he couldn't imagine her taking anything from a guy like that; he wanted to yell at her. He couldn't understand it at all when she put her hand up to her cheek and began to cry weakly.

Then Millie said: "You promised, you know you promised."

"I was a fool," he said

"Then what did you come here for?"

"I don't know. "

"You were going to tell Ma."

Millie turned her head away from him and Muddy shrugged, and then slowly and clumsily let his hands fall on Millie's shoulder. "All right," he said, "I'm sorry, Millie."

Jimmie, trembling and angry, heard his mother coming up the front steps. He hurried back to the kitchen and waited. Mrs. Stevens, a short woman, almost shapeless in her heavy cloth coat, with firm thin lips and steady pale-blue eyes, said, "What's the matter, Jimmie?"

"Millie's in there with Muddy Maguire."

Her face got red. "In this house?" she said.

He followed his mother to the front room. Millie, resting her head against Maguire's chest, was crying quietly, both her arms around his neck as if he had become very precious to her.

Mrs. Stevens had never wanted her daughter to belong to any man, and now she said harshly: "Millie, what is this? What's the meaning of this?"

"We wanted to speak to you, Ma," Millie said timidly

Mrs. Stevens, a severe, rigid woman, had expected Millie to stand up and move away from Maguire when she spoke to her, and now she was startled to feel that Millie and this fellow were drawing closer together as they stared at her; the emotion that held Maguire and Millie together seemed suddenly to touch Mrs. Stevens and puzzle and weaken her. She stood there, getting ready to speak, yet all the severity and grimness in her own way of living seemed unimportant now. Gravely she realized why they were waiting for her, and why Millie wanted to talk to her. "Millie, my dear," she said, bending down to her daughter.

"We just want to have a few words with you, Mrs. Stevens," Maguire said with an awkward indifference.

"Go out and close the door, Jimmie," Mrs. Stevens said, trying to conceal her agitation.

Jimmie was disgusted with his mother. When Maguire had spoken to her so casually, so sure of his relation with Millie, Jimmie had expected his mother to scorch him with her sharp tongue, and yet, as he closed the door Jimmie heard his mother talking calmly, and only at times resentfully. He heard the mumbling and murmuring of their voices, and he could tell, by the few words he made out, that his mother would agree to let Maguire marry Millie.

He went back to the kitchen and put his elbows on the white enameled table. "What's the matter with Ma?" he thought. "She should spin that chuckle-headed sap on his ear. What's got into her? Ma should do something."

As he sat there he remembered the jaunty aloof independence of Millie as she had passed the fellows on the corner that evening, and he realized she must have known she was going to meet Maguire. He began to think of her passing; it seemed tremendously important that she should keep on passing. The more he thought of it the more eager he was, and the more pleasure he got out of thinking of her going by, always aloof and beyond them, clean, with too much class, leaving them with nothing else to do but look after her and croon songs and wish they had enough money to take her out.

THIS MAN, MY FATHER

The week I was given a good position in the broker's office, I moved into a fine new apartment and wrote to my father and mother in Windsor. I hadn't seen them in five years, and I asked them to come to New York.

At the station, they came up the iron stairs from the trains very slowly. When my mother looked up and saw me waiting, her round worried face suddenly wrinkled in smiles. By the slow steps she took and the way her hand kept gripping at the rail, I knew her bad leg and her heart must have gotten worse.

For twenty-five years my father had been a letter carrier in Windsor and he had just been retired on a small pension. While I was kissing my mother, whose arm as she held me trembled, my father, now a stout, white-haired man in a blue serge suit, stood to one side fumbling shyly with his heavy gold watch chain. I had never felt close to my father. When I was a kid, he got excited easily and often shouted at everyone in the family. Even now while we stood together in Pennsylvania Station, I wondered why I had been so delighted to see his face and I tried to figure out why he had looked so glad to see me.

Afraid he might say something affectionate, I said quickly, "Is Thelma getting along better with her husband?"

"Oh, son, son, the way that turned out," my mother said, taking me by the arm on the way to the taxi. "Your sister has had to come to our house for things like vegetables and canned food. That man never was any good."

"That business will stop right now," my father said firmly. "We'll have a hard enough time ourselves living on my miserable pension."

When we were going into my apartment house on lower Fifth Avenue, the uniformed doorman opened the door for us, and my father, making a low bow to him, said, "Thank you very much."

At once I remembered that my father, all his life, had made such humble gestures to strangers. Yet the doorman did not seem to be startled; he even smiled in a new bright way. But when we got into the elevator and my father made the same deep bow to the attendant, I was annoyed at his humility. My mother nudged him. Knowing she had more pride, he looked at her anxiously, and she tried to tell him by her fierce expression that he wasn't to shame us. In those few moments in the elevator while I was annoyed and my father, rebuked, grew irritable, we quickly reestablished the old relationship among us.

Before my father got his letter-carrying job we had been very poor, and when I was a kid I used to long for a time such as this when I'd be making money and they'd be coming to see me, so I sat down in the apartment with contentment while they looked around. My father started examining the woodwork and the way the walls were finished. My mother looked at the material in the window drapes. When they started calling to each other and pointing at things like children, I felt a little like crying.

"I guess it costs an awful lot to live here, son. Are you sure you can afford it?" my mother asked.

"I'll be able to from now on. It took a long time waiting, but I was sure it was coming," I said.

With her arms folded across her chest and a worried expression on her face, my mother looked around and said, "I hope you didn't move into this place just because we were coming." Then, she took a deep breath and turned suddenly and looked at me, and it was as though all the hope she had ever had for me, her son, while I was growing and while I was away from her, was justified in that moment while we smiled at each other.

My father, making clucking noises with his tongue as he rubbed his hands on the woodwork of the mantel, turned and said, "How much are you paying here?"

"A few hundred a month. It's a small place," I said.

He straightened up, glared at me with his face flushed with indignation and burst out, "You must be crazy, man. I hope you're using your head and know what you're doing with your money. I hope you've got more sense than you used to have and you're not making a fool of yourself." While he wagged his finger at me, I felt that old hostile resentment rising in me.

"Joe, Joe, have you no sense?" my mother said to him sharply. "Why should you talk to him like that? Be quiet. He knows what he'll be able to afford." While my father, flustered and ashamed, tried to smile at me, I began to laugh out loud. The thread of a sudden, silly, familiar passionate quarrel among us had made me feel I was at home again.

"Come on, let's go out. I've been waiting to show you the town," I said.

My mother looked down at her ankles, but she got up willingly. Then she sighed and sat down, saying, "I'd love to go, but couldn't I have a little rest first? Couldn't you and your father go?"

My father said rapidly, "He doesn't want to go just with me, isn't that right?" and when I nodded he was even more agitated. "Come on, Helen, come on," he pleaded. "I'll walk as slow as you want. We'll come back as soon as you start to get tired."

Feeling the shyness between us, my mother laughed and said, "Oh, go on. It'll do you both good to have a walk before dinner."

My father looked at us with his blue eyes, seeing us both together and close to each other, then he said quietly, "All right, I'm ready," and he buttoned up his coat and put his hat on the back of his head.

I felt cheated as we went out together. I had looked forward to hearing my mother's burst of enthusiasm as I showed her the town. But my father was following me a few steps behind and in a way that only annoyed me. He didn't make his low bow to the doorman either. Maybe what really annoyed me was that the elevator attendant and the doorman had smiled at my father and said, "Good day, sir," more respectfully and cheerfully than they had ever done to me.

My father was looking up the avenue at the way the line of buildings cut like a cavern into the horizon. Certain it was making him feel humble, I said lightly, "Quite a city, eh? Makes you feel a little strange?"

He seemed to be puzzled about something, then he said quietly, "No, it isn't that it seems strange. It doesn't seem half as strange as I thought it would."

I had counted on him being wide-eyed and wondering, and I said a bit tartly, "Well, I got a big kick out of it the first time I looked around."

"I mean it reminds me of London," my father said. "It's different of course, but it gives me some of the same feeling, maybe it's just the big-city feeling London had."

I had forgotten that my father had been born in England and had come to Canada when he was twelve years old. Again, I felt cheated and didn't know what to say to him.

"I'd love to see Wall Street. Could we go there?" he asked.

We took the subway downtown, and as we walked through the narrow streets of the financial district my father's growing wonder and complete childish acceptance of everything I told him made me forgive him for not being so surprised in the first place. He began grabbing at my arm and pointing at things. Once he asked me the name of a big new building, and when I couldn't tell him, he darted across the street, peering at the brass plate near the door, and came bouncing back through the traffic, with me standing there sure he'd be killed, to report briskly and made me feel helpless.

But it was when we were down at the waterfront, looking across the river at the tugboats and the sunlight on Brooklyn, that we really began to feel closer together. My father had been sniffing the air, smiling to himself and peering in seamen's taverns we passed as we walked along. Suddenly, he took an extra sniff, his face wrinkled up in a wide grin, and he stood still, crying out, "It smells like a fish market!" We were at Fulton Street and the smell of fish was very strong now. On the road, there were little bonfires of refuse. Grim, old, slow-moving seamen passed us on the sidewalk. "Yes, sir, it's a fish market," my father repeated.

"Sure it's a fish market, but what about it?"

"I haven't smelt anything like it in years."

"It's just a stench to me. Let's move along."

"Isn't it lovely? It reminds me of Billingsgate in London," he said. "When I was a boy I often used to go down to the fish market." Turning, he got the smell of the fish market again, looked across the river, took a deep breath and was delighted.

"Why didn't you ever mention being a kid in London before?" I asked.

"I must have forgotten it. It seems such a long time ago," he said.

I felt suddenly that I knew little or nothing about my father as we cut up through the lower East Side. But we began to share in the discovery of broken-down poolrooms; we liked the swarm of Italian, Chinese and Jewish faces that passed us. And it was not nearly as strange for my father, the man walking beside me in the good, freshly pressed blue serge suit and the hat on the back of his head, the postman from Windsor, as it was for me — foreign faces, bright colors, dirty streets, the odors of a seaport he had long ago forgotten, all had come alive for him down there by the waterfront. Again and again he said, "When I was a boy," and the softness and innocence of his voice made me full of wonder, because I had grown up thinking him irritable and loud with excitement. "This is what he was like when he was a kid," I was thinking. "Maybe he's always had an easy mild way with him like this, and we haven't known it. When he was a kid I would have liked him." Feeling years older than my father I took his arm, but when we crossed the road I knew I was restless about something.

"Are you tired?" I asked.

"Me tired? I could walk miles."

"How about going into the lunch wagon there for a cup of coffee?"

"Whatever you say," he said, and we went into the lunch wagon that was on a corner near a garage.

My father always ordered raisin pie with a cup of coffee, and I remembered how fond he had always been of it. While I watched him eat with his head down and his hat almost slipped off the back of his head, there remained in me that mixed-up feeling of being with a kid yet being with my own father.

He was so hungry I knew he hadn't had anything to eat on the train, but he looked up suddenly and said, "When I get back home I wish I could get some little thing to do."

Surprised, I said, "Why, you'll be all right. You'll have your pension and I'll be able to help some now. It's going to be different now because I'm in the money."

"But I'd like it better if I didn't have to be a drag on somebody else. Why shouldn't I be able to look after myself?"

"All right. Maybe I'll be able to set you up in something soon."

My father was looking at the man behind the counter, a little runt of a man whose face was half hidden behind the steam from the coffee boilers, and he whispered, "I'll bet a dollar I'm twice as active as your friend there. Why couldn't I open a place like this back home?"

While my father went on watching the withered-faced man behind the counter rubbing a few cups with a towel, I began thinking again of his childhood in that other city, London, so far away from the lunch wagon. Then I heard him say quietly, "As long as I could make enough to give me the feeling I was working. It's terrible to feel there's nothing for you to do." The way he spoke, the stillness I felt in him when he had finished, made me realize how frightened he had been growing day after day. While I had been sitting there dreaming of the beginning of my father's life, he had been sitting beside me dreading the end of it. It made me unhappy. We went out and started to walk again.

The street lights were lit when we got to Washington Square. My feet were tired, yet I did not want to get home because I knew I was not satisfied. I could not understand my restlessness. Before we went in we stood together looking up the avenue at the flow of lights in the twilight, and my father said, "It's certainly nice here. It's hard to imagine a nicer place."

It was dark in the apartment and we thought there was nobody there, but when we listened we heard the sound of heavy breathing. I turned on the light, and my mother, who had been sound asleep, sat up, startled, crying, "Joe, Joe," feeling around on the bed for my father. "Where am I?" Then she stared at us, swallowing hard as she tried to smile. "I was frightened," she said.

We were both grinning at her, and maybe she felt we were sharing some secret, for she rubbed her eyes and said, "Look at the two of you. What have you been doing?"

"Just walking," I said.

"I was down on Wall Street," my father said. "I looked across the river and saw Brooklyn, and it was beautiful in the sunlight."

She felt something between us that aroused her and she said, "What were you talking about?"

"Nothing, nothing at all," I laughed.

She was a terribly curious woman and she pleaded, "Please tell me," but when I only shrugged she turned to my father and brightened and said, "I had such a good feeling before I fell asleep. I was thinking of the way we worried about the children, and all the times I tried to give Harry here a little good advice. It felt so good to be here with him and see how he was getting on."

"That's right," my father said energetically. "He can't say we both didn't give him good advice."

"Both of us?" she jeered at him. "Why, Thelma was always your pet. You were scared to open your mouth to Harry for fear he'd leave home, and it was only when you got mad that you shouted at him."

My father's neck reddened in the old way as he prepared to become desperately apologetic, and my mother went on, laughing at him. "Son, can you ever remember your father quietly insisting that you pay attention to what he had to say?"

I shook my head and said, "No, I can't"

But when I saw my father looking over at me with that baffled, helpless expression I cried out, "For heaven's sake, mother, leave him alone. Let's not start running him into the ground while he's here."

The loose skin around my mother's throat was working up and down, and her eyes grew desolate. "I'm not trying to take the credit for your success," she said. "You never used to speak to me like that. I guess you've grown away from me a little," and she got up slowly to put on her hat and go out with us.

"It's nothing, I was tired," I said, trying to soothe her, but my father, who had been sitting still, suddenly smiled at me.

While he smiled like that I felt him walking beside me; I felt that mystery of having been close to the boyhood of a man who was now old and who was sitting beside me smiling at me. I had seen the innocence of his childhood restored to him for a little while. As I kept looking at him the restless excitement and wonder were growing in me. I had a great hunger to know of the things that had delighted him, the things he had hoped for when he was a kid far away in London and happy, before he ever thought of Canada or heard of Windsor — this man, my father, whom I had found walking down near the Fulton Street fish market.

THE LUCKY LADY

When Charlie Springer lost the third race, he looked so crushed and angry that Harriet, standing beside him at the rail, slipped her arm under his but he scowled and made her feel that everyone was unfairly against him.

"It's the hot day, Charlie," she said. "Everything just drags along."

He muttered at the big fat man who had leaned against him. "I haven't got room to move. I can't see those beetles I bet on."

"Cheer up, Charlie. There's always the right race."

"Oh, sure, sure," and then he said irritably, "Don't you ever wear anything but that white suit, Harriet?"

"Why, you always said you liked this suit, Charlie." And it was true. When she had first met him and had worn the suit, he said that it went so well with her blond hair and long legs he felt like a rich man walking along the street with her. "Only last night you said the suit still looked good, Charlie."

"What's the matter with wanting you to look different sometimes?"

"Because it's unfair, Charlie."

"It was just a crack. Nothing looks right today," he said.

"I've got nothing else to wear," she said, and wondered why the sun glinting on the gray in his hair made him look so much older than when he had come into Mr. Striker's office to sell some oil stock, and had met her. "I'm broke and you know it, Charlie," her mouth trembled, for she was ashamed to remind him again that she was broke, always broke from lending him money.

She was so fond of him because from the beginning he had been able to make her feel valuable and he had come upon her, after years of shopping around as a salesman and small promoter, knowing at once he needed her, and all the borrowing from her had only been their recognition of his need of her. But his irritated glance had also touched a secret fear that all the giving on her part only made him feel she was forever committed to him.

"Do you think I like looking shabby, Charlie?" she said. "I was to have a new dress for today. Remember? You promised to pay me back something so I could get the dress."

"I know I did, Harriet," he said quickly, and he looked ashamed. "I know you are broke. I know it's my fault. I know you have to get a dress. But I thought with a couple of sure things today I could make a killing. I guess I mentioned the suit because the dress is on my mind."

"I know I look shabby. I know it."

"Play along with me, baby. The trouble is you're always on my mind." It was just the right thing to say; it touched all her affection for him. "The first little windfall goes to you, Harriet," he said, and he slipped his arm around her waist and abused the jockeys and the backstretch touts who gave him tips, and he sounded like himself and made her feel again that everything she wanted was within her reach.

"I'm not betting the next race," he said. "But in the fifth it's got to be Black Pirate. I got it straight from Jonesy. The fifty we've got left goes on Black Pirate right on the nose." Suddenly he turned to her, deeply reflective. "Are you feeling lucky, baby?"

"Sure, I'm feeling lucky."

"Why not?" He was serious. "Nearly everything good that's come my way has come though you, Harriet. That's a fact. We need a break. If anybody can do it you can, Harriet. Here, you put the dough down and change our luck." He handed her the bills. "The fifty on Black Pirate. Right on the nose. Then you'll get yourself a whole new outfit."

"But if Black Pirate should miss?"

"It's not my day, baby, it's yours."

"Yes. Why not, Charlie?" She laughed, and her hand went out to him affectionately, for his conviction that luck could come to him only through her moved her, made her feel again that he really knew how valuable she was in his life. "I'll get moving now so I won't have to line up."

"Take it easy. There's still the fourth race."

"Here we go," she said, and laughed and kissed the bills in her hand, then pressed the bills to his lips; she had a lovely glow as she left him.

On her way to the wicket, when she was passing the clubhouse gate, she had to circle around a group of men, and then she bumped into a shabbily dressed old woman wearing a long gray out-of-season topcoat and a shapeless black felt hat, who had a newspaper-wrapped parcel under her arm. The little old woman had been standing there, mutely staring at the brilliant sunshine on the infield's green grass, and at the horses and the stable ponies moving up the track to the starting post.

"Oh, excuse me," Harriet said, for in bumping her she had knocked the parcel to the ground, where the newspaper wrapping opened and showed a pair of battered old shoes. "I'm sorry," Harriet said, and as she picked up the parcel she folded the paper carefully around the shoes.

"It's all right, Miss. Thanks," the woman said, taking the parcel, and then as Harriet turned she heard her call, "Oh, Miss . . ."

"Yes?"

"Maybe you could tell me something," the little old woman said nervously; and then she nodded and seemed to have made up her mind that Harriet had a good face. "It's about this," she said timidly and fumbled in her old handbag. "See," and she handed Harriet a single slip from an office memo pad. "Can you make it out?"

"Bright Star. The fourth race," Harriet read aloud from the writing in the small pinched hand. "Why, it's the fourth race coming up."

"And I was to hand this in at the wicket," the woman said, looking frightened as she took a ten-dollar bill from the old handbag.

"The ten on Bright Star?" Harriet asked dubiously, for it was plain the woman couldn't afford to lose ten dollars. "I've a friend who knows, and on the way to the track I heard him say Bright Star couldn't win a boat race."

"But Mr. Wilkie said—"

"Who's Mr. Wilkie?"

"In the building. The office building where I clean. Mr. Wilkie worked late last night. Often he talks to me. He wrote this down and gave me the ten dollars and said to be sure and make a bet for myself, and I came here on my way to work.

"Well, never look a gift horse in the mouth, as they say," Harriet said, shrugging. "The wicket is right over there, and I'm on my way there. You can come with me but you'll certainly have to hurry."

"Wouldn't you do it for me, Miss? I feel safer standing right here," she said and she handed Harriet the bill.

"But you shouldn't trust people like that," Harriet said. She was reluctant to take the bill, for the woman's tired wrinkled face told her how much the ten dollars meant to her. "Well, stay right here then. Don't move. Oh, my goodness, the horses are on the track," and she rushed to the wicket and got the money down just before post time, and then stood there a moment wondering if she shouldn't also put down the fifty Charlie had given her to bet on Black Pirate in the next race, but she was afraid he would abuse her for being a fool.

The crowd roared as the horses broke from the post, but she couldn't follow Bright Star; she didn't know the horse or the number. All she could do was stand there and listen to the voice on the loudspeaker, "It's Shoemaker, Ivy Green and Jackanapes. It's Shoemaker and Ivy Green," and think what a ten-to-one shot, a windfall like that, might do for a little old woman. It could make her feel her life had changed magically. Harriet closed her eyes and began to make a little prayer.

When she opened her eyes the horses were on the far turn. "It's Ivy Green by a half, and Dipsy Dipsy. Ivy Green and Dipsy Dipsy and on the outside, Bright Star." Then, in the crowd's roar as they hit the stretch, she couldn't hear the voice, and the race was over, and she was watching the numbers go up on the tote board, and the man next to her cursed and said, "Goddamn Bright Star goes off at ten to one! It's a boat race!" Harriet trembled, then she moved toward the wicket and was the first to hand in her ticket, and she got a hundred dollars.

She made her way toward the clubhouse gate, and as soon as she saw the little old woman, rooted to the spot as if she had been afraid to move an inch, she began to laugh and wave, but the woman, watching blankly, didn't see her until she was only a few feet away. "You won! You won! Imagine!" Harriet cried, waving the bills.

"Did I?" she asked blankly. "How much did I win?"

"A hundred dollars. Look."

"A hundred dollars," she repeated with a frightened smile. "Oh, dear."

"Here, put it in your purse."

"Yes, Miss," and she did, but the clasp on the old purse was so loose it worried Harriet. "Look," she said, taking the woman's arm, "you can't carry that money in that purse. Where are you going?"

"To work." Harriet's pleasure was mixed with nervous concern; all that mattered now was that the woman should get home safely with her money. Still holding her arm firmly, she walked her out the gate to where taxis were waiting at the curb.

When they stopped by a lamppost she said, "I'll tell you what we'll do. You'll have to take a taxi. Wait. Lean against that post and give me the money." When the little old woman had dutifully handed the money to her she knelt down and pretended to be fixing the lace on the woman's shoe. But she drew the shoe off. Separating one ten-dollar bill from the roll, she made an insole out of the rest, laid it in the shoe and laced it up.

"Remember now," she insisted urgently, "don't change your shoes when you get to work. Don't touch that shoe till you get home. Understand?" And she didn't stand up till the woman nodded like an excited conspirator.

"Now take this ten dollars and pay for the taxi," she said, handing the bill to her, and then she beckoned to a driver.

"Thank you, Miss. God bless you," the little old woman said when she was in the taxi. They smiled at each other mysteriously. The woman's tired eyes were bright as a young girl's. As the taxi pulled away, Harriet stood there glowing with satisfaction, for the woman's luck seemed to be flowing around her and in her. She felt light-hearted, carefree and young, and could hardly turn away.

Suddenly, she remembered Black Pirate in the fifth and she ran, frightened, through the gate. The race was on, and she knew Charlie would be down there at the rail, all keyed up, thinking the money was on Black Pirate. She couldn't get her breath. She didn't know what had happened to her. Charlie would never understand what had happened.

"It's Golden Arrow, Moonglow and Funny Face," she heard over the loudspeaker, and she closed her eyes, unable to listen. Then the race was over and it was still Golden Arrow, Moonglow and Funny Face, and she sighed and felt weak.

"Why, I've saved the fifty dollars," she thought, making her way to the rail. "Maybe it's my share of that little old woman's luck." It was a windfall, Charlie would see that it was an incredible windfall. He would laugh, and then wonder, and then he would see that it was intended so she could get the dress. He was waiting by the rail in his expensive light summer suit with the pale blue check, and he was watching her glumly.

"What's the matter? How can you smile?" he asked sourly, while she was still six feet away. "It's your funeral, too."

"Wait a minute, Charlie. Wait a minute. It could be a lot worse."

"Sure. I could have broken my neck. My dough's all gone."

"It isn't gone, Charlie. Look," and she opened her purse.

"What is this?"

"I didn't bet on Black Pirate."

"You didn't?"

"No," she said and she laughed and felt breathless. "I was too late. Oh you'll like this, Charlie. Just as if — well, as if we were being looked after. I got talking to a little old woman and I didn't get to the wicket. So you see, you were right. Luck was with me. If you'd done the betting yourself we'd have blown the fifty, wouldn't we, and now here it is," and again she laughed and wanted to tell him about the little old woman, and she did.

"Well, I'll be damned," he said, grinning. "So here we are right back in the ball game. Let's have the dough."

But she hesitated, waiting for him to remember and say, "No, you really saved this money. I would have thrown it down the drain. I guess it's the money for your dress all right. What a way to get it," and she tried to prompt him a little. "You know I'm broke, Charlie, and I thought . . ."

"Ah, now, sweetheart," he said, making a big joke of it.

"Charlie, I do need it."

"But you wouldn't be a lovely little burglar, would you?" he asked, laughing. "Let's have it and we'll use it to get some real loot. Why, what's the matter?"

"It was yours all right. Oh, it isn't just the money, Charlie."

"No? What else?"

"Oh, I don't know . . ." But she couldn't go on. "Here, take it," she said, and she thrust it at him.

But he knew that something was wrong and while he hesitated uneasily she had a moment of wild hope as, half-ashamed, he struggled against being who he was. He took her arm and gave her a little pull to him, and he told her with the pressure of his fingers on her arm that all that was generous and just and affectionate in his nature made him feel unhappy and ashamed; then all his habit of indulging himself with her seemed to weaken his remorse. "Don't you see, darling, this fifty is meant to give us another chance?" This familiar expression of his hopefulness put an ache in her heart because, for so long, she had shared his hopefulness.

As he reached for the money, she knew he couldn't help himself. He was just being himself with her, as he always would, taking a little more every day, taking and taking and putting nothing back in her heart, and worse still, taking away that kind of young light-hearted happiness she had felt standing at the curb, and he always would do this; he would keep on doing it until she was empty and old.

"Yes, sir. This is going to be the fifty that does the trick for us," he said, trying to feel at ease with himself. "Let's see what I've got for the next race. I think our luck has really changed."

"I think it has," she said softly, and as she stood beside him she thought of the little old woman in the taxi, and, staring across the green infield in the sun, she knew that she would be halfway to work. She remembered how she had hoped the woman's life would change, and now, following the taxi in her mind, she suddenly felt herself, too, whirling away from the track, with the incredible good luck that had come just in time to take her out of Charlie's life.

A Couple of Million Dollars

*T*he well-dressed big man with the puffy-eyed face
turned suddenly on the street and grinned at a shabby
man who was buying a newspaper. The big fellow said,
"Why it's my old friend Max Seagram."

"And you're Myers."

"Sure I'm Myers," he said. It was a cold day in the early
winter and Max was wearing a threadbare, light spring coat.
"Don't tell me you're not doing well," he said, still grinning.

"The truth is I'm flat on my back."

"What were you doing?"

"I was in advertising in Chicago and I thought I might
catch on here, but no luck so far," Max said. He was staring at Myers' grinning face. Ten years ago in Chicago, they
had worked together till Myers had been left a couple of
million dollars by an uncle who had owned a shirt factory.
"What are you doing yourself?" Max asked uneasily.

"Nothing, absolutely nothing. Come on over to the Wal-
dorf and have a drink with me." As he slipped his arm under
Max's and they walked along the street, he whispered,
"How would you like me to put a little money your way?"

"Doing what?" Max asked.

"Keeping an eye on my wife."

"You're kidding."

While Myers hung on to his arm and talked about his wife, Max felt sick with humiliation. "It sounds easy enough," he said, "but I thought you meant a decent job."

Something about Myers frightened Max: something that made him let his arm hang heavy at his side till Myers dropped it and pulled his own arm away.

Going into the bar at the Waldorf, Myers said, "All I want you to do is find out who the guy is she's hanging around with, and that'll be easy because she makes no bones about going out by herself in the evening."

"What'll you do if you catch her?"

"It'll make a nice beginning, just to catch her," Myers said.

As they had one old fashioned, and then another, Max, ashamed of his shabby clothes, could do nothing but listen and stare stupidly at Myers. "I'll show her to you when she's coming out in the evening sometime," Myers said, pulling at his nose with his thumb and forefinger and grinning shyly. Then he took out his wallet, his eyes on Max's frayed threadbare coat cuffs that Max had tried to darken that afternoon with ink, and a bill slipped from Myers' hand and dropped to the floor, underneath the table. Without looking down, Myers beckoned a waiter and pointed to the floor; he kept on grinning and whispering. The waiter picked the bill up and bowed. Myers waved his hand irritably and said, "Don't bother me. Keep it!"

It was a stupid gesture, an insult to everybody in the place.

"Here's fifty," Myers said. "That'll keep you going, won't it?"

"Listen Myers, how long have you been married?"

"Five years. But only two years to this one."

"So I wouldn't know her at all?"

"You might. She was in a show when I met her."

"When do I start?" Max said, holding the money.

"Why not take a shot at it tonight?" Myers said. "I can tip you off when she's going out."

Around nine, opposite the Myers' apartment house on Park Avenue, Max walked up and down. The cold wind blew against his legs. He tried to get a look through the doors along the black-and-white tiled hall as people in evening clothes came out. The giant doorman in the blue uniform was intimidating and he ducked his head and mumbled, "Some buddy! He puts me to work but he never thought of asking me around to see him."

Mrs. Myers was a slim woman with a little green hat, a mink coat, and she had a tall showgirl's shape and a soft glowing complexion. She looked so rich that Max had a wild longing to brush against her, and it was easy following her. Sometimes she met a woman friend. Sometimes she went alone to the theater. There were times when he was close enough to touch the soft fur of her coat. Once, he lost her for a while in a crowd and was terrified.

Every evening, he met Myers at the cocktail hour at the Waldorf and had a drink and reported, "Nothing doing, nothing at all."

Myers was disgusted. "You're not slipping, are you? Look here, Max, you're sure I can trust you?"

"Check it yourself."

"Never mind. She's fooling me and I'll get her. I never miss. Just pin that in your hat, Maxie." They sat for an hour, drinking.

Always, after his third or fourth old-fashioned, his voice grew milder, his face softened, and he asked about the troubles Max had been through with a gentle considerate charm; but a drink later, his voice changed, he started tossing money around at the waiters who winked at each other and grinned, and Max got jittery again.

"You're lousy with dough and don't know what to do with it," Max blurted out.

"Wrong, wrong, wrong again. You haven't learnt anything, Max," he jeered. "I do it because it amuses me."

"But the waiters laugh at you and know you're a sucker."

"I'm a sucker?" He chuckled, wrinkling his puffy eyes. "I'll let you in on something, Maxie. They know I'm a sucker, but what do I know about them? I know how to make everybody here get down and rub his nose in the mud. I make suckers out of them every day." His voice rose, men standing at the bar looked over at him, and there was a frantic, frustrated bitterness in him. "Sure, I can turn this place into a madhouse damned quick and any time I want to. I know all about them. I know what they want and I've got plenty of it, hee, hee, hee, hee."

"Go ahead, have a big belly laugh," Max said. "It's a mighty nice big feeling, crawling with coin, but listen, I got a brother in Chicago who never made more than you throw away in a week."

"What are you getting sore about?" Myers said, suddenly soft and soothing. "You want me to subsidize your whole family? I can do it."

"I don't want anything like that," Max said, afraid he was going to cry.

"Then what are you sore about?"

"Nothing you'd understand."

"Here, you're doing fine, here's fifty bucks, sooner or later she's going to make a break and you be on the job," Myers said, tossing some bills across the table to Max, who stared a long time before he picked them up.

One night, when he was following her, Mrs. Myers got out of her taxi on Fifth Avenue at Thirty-fourth Street and he hurried after her and almost ran into her as she stepped out from a doorway.

"Well, and who are you, anyway?" she said. "And just what do you want?"

"I don't know you, lady, I don't know what you mean," he said.

"You've been following me for a couple of weeks. You're working for my husband, I presume — well, tell him it's no good. Next time, I'll simply have you arrested," and she turned and started to go down the street.

"Just a minute," he called desperately.

"What for?"

"Don't go like that, please, you don't understand. I used to know him years ago."

"You knew him in Chicago?"

"I grew up with him. Nobody knew him better."

"Maybe, if you don't mind . . ." she hesitated. "Maybe you could tell me a few things . . ."

"Sure. Look, I've been wanting to talk to someone about him," he said. "I used to work in the same office with him, only he worked twice as hard. I used to loan him money, we used to go to the ball games together and when we were kids my mother liked having him around because he was hard working." He was so excited to be walking with her, feeling her coat brushing against him, and watching the light touching her fine smooth skin that he broke off and began to apologize for following her. "I was broke, I had to do something. Myers knew I'd take the job."

She walked beside him with her head down, troubled by her own thoughts, and when they were as far as Madison Square, she stepped out to the curb, waved her arm suddenly to a passing taxi, wiped away a few flecks of snow from her face with her gloved hand, and said, "Look here! If he's paying you, you'd better let him go on. You need the money."

"But I'll have to keep following you."

"It won't bother me like it did," she said, "don't worry about it." Her face was lovely in that light in the snow. "You're very nice, you know," she said, and the wheel of the cab spun and sprayed the snow over the sidewalk, some of it catching his pants cuff, and she was gone.

The next time he saw Myers he said, "I'm not going to take any more of your money for this thing. It's no good, so I'm quitting."

"How did it go last night?"

"The same old thing. Nothing happened."

"Then you're missing out, man. She was excited about something when she came in," Myers said. "Listen, you're my old pal, eh, Maxie? Look! Let me loan you some money. Don't figure I'm paying you for the job. You can pay me back when you want to. What do you say?" He grinned. "Let's you and me have dinner tonight."

"With me in these clothes?"

"You don't need to dress if you're with me. I don't," Myers said.

During the dinner in the hotel Max asked Myers what had happened to him since he'd come into the money ten years ago, and Myers said he had stopped working immediately, gone to Paris and had lived there for two years doing everything rich Americans were supposed to do, until he got so bored he pulled out of Paris and settled down in London. But he had come to hate the English and went to the Far East, to Shanghai, and later to Bombay, and then to the golden temple of the Sikhs at Amritsar, and then he had lived for a month in Moscow and grew to hate the Russians.

After dinner, they went to a nightclub. The hatcheck girl beamed, the captain fussed, trembling with eagerness, the manager came and asked if he was pleased with his table, and lovely girls in the floorshow kept smiling at him wistfully. Yet, he didn't give anyone a tip and didn't pay his check when they went out.

"Do you own a piece of this place, or what's the set-up that you don't have to pay?" Max asked.

Myers grinned. "It's more fun this way," he said. "You know what a sucker's game the nightclub racket is for anybody with a little dough. I figured that out a long time ago."

"Then do you pay?"

"Sure, I pay plenty, but I fixed it with them so I pay for everything at the end of the month. Then I owe them a hell of a lot and keep putting it off a long time and they hop around like cats on a hot brick. I get full value for my money."

One night, Max followed Mrs. Myers to a little Russian place in a cellar on West Twelfth Street, and she came up to him with her hand out, as if they had become old friends since they had walked in the snow. "I've been terribly restless," she said, "I've got to talk to somebody."

"What's the matter, Mrs. Myers?"

"It's not safe, I know, to talk like this. It's crazy."

"Sure it's safe," he said, anxious to soothe her.

It was warm in the little café, there was the smell of wine and food and a Russian girl playing a guitar and singing, and when they sat down in a corner at the end of one of the long wooden tables and she started making little patterns with her finger on it, he was sure she was very lonely.

"I don't know anybody who knew him years ago when he was different," she began.

"But what's worrying you now?"

"Nothing, nothing. I just go over and over it." Looking at him helplessly, she blurted out, "You don't understand. I'm scared. He does nothing. He works at nothing. He looks and looks and looks for something to amuse him and I don't know if I amuse him, or bore him, too. I don't know if he wants me, except I'm something he owns."

"Maybe I'm helping make you feel that way," he said. "I'll tell him I won't follow you any more."

"No, that's no solution."

"What do you want me to do?"

"Nothing, nothing. Let's be friends, that's all. You're sweet to listen to me," she said. Her green felt hat was low over one eye, and he could see the smooth sweep of her golden-red hair to the curve of her neck, and she was so close to him, so eager for warmth and friendliness that he had to catch his breath.

"Why don't you leave Myers?" he blurted out.

"I'm scared to."

"But I know what you're really like," he said. "You should be bouncing around having some fun."

"Maybe so," she said, shrugging. "Maybe I'm used to things now. You get used to all kinds of comforts. They become a dear part of your life." There was a weary resignation and something hard and cynical in the way she spoke. "Besides, there are times when he seems charming."

"After three or four old fashioneds?"

"You've noticed it yourself," she said.

Her lovely face, the shape of her breasts, had gotten into his sleep. He began to see Myers' face drifting through the streets, grinning his shrewd and calculating grin at hundreds of people, estimating them all. One night he rushed into the Waldorf bar, stood a moment at the door staring at Myers' broad back, and then began to tremble. Myers had turned, his arms open.

"What's the matter?" Myers said. "Come on and sit down."

"There's nothing the matter with me."

"Why did you stand there pop-eyed watching me?"

"Because I want to tell you—"

"That I'm a little too fat, but it's just an alcoholic fatness . . . A little too fat," and Max felt a little edge of malice in Myers' laughter.

"I'm getting a job in an advertising agency," Max said. "In a few days. I don't need to take any more of your money, I didn't do anything for you anyway."

"Sure, you've done lots for me," Myers said.

"OK, but I'm through now, and thank God I can quit. I know you've no use for me," he said.

Myers started to laugh. "Aw, come on down off your high horse. You're not working yet, what's the matter?" And he took out his wallet.

"No, it's no good, if I stay I'll quarrel with you," Max said, and he slapped Myers on the shoulder, tried to smile, and rushed out.

At the café on Twelfth Street, he ran down the steps, stopped abruptly, and looked around as though someone were chasing him. Mrs. Myers, sitting in the corner at the end of the long table, waved to him as if she were expecting him, but he was out of breath and could hardly speak.

"You've been running. What's the matter?" she asked. "Let's sit here and talk. Talk about anything."

"No. I just left him. It's not safe," he said.

"How do you know?"

"The way he grinned at me. He's watching me. He can't stand me, I can tell."

"It's not true," she said. "He let your name drop the other night, and he felt warmly for you. I'm sure he did."

"He let me drop?"

"Yes." Her eyes widened with excitement. "Oh, you're so sweet," she said, "You're a darling," and then he saw the bones whiten in her hands as she gripped at the edge of the table, and then she stood up. "You're right," she whispered. "He's followed you."

Myers came toward them looking like a contented and vindicated man enjoying a secret happiness. In a sprawling manner, he sat down with them and grinned into their faces.

"Aren't you glad to see me?" he asked. "And me thinking it was time we had this little get-together."

"Stop your stupid grinning," Max said.

"I must get out of here," Myers' wife said.

She hesitated, and then got up and went as far as the counter. White-faced and watching, she waited there.

"Well, you couldn't resist horning in on what didn't belong to you, eh?" Myers jeered at Max.

"Nothing's gone on, Myers."

"Why'd you drop my arm walking along the street the day we met?"

"I didn't."

"Sure you did. I knew you didn't like me, and I didn't like you either, even when we were kids."

"No, you're wrong," Max said. "And you're wrong about everything. You think you found out everybody's cheap. You despise everybody."

Myers' face seemed to grow heavy. In the other corner, the Russian girl playing the guitar began to sing. Myers raised his wife's glass and looked through it at the light. He put it down carefully on the table. He blinked his eyes at Max. "You think you can touch what I want," and he shot out his fist, hitting Max hard on the jaw, smacking his head back against the wall. Myers swung again, tipping over the table to get close to him, pinning Max against the wall; he let him have three hard short shots and then he stepped back and let him roll under the table. "You touched what I want." People crowding around were frightened by the leering arrogant expression on Myers' face. "Get up, stooge," Myers yelled.

Pushing her way through the crowd, Mrs. Myers knelt down beside Max. He whispered, "I just wanted to help you."

"You have, you have," she whispered.

Max went to reach for her arm, but she turned away and was looking at Myers with an expression of grief and tenderness. "Come home, come home," Max heard her say as she stood up, and then she looked back down at Max and shook her head as if she were about to cry, but not for him as he lay there on the floor, tasting the blood in his mouth. Stunned, he wondered if all along they had needed someone like him to hold them together. When Myers turned away and took a few steps with her, holding her arm, and started to go with his head down, someone slyly tripped him and he stumbled, nearly sprawling, and he looked around with a dreadfully surprised look on his face, feeling the contempt everybody had for him, but he straightened himself and hurried out with his wife, and they were arm in arm.

THE BLUE KIMONO

*I*t was hardly more than dawn when George woke up suddenly. He lay wide awake listening to a heavy truck moving on the street below; he heard one truck driver shout
angrily to another; he heard the noises of doors slamming,
of women taking in the milk, of cars starting, and sometime
later on in the morning, he wondered where all these people went when they hurried out briskly with so much assurance.

Each morning he wakened a little earlier and was wide
awake. But this time he was more restless than ever and he
thought with despair. "We're unlucky, that's it. We've never
had any luck since we've come here. There's something you
can't put your hands on working to destroy us. Everything
goes steadily against us from bad to worse. We'll never have
any luck. I can feel it. We'll starve before I get a job."

Then he realized that his wife, Marthe, was no longer in
the bed beside him. He looked around the room that seemed
so much larger and so much emptier in that light and he
thought, "What's the matter with Marthe? Is it getting that
she can't sleep?" Sitting up, he peered uneasily into the
room's dark corners. There was a light coming from the
kitchenette. As he got out of bed slowly, with his thick hair
standing up straight all over his head, and reached for his

slippers and dressing gown, the notion that something mysterious and inexorable was working to destroy them was so strong in him that he suddenly wanted to stand in front of his wife and shout in anger, "What can I do? You tell me something to do. What's the use of me going out to the streets today? I'm going to sit down here and wait, day after day." That time when they had first got married and were secure now seemed such a little faraway forgotten time.

In his eagerness to make his wife feel the bad luck he felt within him, he went striding across the room, his old, shapeless slippers flapping on the floor, his dressing gown only half pulled on, looking in that dim light like someone huge, reckless, and full of sudden savage impulse, who wanted to pound a table and shout. "Marthe, Marthe," he called, "what's the matter with you? Why are you up at this time?"

She came into the room carrying their two-year-old boy. "There's nothing the matter with me," she said. "I got up when I heard Walter crying." She was a small, slim, dark woman with black hair hanging on her shoulders, a thin eager face, and large soft eyes, and as she walked over to the window with the boy she swayed her body as though she were humming to him. The light from the window was now a little stronger. She sat there in her old blue kimono holding the boy tight and feeling his head with her hand.

"What's the matter with him?" George said.

"I don't know. I heard him whimpering, so I got up. His head felt so hot."

"Is there anything I can do?" he said.

"I don't think so."

She seemed so puzzled, so worried and aloof from even the deepest bitterness within him, that George felt impatient, as if it were her fault that the child was sick. For a while he watched her rocking back and forth, always making the same faint humming sound, with the stronger light showing the deep frown on her face, and he couldn't seem to think of the child at all. He wanted to speak with sympathy, but he burst out, "I had to get up because I couldn't go on with my own thoughts. We're unlucky, Marthe. We haven't had a day's luck since we've come to this city. How much longer can this go on before they throw us out on the street? I tell you we never should have come here."

She looked up at him indignantly. He couldn't see the fierceness in her face because her head was against the window light. Twice he walked the length of the room, then he stood beside her, looking down at the street. There was now traffic and an increasing steady hum of motion. He felt chilled and his fingers grasped at the collar of his dressing gown, pulling it across his chest. "It's cold here, and you can imagine what it'll be like in winter," he said. And when Marthe again did not answer, he said sullenly, "You wanted us to come here. You wanted us to give up what we had and come to a bigger city where there were bigger things ahead. Where we might amount to something because of my fine education and your charming manner. You thought we didn't have enough ambition, didn't you?"

"Why talk about it now, George?"

"I want you to see what's happened to us."

"Say I'm responsible. Say anything you wish."

"All right. I'll tell you what I feel in my bones. Luck is against us. Something far stronger than our two lives is working against us. I was thinking about it when I woke up. I must have been thinking about it all through my sleep."

"We've been unlucky, but we've often had a good time, haven't we?" she said.

"Tell me honestly, have we had a day's luck since we got married?" he said brutally.

"I don't know," she said with her head down. Then she looked up suddenly, almost pleading, but afraid to speak.

The little boy started to whimper and then sat up straight, pushing away the blanket his mother tried to keep around him. When she insisted on covering him, he began to fight and she had a hard time holding him till suddenly he was limp in her arms, looking around the darkened room with the bright wonder that comes in a child's fevered eyes.

George watched Marthe trying to soothe the child. The morning light began to fall on her face, making it seem a little leaner, a little narrower and so dreadfully worried. A few years ago everybody used to speak about her extraordinary smile, about the way the lines around her mouth were shaped for laughter, and they used to say, too, that she had a mysterious, tapering, Florentine face. Once a man had said to George, "I remember clearly the first time I met your wife. I said to myself, 'Who is the lady with that marvelous smile?'"

George was now looking at this face as though it belonged to a stranger. He could think of nothing but the shape of it. There were so many angles in that light; it seemed so narrow. "I used to think it was beautiful. It doesn't look beautiful. Would anybody say it was beautiful?" he thought, and yet these thoughts had nothing to do with his love for her.

In some intuitive way she knew that he was no longer thinking of his bad luck, but was thinking of her, so she said patiently, "Walter seems to have quite a fever, George."

Then he stopped walking and touched Walter's head, which was very hot.

"Here, let me hold him a while and you get something," he said. "Get him some aspirin."

"I'll put it in orange juice, if he'll take it," she said.

"For God's sake, turn on the light, Marthe," he called. "This ghastly light is getting on my nerves."

He tried talking to his son while Marthe was away. "Hello, Walter, old boy, what's the matter with you? Look at me, big boy, say something bright to your old man." But the little boy shook his head violently, stared vacantly at the wall a moment, and then tried to bury his face in his father's shoulder. So George, looking disconsolately around the cold room, felt that it was more barren than ever.

Marthe returned with the orange juice and the aspirin. They both began to coax Walter to take it. They pretended to be drinking it themselves, made ecstatic noises with their tongues as though it were delicious and kept it up till the boy cried, "Orange, orange, me too," with an unnatural animation. His eyes were brilliant. Then he swayed as if his spine were made of putty and fell back in his mother's arms.

"We'd better get a doctor in a hurry, George," Marthe said.

"Do you think it's that bad?"

"Look at him," she said, laying him on the bed. "I'm sure he's very sick. You don't want to lose him, do you?" and she stared at Walter, who had closed his eyes and was sleeping.

As Marthe in her fear kept looking up at George, she was fingering her old blue kimono, drawing it tighter around her to keep her warm. The kimono had been of a Japanese pattern adorned with clusters of brilliant flowers sewn in silk.

George had given it to her at the time of their marriage; now he stared at it, torn as it was at the arms, with pieces of old padding hanging out at the hem, with the light colored lining showing through in many places, and he remembered how, when the kimono was new, Marthe used to make the dark hair across her forehead into bangs, fold her arms across her breasts, with her wrists and hands concealed in the sleeve folds, and go around the room in the bright kimono, taking short, prancing steps, pretending she was a Japanese girl.

The kimono now was ragged and gone; it was gone, he thought, like so many bright dreams and aspirations they had once had in the beginning, like so many fine resolutions he had sworn to accomplish, like so many plans they had made and hopes they had cherished.

"Marthe, in God's name," he said suddenly, "the very first money we get, even if we just have enough to put a little down, you'll have to get a decent dressing gown. Do you hear?"

She was startled. Looking up at him in bewilderment, she swallowed hard, then turned her eyes down again.

"It's terrible to have to look at you in that thing," he muttered.

After he had spoken in this way he was ashamed, and he was able to see for the first time the wild terrified look on her face as she bent over Walter.

"Why do you look like that?" he asked. "Hasn't he just got a little fever?"

"Did you see the way he held the glass when he took the orange juice?"

"No. I didn't notice."

"His hand trembled. Earlier, when I first went to him, and gave him a drink I noticed the strange trembling in his hand."

"What does it mean?" he said, awed by the fearful way she was whispering.

"His body seemed limp and he could not sit up either. Last night I was reading about such symptoms in the medical column in the paper. Symptoms like that with a fever are symptoms of infantile paralysis."

"Where's the paper?"

"Over there on the table."

George sat down and began to read the bit of newspaper medical advice; over and over he read it, very calmly. Marthe had described the symptoms accurately; but in a stupid way he could not get used to the notion that his son might have such a dreadful disease. So he remained there calmly for a long time.

And then he suddenly realized how they had been dogged by bad luck; he realized how surely everything they loved was being destroyed day by day and he jumped up and cried out, "We'll have to get a doctor." And as if he realized to the full what was inevitably impending, he cried out, "You're right, Marthe, he'll die. That child will die. It's the luck that's following us. Then it's over. Everything's over. I tell you I'll curse the day I ever saw the light of the world. I'll curse the day we ever met and ever married. I'll smash everything I can put my hands on in this world."

"George, don't go on like that. You'll bring something dreadful down on us," she whispered in terror.

"What else can happen? What else can happen to us worse than this?"

"Nothing, nothing, but please don't go on saying it, George."

Then they both bent down over Walter and they took turns putting their hands on his head. "What doctor will come to us at this house when we have no money?" he kept muttering. "We'll have to take him to a hospital." They remained kneeling together, silent for a long time, almost afraid to speak.

Marthe said suddenly, "Feel, feel his head. Isn't it a little cooler?"

"What could that be?"

"It might be the aspirin working on him."

So they watched, breathing steadily together while the child's head gradually got cooler. Their breathing and their silence seemed to waken the child, for he opened his eyes and stared at them vaguely. "He must be feeling better," George said. "See the way he's looking at us."

"His head does feel a lot cooler."

"What could have been the matter with him, Marthe?"

"It must have been a chill. Oh, I hope it was only a chill."

"Look at him, if you please. Watch me make the rascal laugh."

With desperate eagerness George rushed over to the table, tore off a sheet of newspaper, folded it into a thin strip about eight inches long and twisted it like a cord. Then he knelt down in front of Walter and cried, "See, see," and thrust the twisted paper under his own nose and held it with his upper lip while he wiggled it up and down. He screwed up his eyes diabolically. He pressed his face close against the boy's.

Laughing, Walter put out his hand. "Let me," he said. So George tried to hold the paper moustache against Walter's lip. But that was no good. Walter pushed the paper away and said, "You, you."

"I think his head is cool now," Marthe said. "Maybe he'll be all right."

She got up and walked away from the bed, over to the window with her head down. Standing up, George went to follow her, but his son shouted tyrannically so he had to kneel down and hold the paper moustache under his nose and say, "Look here, look, Walter."

Marthe was trying to smile as she watched them. She took one deep breath after another, as though she would never succeed in filling her lungs with air. But even while she stood there, she grew troubled. She hesitated, she lowered her head and wanted to say, "One of us will find work of some kind, George," but she was afraid.

"I'll get dressed now," she said quietly, and she started to take off her kimono.

As she held it on her arm, her face grew full of deep concern. She held the kimono up so the light shone on the gay silken flowers. Sitting down in the chair, she spread the faded silk on her knee and looked across the room at her sewing basket, which was on the dresser by the mirror. She fumbled patiently with the lining, patting the places that were torn; and suddenly she was sure she could draw the torn parts together and make it look bright and new.

"I think I can fix it up so it'll look fine, George," she said.

"Eh?" he said. "What are you bothering with that for?" Then he ducked down to the floor again and wiggled his paper moustache fiercely at the child.

WITH AN AIR
OF DIGNITY

*T*he Langleys, a highly respected, well-off family, lived
in a big red brick house on the outskirts of the prairie
town. Old Mr. Langley had been the bank manager until he
suffered the stroke that left him crippled. Living with him
was his housekeeper, a pretty young woman named Rita, a
stranger in town from the east, who was working her way
to the west coast, and the Langley children — Pauline, the
town librarian, and her brother, twenty-two-year-old Steve.

When Steve was eighteen and a little wild, he had refused to go to school and had hung around the poolroom and
the dance hall with big Kersh and his friends. After the furniture store had been robbed, Steve, under police question-
ing, admitted he had heard Kersh planning to break into the
store. Kersh had been sent to jail for three years. Steve,
changing his life, had gone on to the university in Saskatoon
and was now working in the bank. When Kersh got out of
jail he came back to town and whenever he got drunk he
went looking for Steve and when he found him, even if it
was at the entrance to the bank, he beat him up.

Kersh was a long-nosed truck driver with pale hard
eyes who was over six feet tall. Steve was only five foot

eight and he had small hands. When Kersh came after him yelling, "All right, pigeon, get out of town," Steve would battle him but he always looked like a slight freckle-faced boy with despair in his eyes. Kersh had beaten him in a restaurant, he had beaten him out on the street, and once in the snow in front of the Langley home. The police had thrown Kersh in jail for a week, but everybody knew Kersh would keep on beating Steve Langley.

On a Saturday afternoon, Rita Whaley, the stranger among the Langleys, saw Kersh's old car turning in from the highway. She was in her attic room standing by the window brushing her hair, letting it hang loose on her shoulders in the long bob she used to wear back east. There was bright sunlight glistening on the banked snow on the Langley drive and from the high window she could see the way the road ran for miles beyond the town into the vast prairie snow. There was sun and mist and dryness in the air, yet it was very cold, twenty below zero.

As the car stopped in the drive, Rita watched Kersh lean back surveying the house. He was wearing a leather jacket and a brown cap. He was not alone. Whitey Breaden, in the front seat with him, was a slow-witted fellow in a moth-eaten coon coat, who worked in a garage and had once dreamed of being a professional boxer. Kersh always brought someone along with him, an audience. Kicking the car door open, he stumbled out and stood staring at the house with all his half-drunken arrogance.

Kersh's big grin made Rita feel sick, for Steve Langley had become important to her. Unlike Pauline, he treated Rita with a gentle respect, as if she were a fine friend of the family and not just a stray working her way to the coast. Maybe he understood that in Montreal she'd had a bad time, but his courteous respectful manner, filling her with gratitude, seemed to caress and restore her. With Kersh out there now she knew what was going to happen, so she rushed downstairs.

Mr. Langley was in the wheelchair by the grate fire, and beside him in the rocking chair, Pauline was stitching the hem of a dress. Steve, peeling an orange, was thinner, nervous, and more serious these days. Everything was warm and peaceful. "Kersh," Rita blurted out. "It's Kersh."

"Where?" Steve asked, his face white.

"Out there in the car with a pal."

The orange slipped from his hands and his eyes grew despairing as he watched it roll to the floor. Then, as he looked at his sister, her face seemed to fascinate him. "Steve, what'll you do?" Pauline whispered.

"I don't know," he said helplessly. "Lock the doors, I guess. Yeah, lock the door, Rita." Sitting down, he took a deep breath and closed his eyes. "The drunken lout," his sister cried fiercely. "To come right to our home. All right. I'll have the police out here in ten minutes."

"We've already tried that," Steve said lifelessly. "A fine exhibition."

His father watched him. Old Mr. Langley had lost the power of speech but he followed everything with his lively eyes. The stroke had caused a curl to his lip and Steve could never be sure if the curl was also contempt.

"Hey, Langley," Kersh yelled. "Come on out. I want to see you."

"Don't say anything," Steve said.

"What if he tries to come in?" Pauline asked. "I'm frightened, Steve."

"If he's good and drunk he'll go away."

But Kersh had begun to pound on the door. "Come on out here, little pigeon," he roared.

"Steve, don't," Pauline cried.

"I'll get him out of here. I've got to."

"No. Please Steve. My God. Not again. This is our house, our home," Pauline pleaded.

"I'm not afraid of him. I'm not," he said doggedly. Then he swung around to his father who sat so motionless in the wheelchair. The crippled man still looked like a dignified figure with his white hair and his neat black coat. Before he had been stricken old Mr. Langley had been a tall powerful man with a commanding presence and Steve had always had great respect for him. His father's eyes were bright and critical.

"I'm not afraid of him, don't you understand?" he said, making an angry apology to his father. "I'm just not big enough. I can smack him again and again. And then what? I can't go on."

When his father turned away, Steve looked at his sister who nodded sympathetically, and then at Rita Whaley, who tried to hide her concern with a nervous shy smile.

"Hey, Langley," Kersh yelled. "I'm right here on your doorstep. Come on out. Or maybe I should come in."

"If he tries to come in," Steve whispered, going slowly to the window, "I'll kill him. Somehow I'll kill him. I've got a right to kill him."

There was a heavy frost on the windowpane and Steve breathed on it and began to rub away the frost so he could look out. Then he saw Whitey Breaden's face at the lowered window of the car. Whitey was waiting with a big derisive grin. Kersh was over to the right of the path, scowling, blinking because the sun on the snow dazzled him, and then he lurched suddenly in the snow, going down on one knee cursing. In the cold bright sunlight his heavy red face shone with so much mean drunk brutal contempt that Steve's right leg began to shimmy and he couldn't control it. He turned with a crazy smile and left the others and hurried upstairs to his room. He got the twenty-two he used to hunt rabbits with and came down to the window again.

"You big fool, Steve," his sister cried out. "Oh you big fool."

"Get away," he said as she came close to him.

"It'll only make it worse for you, Steve," she cried.

"I'd shoot him like a rabbit," he said.

"Hold on to yourself, Steve," she said.

"Maybe I could talk to him," Rita said.

"Keep out of this, Rita," he said.

"No, listen, Steve," she cried, "a girl can do things with a guy like that." She touched his arm gently. She had an apologetic smile, as if she felt her confidence in her ability to handle Kersh revealed an aspect of her life she had tried to hide from them.

"I know how you feel, Steve," she said. "I can get him to go away."

"Forget it," Steve said.

"I know Kersh," she said.

"Yes," Pauline said. "Rita knows Kersh. Kersh knows her."

"What're you talking about? I said no," he said.

"Steve," Pauline said. "This is nothing to her."

"Pauline," he shouted.

"It's all right, Steve," Rita said, fussing with her hair. She got her muskrat coat from the peg in the hall and went out.

Steve peered through the spot on the windowpane that he had rubbed clear of frost. He waited until she came into the sunlight. She was holding the collar of her coat tight across her throat, taking slow delicate steps in the snow because she had on low shoes. A bright sun glowed against a shimmering prairie mist.

While Kersh waited, Whitey Breaden got out of the car and stood beside Kersh as she came to them with an easy smile. Then, the three were talking and she looked like a little girl beside Kersh in his leather jacket. Kersh pointed at the house, laughed and patted Whitey on the back, and then he took Rita's arm in a confidential gesture. She shrugged, hesitated, and looked back at the house. Suddenly she left them and came in quickly.

"I knew he wouldn't go," Steve said to her.

"They'll go all right," she said.

"No, they're not going."

"Well," she said awkwardly. "Kersh wants me to go into town and have some dinner with them. I don't know. What do you think?"

"If it's just a matter of going to town," Pauline said quickly, "then why not?"

"Maybe I can talk some sense into Kersh," Rita said.

"You're crazy," said Steve.

"No, go ahead, Rita," Pauline said.

"I'll change my dress," Rita said, and hurried upstairs.

Steve and his sister, silent with their father watching, were suddenly embarrassed. But Pauline, a severe proud girl, said irritably, "I'm not worried, Steve. A girl like Rita can always handle a man like Kersh."

"A girl like Rita?"

"Yes, a girl like Rita can look after herself. She won't stay with us long. It's not as if she belongs here with us."

Rita was coming downstairs in a green dress and she had a lot of lipstick on. Hurrying to the hall, she stepped into her overshoes, but as she knotted the lace on the right shoe, she looked up and paused as if she suddenly understood what they were saying about her.

"If you're worrying about me it's a mistake," she said. "It's nothing. I'll be back in an hour or two."

Steve and Pauline watched her get into the car with Kersh. When the car turned out to the road, Steve, wherever he moved, was sure his father's eyes were on him. An hour passed, and then it was dinnertime. He could not eat, nor could he read after dinner. He found himself saying, "She knows Kersh. Rita's been around." He went up to his room and stood by the window watching the road in the long lonely prairie twilight. His hurt bewildered him.

Finally, he began to get dressed and in a slow methodical fashion he shaved carefully, put on a clean white shirt and his best blue suit. He wanted to look like an important man who didn't belong in Kersh's world. When he went downstairs where his father was dozing by the fire, he saw how the hot coals were throwing a fiery reflection on his father's broad calm forehead, and he frowned. He put on his overcoat and the expensive fur cap they had given him at Christmas and went out and along the road to town walking slowly.

In the night air, there was a shining winter brightness and great height to the darkness, with a sweep of yellow-green and red northern lights across the sky. His feet crunched on the frozen snow. It sounded as if he had on squeaky new shoes. A freight train moaned in the long night. Down the road, the cluster of lights in the center of the town shone and then the houses were closer together and he began to walk faster, as if he had made a plan. But he had no plan at all.

The quiet street led to the park in front of the big white hotel and a row of stores was across from the park, all closed with no lights except in one narrow window, Mike's restaurant. When he got to the window, he peered in: Mike was at the counter with his pointed bald head and his moustache, sitting on one of the row of counter stools with the torn leather seats, and back in the corner by the kitchen, at the end table, Kersh, Breaden and Rita and a barber named Henry Clay were joking and laughing. Kersh was the first to see Steve come in and he frowned and scowled and stood up slowly. "Mike," he called. "You were closing up, weren't you?"

"I want no trouble, Kersh," Mike said.

"You said you were closing up."

"I'm closing."

"Go ahead, then."

"What's the game, Steve?" Rita said, her face flushed. She was ashamed that Steve had found her laughing. "I thought you wanted to keep away, Steve," she cried. "So why don't you?"

"I was passing by," he said. "I thought you might want to come along with me." In his good clothes, he looked like a serious young man.

"Listen, pigeon, beat it," Kersh said, grinning at Whitey Breaden who smirked and took out a nail file and began to clean his nails. "Or maybe I don't make myself clear, Mr. Langley?" he added.

"I'll go in my own time, when Rita's ready," Steve said.

"I try to make you understand I feel lousy about my whole life when I see you, pigeon," Kersh said. He had had a lot to drink and his pale blue eyes were half shut. "Okay," he grunted, "it's always a pleasure." He slapped Steve viciously on the mouth and then he waited. "Come on, hit me," he said. "Come on, come on."

"No, I'm not going to hit you, Kersh."

"So what's this?" Kersh asked, and when Steve saw the confusion in the pale blue eyes his heart leaped. "So now the punker's yellow," Kersh said. "See, now he's yellow."

"He was yellow three years ago," Whitey said. "A yellow pigeon."

But Kersh didn't like Steve's tight superior smile as he held his hands straight at his sides.

"Superior little punk, eh," Kersh yelled and grabbed Steve by the collar, choked him, slapped his face, and kept on slapping in a frantic eagerness to make Steve raise his hands and resist, but his hands didn't come up, and Kersh, slamming him against the wall, grunted, "Grin at me you bastard, grin."

"You're making a big mistake, Kersh," Steve whispered.

"How can a guy take it?" the barber said, and Rita stared at Steve.

"Here," Kersh coaxed, thrusting out his own jaw eagerly. "Hit me here."

"I don't need to," Steve gasped.

"Hit me right here, baby," Kersh pleaded, tapping his jaw delicately with his forefinger.

"I don't need to. No."

"So what's this?" Kersh blurted out. Blinking his eyes, he looked at the others to see if they felt he was being mocked. He was enraged. Then he smashed Steve on the jaw; he smashed him again and waited, but the crazy smile remained on Steve's face, and he would not back away. His fine fur hat had been knocked off, his white shirt was flecked with blood from his mouth, and there was a silence, a silence that embarrassed them all, and then Steve touched his swelling eye with his hand, swaying a little as he tried to smile. Rita put her hands over her face. She started to cry.

"It's a gag," Kersh whispered, feeling the others withdraw from him. Bewildered, he cracked Steve on the jaw and watched him slump to the floor.

"It's not right, Kersh," Mike protested. "That's not right."

The barber, who had got up, leaned over the table and looked down at Steve. "It's wild," he said softly. "Very wild."

"Shut up," Kersh yelled as Steve, raising himself on one knee, wiped the blood from his mouth.

"What's the matter with you, Kersh?" Steve whispered.

"Me?" Kersh yelled. "What the hell is this?" and went to hit him again, but stopped suddenly. A sick look came into his eyes. "The guy ain't right in the head, I sucker myself hitting him," he said slowly, turning his back on Steve and appealing to the others. "Did I go after him? He came after me. The broad wanted to come along. All I want is that the guy should keep away from me."

"I'll tell him," the barber said.

"Come on, let's blow this joint," Kersh said. He wanted to swagger but he was afraid the others weren't going to come with him. "So what about it?" he asked.

"Yeah," the barber agreed. "I think we should go. Come on Whitey."

As they went out, Mike said, "I kinda think that guy won't bother you again, Steve."

"I don't know," Steve said, sitting down and straightening his collar.

"A guy like Kersh ain't used to feeling like a punk," Mike said.

Going to the counter, Mike poured a cup of coffee and brought it to Steve. Rita had dipped a handkerchief in a glass of water and was wiping his face. "You don't look so bad, Steve," Mike said. "Are you all right?"

"It's nothing," Steve said, gulping down the coffee. Neither he nor Rita spoke. When he had put on his fur hat he said, "Come on, Rita," and he smiled at Mike and they went out.

The cold air stung the cuts on his face. He noticed Rita had forgotten to put on her gloves. "Put on your gloves, Rita," he said.

Walking in step, she kept her head down. It was a long time before he realized she was crying.

"Hey, what's the matter?"

"Nothing." Stopping, she took out her handkerchief and wiped his mouth. "That blood is drying in the cold," she said. "Look, I know I can't stay around your place any more."

"You can stay as long as you want."

"No. Not in that house with your sister. She thinks she knows what I was. She's sure she knows what I am. Well I don't want it. I won't have it. Anyway, I was going to the coast, wasn't I, so — now I'm on my way."

Then, as they walked along in silence, her grip on his arm tightened.

"I still can't figure out why you came after me," she said.

"Well, I got thinking."

"You've got your good suit on. You got all dressed up to come after me."

"What else could I do?"

"But to stand there and be beaten?"

"Beaten? Who was beaten? Not me!" As they walked in step, their shoes squeaked in the hard snow. The street was long. It ran into the prairie, and the prairie into the cold sky. They were both watching the ribbons of light on the rim of the prairie sky.

THE WAY IT ENDED

*A*s they sat around the table in the little room the detectives used in the neighborhood police station, Hilda Scranton told the detective who had found her working as a waitress in Detroit, and Miss Schenley, the social worker, that they were wasting their time; her mother wouldn't dream of complaining that she was incorrigible.

She was a big girl for her age, sixteen, not really pretty, yet with a wide, attractive mouth, good eyes and thick black hair. She was sure that in her yellow summer dress she looked like a full-grown woman and she tried to act like one, but it was a hot night, and as the little beads of moisture appeared on her forehead and upper lip and her make-up wore off she became just a defiant, worried girl. "If you were my daughter," the solemn, graying detective said, "and you ran off like that, I'd spank you until you couldn't sit down." But Hilda knew he had decided that she was just another wayward girl, and she knew too that he watched the way her dress tightened across her breasts when she moved, so she lowered her eyes and smiled demurely, embarrassing him.

She didn't want them to see that she was really listening for the sound of her mother and dreading it, for she was afraid her mother would stand there grimly and say, "This is the end. I've tried everything — everything, and I can't do anything with her," and then she didn't know what would happen to her. So, as they waited she tried to make a friend out of Miss Schenley, the neat, thin, social worker. Miss Schenley was a trained psychologist and she said she wanted to be helpful and understanding. Turning to her with a graceful little motion of her hand, Hilda opened her eyes wide and in good, soft, polite language and with an air of troubled, intelligent reluctance tried to explain the difficulty she had had with her mother, and why she had run away, and in a little while she was sure she could use Miss Schenley as a protection against her mother.

There was nothing she wasn't ready to tell Miss Schenley, and she did, though, of course, not exactly everything, because Miss Schenley really wanted to know only why she didn't get on with her mother. She had to get it all in before her mother came, for Miss Schenley understood there were certain things her mother couldn't believe; her mother still thought of her as a child. It had gotten worse in the last year, since her father had died. She felt smothered by her mother's concern and she had no chance to have any life of her own.

Then, the desk sergeant in the outer room called to the detective who got up and went out, and Hilda heard her mother's voice, and Miss Schenley frowned and meditated. "Well, here she is, Mrs. Scranton," said the detective. Hilda wanted to meet her mother with a bold, unyielding look, but her mother had on the old blue two-piece dress with the white bow at the throat, the dress Hilda had discarded. And she looked so much older than she had looked just a week ago. Hollow-eyed and tired, her hair untidy, she showed in her face everything she had been doing the last week and the last year; the waiting at the window, the telephoning, the little prayer, the restless nights and the anger. She seemed to stand there with her jaw trembling, heaping it all on Hilda.

"Hilda, are you all right?"

"Of course I'm all right, Mother," she said, but she turned away, feeling angry and humiliated.

"Sit down, Mrs. Scranton," the detective said, pulling a chair out for her.

"Hilda and I have had a fine long talk," Miss Schenley said cheerfully. "You know, Mrs. Scranton, I like your Hilda."

"Yes, she's quite a likeable girl."

"And I don't think there's anything basically wrong with her."

"Of course there isn't, Miss Schenley. Hilda's a little reckless and careless, but she's not a bad girl, and I'm sure she'll settle down."

Hilda didn't like the way they were talking about her as if she weren't there, but then Miss Schenley said, "However, the fact is Hilda doesn't want to go to school and she doesn't want to live at home."

"All that has happened only in the last year," her mother said, but she sounded too anxious, as if Hilda had been misunderstood and she wanted only to protect her. "She'll grow out of it, Miss Schenley."

"Mother, please," Hilda said resentfully, "don't talk about me as if I were a little child."

"Well, in many ways you still are a child," she said calmly.

"But in other ways Hilda is quite a big girl," Miss Schenley said patiently, "and it makes it hard for her," and she smiled at Hilda. It proved she was on her side and Hilda could hardly conceal her satisfaction. "I've got quite a bit of Hilda's history from her," Miss Schenley went on, "and I'm wondering if the whole trouble may not be that you worry too much about her."

"Of course I worry about Hilda, I'm her mother."

"But I mean about every little thing — her clothes, her parties, her music, her friends, her language."

"But I'm the only one there is to be concerned," Mrs. Scranton said with a patient smile as if she had just perceived that Miss Schenley was hard of understanding. It irritated Miss Schenley and Hilda said quickly, "Oh, Mother. Miss Schenley is a psychologist," and her mother nodded apologetically.

"And those boys in the park," Miss Schenley said. "Why don't you trust Hilda with them? Try it, why don't you?"

"Those boys. You don't know those boys. Trust my daughter with them in the park at two in the morning? Why, that would be shameless."

"Well, the boys won't come to the house if they're going to find Hilda sitting in your lap, Mrs. Scranton. Naturally she prefers the freedom of the park, don't you see?"

It was just what Hilda wanted Miss Schenley to say, but the tone in which she said it and her patient smile made Hilda feel cheap, and she had to avoid her mother's eyes as Miss Schenley went on. "It may be that Hilda expects to find you living in her pocket, eating her life up. If I were you I'd try and stop worrying about her. I'd say, 'All right, don't go to school: get a job,' and see how it works out."

"But you don't know Hilda. You don't know her at all." Her voice broke for she was outraged and ready to lose control of herself. "Why, she'd stay out all night."

"Not if she had to go to work in the morning. Once you make up your mind you're not going to do any more worrying . . ."

"Not worry about Hilda? Why, till the day I die . . ." But she faltered and looked bewildered, and Hilda wanted to speak to her but there was nothing to say.

"You see, Mrs. Scranton," Miss Schenley said easily, "it's just possible you may be a little too possessive about Hilda."

"Possessive?"

"Oh, thousands of mothers are possessive about their daughters, just because they love them. And they give them no chance to feel responsible. Maybe you like worrying . . ."

"Like worrying?" The hurt surprise in her voice worried Hilda. Her mother seemed to be wondering if she had some flaw in her nature that would make any daughter feel smothered, and her eyes filled with tears and she blurted out, "In heaven's name, Hilda, what have you been saying about me?"

"Nothing that isn't true," Hilda muttered, as her mother stared at her blankly. She wanted to say more but she could not get her breath and she concentrated on the detective's cigar butt on the ashtray, then hated him for sitting there listening, and for some reason she thought of the fine clothes her mother used to wear, and how she used to get her hair done once a week. "You know you do like to worry about me," she whispered.

"Well, the point is," Miss Schenley said soothingly, "Hilda's nature is what it is, and your nature, Mrs. Scranton, is what it is. Maybe you're hard on each other. But Hilda's young. She can change." Miss Schenley paused, and Hilda,

out of the corner of her eye, saw her glance at her mother, pale
and tired in the shabby dress. "Nobody's going to change
you, Mrs. Scranton. It's too late for that. But maybe we can
do something for Hilda."

"The main thing is," the detective said, standing up impatiently, "I can see Mrs. Scranton doesn't want to charge
Hilda with being incorrigible."

"Of course I don't. Of course not."

"Well, she's your daughter. You might as well take her
home now."

"Come on, Hilda," Mrs. Scranton said stiffly. As she
stood up she lifted her head with dignity and put out her
hand to Miss Schenley. "Thank you for trying to be of some
help."

"Sometimes it's good to talk these things out," Miss
Schenley said, and then, as her eyes met Mrs. Scranton's
for the first time she looked embarrassed. "Hilda, for heav-
en's sake, from now on, try and be responsible."

"Yes, Miss Schenley," she said meekly.

Outside on the street that led through the little park to
their home, they fell in step and Hilda waited for her mother
to turn on her and abuse her fiercely. But she didn't turn on
her, she hurried along, her mouth in a thin line, her head bent
with her troubles. Hilda knew all that she was thinking; she
was worrying about what she might have done in Detroit,
and wondering what there was to say to her now.

They reached the little park and went along the cinder
path by the fountain. In the shadows of the bushes in the
corner were benches and they could hear laughter and then
a raucous voice coming out of the shadows. As they walked
along, grim and silent, it was all familiar to Hilda. It was

just like one of those other nights when her mother, after waiting at the window, had come out to wander around for hours. And if she herself had been with one of the fellows in somebody's house until very late, she would come out and hurry along the street, knowing she would encounter her mother, and usually she would see her standing at the corner where she could watch both streets. Her mother would be so relieved to see her that there would be a few moments of silence and in those moments Hilda would talk quickly, "Why are you waiting around? Everybody knows what you're like. Why do you make such a baby out of me?" Then her mother would get control of herself and scold her bitterly. They would walk along, trying to keep their voices down so they wouldn't wake the neighbors. And now, again, her mother was walking her home, ready to call her shameless and ungrateful and a terrible heartbreak.

The sound of their footsteps and her mother's silence became unbearable for she knew how her mother was berating her in her thoughts, and it was unfair that she was giving her no chance to defend herself. "Well, why don't you say something?" she blurted out.

"Say something, Hilda? Why?" she asked lifelessly. "People don't know how I feel. I don't seem to matter."

"I don't know what you mean," Hilda said awkwardly. But everything suddenly became strangely unfamiliar. At first she didn't know what was wrong, and then she realized that her mother, as they walked along, hadn't been brooding over what might have happened to her in Detroit; she hadn't really been thinking of her at all; she had been thinking of herself and her own life. Hilda felt off by herself, and then lonely.

"I must have looked an awful fright back there with those people," her mother said, as if trying to explain something to herself. "Imagine. Too late. Too late. Why, I'm only forty, Hilda."

"Yes, that's right," Hilda, said uneasily.

"Only six months ago Sam Ingram asked me to marry him."

"You didn't say anything about it."

"I thought I should wait until you were a little older. Maybe it's too late now."

"I didn't know," Hilda said, and she was afraid to turn and look at her, afraid she would see that she had never really known what her mother thought about anything, and now it was like walking with someone entirely apart from herself, another woman with a life of her own.

"I should have fixed myself up a little before I ran out," her mother said, stopping by the light and fumbling in her bag for her mirror. "I shouldn't look like this on the street," and she patted back loose strands of hair.

"Put on a little lipstick, mother."

"Yes, I'd better."

"Here, use mine," Hilda said, opening her purse. With a shy gesture she offered her lipstick like a woman offering it to another woman whom she doesn't know very well. Her mother's hand trembled as she marked her lips and Hilda watched the lips come together and then part, moistened and brightened, and in the anxious face she seemed to see everything that had been happening in her own life, all lined there on her mother's face, and a heavy weight seemed to come against her own heart. Then she was angry and impatient with herself, and angry at everything that had been said in the police station.

"That's better. You look fine now," she said, and as they walked on home she felt years older, and knew that something was ended.

LADY IN
A GREEN DRESS

A year ago, when he was at law school, Henry Sproule
walked as far as the city hall square with five or six
fellows from the final year. In the first fine days of early
spring, they walked the wet pavements, carrying their brief-
cases. They went into the cigar and magazine store at the
corner to talk for a few moments with the woman behind the
counter before they separated and went to their law offices.

The woman looked to be about thirty-five, smiling, polite
and always glad to see the students. Usually, she wore a simple green dress that set off her thick blond hair pulled back
into a knot on her neck. The proprietor of the store, a Greek,
was delighted to have the fellows in his store making small
but regular purchases for the sake of trivial conversation with
the woman. Henry, who was red-headed and lanky, resented
the way the proprietor stood rubbing his hands, trying to
make conversation by whispering, "She's a nice woman, ain't
she? But a shame she's so married, eh?"

Henry began to go into the store alone and he talked am-
usingly and wittily with the woman who would suddenly
laugh out loud. She admitted reluctantly that her name was
Irene Airth. Henry pleaded with her to go out with him and

she teased him charmingly as though he were a very young but nice fellow.

In the morning classes at the law school, Henry looked out the window at the new green leaves on the chestnut tree and the blue sky. The city streets were clean. He liked the city in the spring. Soon, after the exams, he would go away to practice law in a country town and suddenly he was aware that he yearned for this woman with the fair hair and green dress. Several times he left the school in the morning and went over to the store to whisper intimately with Irene who was a little embarrassed and puzzled by this sincerity, but she was very eager to see him in the mornings. "I don't think she knows what to do about me at all, that's the trouble," he thought. She told him one morning that she would like very much to have a simple friendly feeling for him. She was so gentle in her explanation and yet so lovely that he left the store abruptly, not knowing what to say.

One night he followed her, remaining a distance behind the neat figure in the light coat with the pretty cape. She walked to the older part of the city where there were many big dilapidated rooming houses. When she was under a street light, he caught up with her and took hold of her by the arm.

"Oh Red, where did you come from?" she said casually and smiled.

"I've been following you."

"Heavens, what for?"

"Nothing at all; just to be with you, Irene," he said.

She was delighted but afraid to encourage him. "I was going into the house," she said.

Arm in arm and laughing cheerfully, they entered one of the houses and went into a large high-ceilinged room on the ground floor. A dressing table and a bed were at one end of the room. She took off her hat and stood in front of the mirror, powdering her nose while Henry fumbled with his hat. Then he noticed that she had on the green dress.

"Is that the only dress you have?" he said suddenly.

"No, I have another good one, but I don't like it so well. I'll talk with you from the kitchen while I make a cup of tea."

Waiting, he wondered how long she had lived in the room, it was furnished so impersonally. Then they sat beside each other to drink the tea, and smoothing her skirt she said suddenly, "You're really a good guy Red, but promise you won't try to fool around with me if I let you stay."

"But why?"

"Because I'm happy as it is, for one thing. Then again, I might like it and I couldn't stand that. Besides, you've got such a nice freckled face."

"Oh, I thought you might be worrying about your husband."

"I do worry about him sometimes."

Her cheeks were flushed. He could hardly keep from putting his arms around her. Cautiously, he said, "Are you in love with your husband?"

"Am I in love with him? Of course I am," she said abruptly.

"Where is he?"

"I don't know."

She was angry and a little bewildered. He thought she was going to cry. "I'm awfully sorry. You've no idea how sorry I am," he said. "I just meant . . . I mean — I don't know what I meant."

Smiling calmly, she said, "You've been very friendly, Red, so there's no reason why I shouldn't explain to you. I haven't seen my husband for eight years, what do you think of that?"

"Where in the world is he?"

"I don't know. It sounds a little funny, doesn't it. Yet I love my husband. I love him more than anyone else. I love all my thoughts of him and the clear bright picture I always have of him in my mind."

Her blue eyes were moist, and she began to tell him that her husband had gone away a few months after they married. "I'll show you a picture of him," she said, and got up to look into a bureau drawer. Then she showed him a small picture of a young man with remarkable eyes and a sneering lip. He was in uniform. "We were married when he came back from the war. We only lived together six months," she said.

"He's a nice-looking guy all right," Henry said.

"Red, if I tell you something will you promise never to tell . . . because I like you so much."

"Sure, I promise. Honest to God."

"Weren't you wondering why he went away?"

"I didn't like to ask."

"He was going to be arrested for embezzlement. He stole money, quite a bit I think. He left me a note saying that no one would ever bother me about it and someday he'd pay back every cent and come back. Of course he will come back . . . if he can. That was eight years ago."

"And you haven't heard from him?"

"No. But I believe there's a good reason for it. I prefer to think that," she said, looking at him steadily.

incredible that he would want to live there. When she rapped on the door her face was glowing with good feeling and concern for him. But when he stood there, white-faced, tired and thin, and with no friendly smile, her mouth opened and she faltered and said timidly, "Well, you aren't that upset just to see me, are you, Alec?"

"I'm not upset at all," he said.

"I only want to talk to you for a minute."

"Why did you come here?"

"It's about that job . . ." she began, but her voice trailed away, for though he was listening, he did not seem to be paying attention to her words.

Then, distressed, he shook his head and said in a worried, impatient voice, "This is no place to come. I live here and I don't live alone, as you know. What's the use?" He blocked the door, his arms folded, yet not looking at her, as if he were afraid that the warmth of her generous nature would suddenly touch him and draw him close to her. "There's nothing to say about the job. I don't want it. That's final. Don't you see?"

"But you were going to take it," she pleaded.

"Sure."

"And when you found out I had something to with it — oh, Alec, you must hate me. Why, why? If it were just for a friend, if it were just for one of my customers, they wouldn't snap at me like that." Then she was suddenly short of breath, because he said nothing to help her. "Alec, you should take that job. I'm not trying to get you to come back to me. But I believe in your talent like I might believe in the talent of someone I hardly knew. Forget there was ever any love between us," she said. "I could still believe you had talent, couldn't I?"

When the stubborn, boyish, unyielding expression that she had seen a thousand times on his face after they had begun one of these little struggles came into his eyes, she brightened and felt a sudden mad eagerness to persuade him as she had so often done. For the girl she felt only restless impatience.

"Let me come in and talk to you, Alec."

"All right, all right," he said, stepping aside.

The room, with its old red-covered plush furniture, its little kitchen cabinet with the figured curtain drawn across it, and the faint but pervading smell of gas, gave her fresh confidence. All she had to do, she thought eagerly as she sat down, was to keep on talking reasonably with him and she could suddenly lift him right out of the squalid place. His generous nature would open up to her, she would hear again the shy laughing apology.

"I don't think you'll go till you've said your piece, so go ahead," he said sighing.

"It's not just what your life is now," she began, looking around the room. "Even if I'm dead you'll want something better than this."

"I'm not taking that job," he said calmly.

"But why? Alec, tell me why."

"It's a free country," he said stubbornly. "A job comes my way and I don't choose to take it. What's the matter with that?"

"Why, nothing at all," she said. Then she couldn't help it, she burst out indignantly, "That's not you talking, Alec."

"No?"

"No, indeed. You're not a petty man," she said. "It's the — well, it's Eva, isn't it? Why can't you both see that I'm not plotting anything? You've listened to her, haven't you? If you love her you should. But she shouldn't make you do a thing that will hurt you just for the sake of taking a crack at me."

"Eva," he called out suddenly.

"All right," the girl called from the bedroom. "I'm coming."

While they waited, and Julia trembled with eagerness to face the girl, every gesture Alec made seemed harsh and unyielding and yet a little desperate: she felt a tug between them and it gave her joy.

Eva came out of the bedroom powdering her nose laconically. She had her hat on and was dressed to go out. "I heard you talking, Mrs. Watson," she said carelessly. As Eva took a last look at herself in her little hand mirror, rubbed her lips together, and then put the mirror in her purse, Julia was shocked. There was going to be no struggle between them. Eva was like a soft feathery little milk-white doll, and as she crossed the room she seemed confident that her soft shapeliness would be looked after by someone no matter what happened. Julia couldn't understand why he did not see the sluttishness in the girl.

"I knew you'd be around sooner or later, Mrs. Watson," Eva said. "I'm sorry I'm on my way out."

"Then you knew more than I did," Julia said, reddening.

"Maybe I do."

"I wish you wouldn't misunderstand why I'm here," Julia said quickly. "I'm not trying to—"

"You're here about that job, aren't you?"

"Yes."

"That's what I meant."

"I mean you're not — I mean I'm not trying to get in your way," Julia insisted.

"You're not getting in my way, lady," Eva said.

"You don't resent my interest?"

"Not that. I wanted Alec to take the job." Then, while Julia waited, feeling dreadfully insecure, as if she were touching something in Alec she had never known, Eva turned to him and said impatiently, "For heaven's sake, why don't you take the job? It sounds like a decent job to me. What do you care where it came from?"

To Julia, it seemed the girl was pleading her case for her and she was sure Alec, looking at Eva's soft shapeliness, would give her anything she wanted, and she couldn't bear it: she lowered her head, she was so ashamed to be there. But Alec said harshly, "You keep out of this, Eva."

"Suit yourself," Eva said. She smiled at Alec. There was acquiescence in her full red mouth. Julia could see she always yielded. Then, looking shrewdly at Julia, and finding nothing dangerously seductive in her aggressive eagerness, she said, "You won't mind if I run along, will you?" She went out.

Humiliated, Julia stared timidly at Alec, and when he only waited, unmoved, she whispered, "Can't you see she's indifferent to you?"

"Maybe she is," he said, shrugging.

"But she doesn't love you."

"I like it that way. Just that way," he said.

"All right," she said. "Only you should take the job unless you hate even the thought of me." She was pleading with him not to destroy all she had left, the memory of the years when they had loved each other. "I'm mixed up," she said. "I don't know why you have this terrible feeling about me."

"Julia, I don't hate you," he said, looking miserable. "I'm not trying to hurt you." Then he seemed to lose his breath. All the love she had given for so long seemed to touch him suddenly and make him mute. But he shook his head, pulling away resolutely. Looking around the mean room with the old furniture and the long faded window drapes as if it were a new life that he had to guard desperately against her, he whispered, "Sure, I've treated you terribly. But, my God, Julia, you've run my life for years. I was smothered. I'm not a child. And even now when I leave you, you keep coming in and out of my life arranging it for me. You can't stop. This job — it's nothing. But it gives me a chance to say no to you." Then he shouted, "I'm saying no, no, no. Stop."

"No to what?" she asked, bewildered.

"Your care for me. Your love," he said.

"My love?"

"There's hardly anything left of me."

"I only wanted you to be happy," she whispered. But she looked so powerless and frightened that he cried out, "There hasn't been anything that's me for years. It's been all you. Every little thing, day after day."

He came close to her and she went to put her arms around him and cry out that he should tell her everything he hoped for and she would share it, but with his eyes he seemed to be begging her to keep away, so she drew back, scared to touch him. She was suddenly frightened by her own eagerness, and her whole life seemed to be full of people she had pushed around, consumed because they liked her. Terrified, she put her trembling hands over her face.

"Julia, don't cry," he said. When she didn't answer he went closer and bent over her.

"Don't touch me," she begged him. "Keep away from me."

"If you think I'm refusing the job just to hurt you . . ." he began.

"No. Don't take it, don't let it touch you," she cried, so self-effacing and so suddenly humble that he stared at her. "I didn't understand," she whispered, but he was shy with her, bending over her, touching her as if she were still the eager Julia, yet a woman he had never known.

FATHER AND SON

*T*he old stone farmhouse stood out sharp and clear
against the dark hill in the moonlight. He walked up the
path a little, then realized that he was walking into the flood
of light from the window. This scared him and he stopped.
"Why did I feel that I had to come?" he thought. "After waiting four years why do I come now? What am I doing here?"
He looked around the little valley, at the huge old barn shad-
owing all the hill and at the little garden beside the house. He
heard the old car that had picked him up rumbling back
through the ruts on the road. There was a heavy mist in the
valley. The soft Pennsylvanian hills rose up clear above the
floating mist and were rounded against the sky.

He was so afraid of his own uneasiness and the valley's
silence that he darted forward through the shaft of window
light and rapped firmly on the door. When the door opened
Mona was there with her hand still on the knob and her little body leaning forward. While all the light was falling on
his bewildered shy face he could do nothing but stare at her
and wait. "Oh, it's you, Greg. We were expecting you sometime soon," she said. "We heard the car coming up and going
away and wondered who it was."

She could not help looking for a long time at Greg Henderson, wondering what had happened in his life to drive him

back here after four years. He was hesitating at the door, tall and dark, in his fine expensive city clothes, but really much older, and the light was on his worried face: it was puzzling to Mona to see him so reticent and lonely looking because she knew he had always been full of eagerness, giving all of himself first to one thing and then to another, full of love, and then getting hurt, and then hard and unyielding and never consenting to go anyone else's way. As he blinked his eyes in the light he had none of the plausible flow of easy words he had had in the old days. He said, haltingly, "I was walking up from the station. They picked me up on the road." He followed her into the big lamplit room with the great open hearth, and for the first time he was able to look at her, her body enveloped in a large white apron. Her long black hair fell soft and thick around her oval face, and she was looking at him steadily with her peaceful dark eyes in a way that made him more uneasy. "I got your letter, Greg, and so you must have got mine."

"Maybe I oughtn't to have come at all," he said.

"Why shouldn't you come, if you wanted to?"

There was the sound of someone moving in the kitchen. A short, broad-shouldered, bony-faced young man with thick light hair appeared holding a pail in his hand. He was wearing a short leather jacket, as if he had just expected to go out, and he stood grinning a little at Mona and eyeing Greg with a frank curiosity.

"You've heard me speak of Greg Henderson, Frank," Mona said.

"Hello, Mr. Henderson," Frank said with a kind of good-humored warmth. There was a broad comprehending smile on his strong face as he put out his hand and said, "Are you hungry? Not at all? You'll be staying the night with us any-way, won't you?"

"I hadn't thought about it."

"Stay the night," Mona said.

"Maybe I'd better stay."

"Come on upstairs, and I'll show you we've got a room," Frank said.

"Little Mike is asleep, but maybe we could take a peek at him when you're ready," Mona said.

Greg followed Frank up the narrow twisting staircase that was built in the thick wall of the old farmhouse, and into a little room with a window, a low-beamed ceiling and a narrow bed. "You'll be comfortable for the night," Frank said. "Feel at home while you're here. We want you to feel at home. Mona has told me all about you." He was speaking in an easy, jolly, friendly way, but the composure that was in his voice made Greg feel his own utter unimportance. Greg was an opinionated, arrogant man with a natural fierceness in his nature, and he could not help saying, "Did she tell you about me?" but then in a panic, without waiting for an answer, he went on: "This is a fine place in the country. A man ought to have such a place. The country is very beautiful but a little melancholy. I felt it in me walking on the road, maybe it was just the darkness and the softness of the hills," and he kept on talking till they started to go downstairs again.

"I was just going down the road a piece to get the milk," Frank explained. "Maybe you'll be wanting to take a peek at Mike with Mona." Picking up the can that he had brought from the kitchen, he went out brusquely, leaving Mona and Greg listening first to his footfalls and then to the sound of his whistling as he went down the road.

Mona smiled in a sympathetic, agreeable way as she said, "You can come and see Mike if you want to." Greg followed her meekly, going upstairs again and tiptoeing into another little room and standing beside her, bending over a cot. There was enough early moonlight flooding the room to show the soft lines of the sleeping boy's face. Mona and Greg bent down together over the bed, and Greg began to feel a strange excitement, then a vast uneasiness like a rising and falling of life within him, as he tried to make out the shape of his own boy's head. It was for this that he had come, after a few years of forgetting and then a short month of restless wondering, and now, bending over the bed and feeling the mother so quiet beside him, he had a wild hope that the great, heavy beating of his own heart might sound so loud in the room it would wake up the boy.

But Mona, with her finger to her lips, was beckoning him, and he tiptoed out behind her and followed her downstairs.

While he walked up and down the room, not daring to look at Mona or speak to her, he felt how undisturbed and peaceful she was as she sat in the rocking chair. Mona had always been so tender when there had been any suffering in him, and yet now when he was most wretched and deeply suffering, she waited, quiet, still, without any emotion. In her peacefulness he could feel how unimportant he had become. He could almost hear her husband saying to her, "A no-account lawyer, a little bourgeois, his little middle-class emotions and his sentimentality, it's no longer important that he once loved you and left you. The poor fool." Greg began to stare at Mona, staring at her white, round, soft face, and then, he went over to her and whispered, "Mona, it's unnatural for you to be so calm with me now," and he put out his hand to touch her.

Her hands had been quiet in her lap and her face had been full of soft contentment, but when he came toward her, reaching out to touch her with his hand, her face took on a wretched fearful look that destroyed swiftly all her calmness and she looked now like she had looked the last times he had seen her and she was saying, frightened, "Don't come near me, don't touch me."

"I won't, Mona. You must forgive me. It's just meanness I was feeling because you were so peaceful and content and I wanted to disturb you." Greg really was ashamed because he knew, too, that it was out of his resentment of her husband's confidence that he was trying to disturb her and trying to assert his own strength. "The boy is feeling fine, isn't he?"

"His health has been good. In the morning you can talk to him and play with him."

"I can have him for hours?"

"As long as you wish."

Then Frank came in with the milk and took off his leather jacket and the three of them sat down to talk. They asked Greg about the city. They were living in the country, but they longed for any bit of news about the city. Frank began to talk about social problems with enthusiasm because it was the subject that had most power over all his thoughts, and he talked at Greg, knowing he had another point of view. His voice rose and he waved his hands, and then his voice softened and he was patient with Greg who hated every word he said. When he interrupted there was a sharp hostile silence between them. In these moments of silence they looked at each other: they realized they were there together, they felt the country silence outside, and they did not like it.

Then Mona said, "Maybe Greg is tired, Frank, after walking most of the way from the station. Maybe he wants to go to bed."

"I'm sorry," Frank said considerately. "Don't let us keep you up. We go to bed early around here, anyway. Are you sure there's nothing we can do for you?"

"Nothing at all," Greg said, and after saying good night to them he went up to the bedroom. But he was so wide awake he could hardly keep still. He stood at the window looking out over the little valley lit by the moonlight. He heard the trickling of water in the nearly dried-up creek, but every other part of the night was dreadfully still. He was thinking that everything that had been hurt deeply in Mona's life had been smoothed out here in the quietness of this mist-laden valley And he was thinking, too, "She never looked as lovely when she loved me as she did sitting there in the chair tonight." It was terrible to feel that once there had been such strong passion in both of them and now he was here, wel-comed calmly by her, as though he were a visitor or a stranger. He wanted to cry out in a loud voice and break the night's calmness, but he threw himself on the bed and rubbed his head in the pillow and groaned within him, feeling it a ter-rible thing that all the ecstasy, all the joy of loving that used to be between them was gone, didn't live at all tonight. Then he heard them coming up to bed. He heard them undressing. They must have lain down together, for soon he heard them whispering peacefully. The whispering between them had a fine evenness, her whispering and murmur blending and made one with the low murmur of his voice. "There's nothing I've held on to. I possess no part of anything that's here," Greg thought. "I don't touch their life at all," and he felt humility and even a little peacefulness in himself.

In the morning he went downstairs with a humble eagerness to see his son, feeling that something mysterious but very gratifying was about to happen. He was shy and smiling when he said good morning to Mona and Frank.

"Mike is in the kitchen finishing his breakfast," Mona said.

"Can I go in?"

"Come on along," she said, and they went together into the kitchen where a dark-haired, round-faced little boy was eating a piece of toast very seriously. His eyes were large and brown and soft like his mother's. He was so sturdy, handsome, and rosy-cheeked that Greg felt a marvelous delight in just looking at him and he said suddenly, "Hello, Mike."

The boy looked at him gravely and then said without smiling, "Are you my uncle?"

"A kind of uncle."

"Mother said my uncle might come and see me today. Aren't you really my uncle?"

"Sure, I'm your Uncle Greg." Greg looked at Mona and they both smiled to each other, then they began to laugh easily. "Will you go for a walk with your uncle while Daddy and I drive into town, darling?" Mona asked.

"All right," the boy said laconically, and he went on eating his toast.

Later on, in a straightforward simple way, Mona and Frank got ready to go to town in order that Greg might be alone for a few hours with the boy. He stood at the door watching them get into the old battered automobile. It was a fine, clear spring day. The car was on the other side of the little garden near the barn and beside a pile of red shale. The ground on that side of the house was covered with this powdered red shale. When the car started, Greg and the boy standing beside him waved their hands.

Speaking soft and coaxing, Greg said to Mike, "Will we go for a walk down the road, maybe all the way down the road to the river? Is it too far?"

"I've often walked that far with my father in the spring when he went fishing. I can walk twice that far. I can walk three times that far."

As soon as they started to walk the little boy put up his hand and took Greg's hand firmly in his. The simple gesture moved Greg more than anything that had happened since he had come. He stared down at the boy's neck as they walked hand in hand along the red clay road, waiting for something mysterious to happen between them.

"Where are you from, Mister?" Mike asked.

"I'm from New York."

"I guess it's too far away to walk there today, eh?"

"Much too far. It's miles away."

"Are there a lot of little kids there?"

"The streets are full of little kids shouting and playing."

"Do you know them? I'd like to see some kids. It's nice here, I like it here, but there are hardly any kids to play with," he said gravely. Then he hesitated, looked up at Greg, wondering if he could be confided in completely. "Would you let me come and see you in New York some time, Mister?" he asked.

Greg let his hand fall with a light gentleness on the boy's shoulder, caressing the shoulder timidly. "I certainly will," he said. But Mike shook his shoulder free of the hand, not that he was offended, but he was simply asserting that he was a boy and not to be petted. Greg loved his unspoiled childish directness. He longed to sit down with him and explain that they belonged to each other, or do some significant thing that would bring a swift light of recognition into the boy's eyes.

Mike was saying, "Do you see that broken fence along there?"

"I see it."

"Would you bet me an ice cream cone I can't jump over it?"

"Sure I will. Do you want a cone, Mike?"

"Well, when we get this far on the road my father always bets me an ice cream cone I can't jump that fence."

"Go ahead then."

The little boy went leaping forward with short strong steps and took a broad jump over the broken scantling that was only a foot off the ground, and he landed on his knees in the long thick grass by the roadside and rolled over on his back, laughing. Greg ran after him and stood beside him, watching him rolling around while he shouted, "I fooled you. You've got to buy me a cone now." Bending down over him, Greg grabbed him and lifted him high in the air, holding him tight while he squirmed with helpless laughter. When Mike was all out of breath, Greg put him down on the ground again.

When they came to the little bridge over the creek and were standing a moment watching the skitters on the surface of the shallow water, Greg turned his head, looking far down between the hills, and he was surprised to see how the valley opened up from this point with the hills and the red barns with the hex signs over the doors and the dilapidated farmhouses flowing wide away into the immense valley of the Delaware that was full of noonday light; and down there the great river shone silver white on the green flat land, and farther beyond the river was cultivated land and maybe town land all rolled into soft blue hills, rising grandly with the color of a new, unknown country that was suddenly touched by the same sunlight that was overhead. Greg kept looking away off with a leaping excitement. He had promised Mona that he would not tell Mike that Frank was not his father, but he could not stop thinking, "Why can't I take him away with me now? Why shouldn't I do it?" Without answering he gripped the boy's hand tight and began to walk faster, still looking ahead far down the valley.

"Isn't it a fine sight over there on a clear day, Mike?"

"That's nothing," Mike said. "From the top of our hill on a clear day you can almost see the ocean."

"The ocean. There's no ocean there to see."

"My father said one day if you could only see far enough you'd see an ocean, and that's the furthest of all away."

"Think of all the towns you'd look over, Mike," Greg said, and they kept on walking fast, going straight ahead. At the little store where the roads crossed in what was called the village, they stopped to buy ice cream and an orange drink for Mike. Behind the counter was a lean, slow-moving man with a completely disinterested expression on his face, who said with surprising amiability, "You've got Molsen's kid along with you, eh?" and he made a very comical face at Mike, who was eating the ice cream greedily.

Then they went on again, going farther down the road, going toward the river and away from the hills, with Greg always holding the boy's hand tight and making him trot beside him. They were off the red clay road and down the flat land where the road was gray and dusty when Mike said, "I'm tired, Mister. Can't we stop a minute?"

"Are you very tired, Mike?"

"I want to sit down," he said.

So they sat down by the ditch a few feet from the road in long grass and weeds covered thick with gray dust, and they didn't say anything, nor were they shy, but Mike merely began to cross his legs at the ankles the way Greg had crossed his. Then Greg, watching the boy, leaned all his weight back on his hands, and Mike did that too, smiling quickly. And after they had looked at each other a while, Greg leaned forward and linked his hands around his knees, whistling between his teeth and pretending to look seriously across the fields; and soon he heard a thin whistle coming from Mike, and glancing out of the corner of his eye, he saw him, too, gravely staring at the fields. This moment became the most beautiful moment that Greg could remember in his life. As they sat there in the strong sun with the dust from an automobile blowing over them, he began to think, "Maybe when he grows up he'll have many little gestures just like mine. Maybe he'll hold his head on one side the way I do, or his voice will sound like mine." But while he was clinging to this fine moment and feeling real joy in these thoughts, he became aware that Mike, bit by bit, was snuggling closer to him, and when he looked down at him he saw that his eyes were slowly closing. He did not know why he was so fearful of having him fall asleep. He dared not let him fall asleep.

"Maybe you'd like to go back to the store, Mike, and get another ice cream cone," he said quickly. They got up and went back along the road, and Mike was walking with the solemn, expressionless face of a tired little boy.

After Mike had had another cone and another orange drink they both sat down together on the edge of the store veranda. Mike said suddenly, "I wish mamma would come," and he kept looking down the road toward the highway. He could not stop his head from drooping and bobbing up and down. It was past his lunchtime. As they sat close together, raising their heads together whenever a farmer or a few city people there for the summer came into the store, Greg was wondering how it was that Mona could be happy with Mike here in these hills. "Don't you get tired of this little place, Mike?" he asked. Mike heard him but did not answer; he was doing nothing but opening his eyes wide and then letting them close slowly. "I'll pick him up and carry him to the station," Greg thought. "Why should I leave him here in this melancholy place to grow up with the socialist wild notions of that arrogant man?" And while he was planning and pondering he felt the boy's head heavy against him. Mike was in a sound sleep. For a long time Greg stared at the boy's closed eyes and at the long lashes touching the cheeks, and then he thought with utter misery, "He was sitting there thinking and talking of Mona. I've no right whatever to take him away from her. I'm nothing to him really." In a kind of panic he picked Mike up and began to hurry back into the hills, saying angrily, "Why does Mona stay away like this and not care what happens to him?" He hurried on, going back to the house, clutching the sleeping boy and feeling more and more wretched.

He was almost in sight of the farmhouse before he heard the honking of a horn behind him. When he stepped off the road and looked back, he saw the Molsens' old car swaying in the ruts. Mona was leaning out, waving her hand cheerfully.

Full of resentment, Greg said, "He's sound asleep. What do you think of that?" and he stared at her as if she ought to give an account of herself to him. But she only said, "The poor little boy," without noticing Greg at all. Frank, who had nodded with his old, good-natured tolerance, simply put out his arms for Mike, lifted him into the car and put him on Mona's knee. Without moving, Greg stood on the road, flustered, knowing only that he had not wanted Frank to take the boy from him in that way, and then he realized that they were wondering why he did not get into the car. So he sat in the back seat, leaning forward, with his head only a foot from Mike's, listening to Mona clucking sounds all over his head: and yet he was utterly detached from them. They did not even ask him where he had been with Mike, for it did not occur to them that anything important could have happened. So he said, "I must leave at once. I ought to have left an hour ago."

"Why didn't you say you had to go? We're so sorry," Mona said.

"It's all right. Everything's all right," Greg said.

"Frank will drive you to the station whenever you're ready," she said.

When they got to the house Greg got out of the car first, and he said eagerly, "Let me carry him, Mona."

"No, I'll carry him. You'll wake him," she whispered.

"Wouldn't it be all right . . ." He intended to say, "Wouldn't it be all right to wake him just to say good-bye?"

but he fumbled, from wanting it so much, and he said instead, ". . . all right just to carry him to the house?"

"Sh, sh, sh," Mona said. Mike's head was moving on her shoulder and he was wetting his red lips with the tip of his tongue. This was while they were going toward the house. Greg kept watching Mike, hardly knowing what to hope for, but anxious for something that would destroy the desolation within him. Once he even coughed, just at the door, and cleared his throat noisily, but there was nothing more for him than that one restless move of Mike's head.

When Greg was ready to leave, he stood at the door with Mona. He wanted to go, to hurry, but he felt such emptiness in going. He wanted to shake hands heartily with Mona, to look at her directly, but his words came slow and groping, "Good-bye Mona. You were good to let me come."

"Good-bye Greg," she said, smiling and calm. "You come any time you want to come."

"I will," he said, trying hard to conceal the dragging emptiness inside him. There was one awkward moment, then he turned and was walking to the automobile; and then he heard Mona speaking in her mother voice, "Did we wake you up, Mike? You still look half asleep." Looking back, Greg saw Mike pushing past his mother standing in front of her, and he was staring after him.

"Where are you going, Mister?" Mike called.

"Back to the city, Mike."

"Good-bye, Mister," Mike called, and he went running toward Greg. Grinning broadly, Greg bent down and caught him in his arms and lifted him high over his shoulders, shaking him and making him laugh again before putting him down. Then he kissed him with a quick eagerness and went on to the car, where Frank was waiting and watching. But before Greg could get into the car, Mike ran up to him again, only this time he stopped short a few feet away, with a puzzled, shy, wondering look on his face, feeling that someone he liked a lot and had felt very close to immediately was leaving him for some reason he did not understand.

This look on Mike's face brought a surge of joy to Greg, and he looked back a long time, half-smiling, wanting so much to believe that the feeling in the boy's eyes came from the same kind of longing that had been in his own heart when he had felt compelled to return to him. This one look, making them both feel there might have been much love between them, was something like what he had waited for when he had watched Mike sleeping.

Greg was smiling when he did finally get into the car. He waved cheerfully at Mona. He sat down beside Frank and looked at him in a direct, friendly way. He almost wished Frank could forgive him for being a professional man who had done well in the last two years. But he couldn't help saying almost triumphantly as the car started, "You certainly have to admit he's a fine boy."

It Had to be Done

In the drive out to the country that night to get the suits Chris had left at Mrs. Mumford's place, he kept telling Catherine she shouldn't have come. He was only going because he needed the suits. It didn't matter whether or not Mrs. Mumford only wanted him to be wearing something she had once bought for him. "She knows I'm going to marry you," he said.

"That's why I should meet her. Then maybe she'll believe it," Catherine said. "You're not ashamed of me."

They were crossing the Delaware and driving through the soft rolling hills, and it seemed to Catherine that they never would be able to stop talking about Mrs. Mumford. He had met Mrs. Mumford five years ago when he was broke and wanted to be an architect, and she was rich and believed in his talent. She had so much enthusiasm he had thought he might be in love with her, even if she was five years older. She got him one job, then another, then had him quit the jobs and go to Europe with her to study. There never was a chance for him to worry about anything. But when he woke up and found she wanted to marry him and had taken charge of his life, he hated himself for getting into it and left her. But she kept track of him and still kept trying to look after him. When she heard he was with Catherine she wrote him that maybe a girl like Catherine, whom he had met at a dance and who worked in a department store, would be good for him for a while. Then she asked him why he didn't come out and get the suits he had left at her place: she said she knew he needed them.

They had turned off the highway and were going up the side road past the little lighted store, and then Chris stopped the car. "Here we are," he said.

"I'll go up with you, Chris."

"I know," he said, getting out of the car. "But it can't do any good, see. I'll only be gone twenty minutes."

"But she'll wonder why you didn't bring me."

"She'd certainly be surprised if I did," he said, pulling his bag out of the back seat.

"That's just it," she said eagerly. "She's sure you would not, no matter how often you write her that we love each other."

"Look, honey," he said, patting her arm. "I don't want to make a visit out of this. I want to get out quick, isn't that right? I'll only be gone twenty minutes." Then he kissed her and went on up the slope, swinging the bag, and his shadow got longer in the moonlight and broke over the car.

When he was out of sight she got out of the car and stood in the road looking around nervously. She had her hands deep in the pockets of her belted coat, and she pulled off her little blue hat and shook her long-bobbed fair hair. She was twenty-one, fifteen years younger than Mrs. Mumford, and as she stood looking back at the light in the little store and then at the way the moonlight touched the stone fences as they curved up over the meadowland on Mrs. Mumford's property, she felt like a timid child. She was thinking that as soon as Chris opened the door Mrs. Mumford would say, "Why, darling, where's your girl?" and no matter what excuse he made she would know that he was ashamed to bring her.

In spite of herself she started to go up the road after Chris, but when she got to the little rippling stone-banked creek she grew afraid. She could go no farther. Staring at the big white house and the lighted windows and the dark high hill behind it, she sat down weakly in the grass. When a cowbell tinkled in some nearby pasture and she heard the swishing sound of the cow moving in the grass and then settling down again by a fence, she felt suddenly lost in a country that belonged to a rich woman, a country where Chris had lived, and that was so beautiful and peaceful that surely as he walked up the road he would be remembering how he had wanted to hear all these little sounds again. Maybe he was remembering and hearing these sounds every time Mrs. Mumford wrote him offering to loan him money and giving him advice about little things and wishing him great happiness like a very noble woman.

"Oh, Chris, we've had such good times. You've said you felt free for the first time in your life," she was whispering to herself, looking up at the house. He had got a job in an architect's office. He seemed to feel like a kid with her. He said he wanted to work and make something out of himself. He said that she would never understand what it was to have someone own your life and smother you and never give you a chance to be yourself. She was trying hard to remember these things, but if he was ashamed of her, then nothing she had given him was good. While he felt that he did not want Mrs. Mumford to see her, he could never really belong to her.

As she got up and began to go slowly toward the house she was frightened. She felt she had to do it, and the loud beating of her heart could not stop her. At the door she faltered, then she rapped weakly. "I was waiting," she said to the maid. "Mrs. Mumford will know me." Then she went into the old white colonial living room, trying to smile and walk lazily.

Chris and Mrs. Mumford were standing together at the long pine table. The open bag was on the table, and Chris was packing his suits in it. As Catherine came in they both turned, startled. Mrs. Mumford was a large handsome woman with jet-black hair drawn back tight from her bold and vivid face, and the white part in her hair was shining in the light. If Chris had only smiled naturally, or come to her to welcome her she would have felt immense relief, but his face reddened as Mrs. Mumford stared at Catherine, then turned, wondering, to him.

"It got chilly outside," Catherine said. "I thought I might as well come in."

"You're Catherine, aren't you?" Mrs. Mumford said.

"Yes."

"Why, Chris," she said, "you said you came alone."

"I didn't want to stay more than a minute," he explained awkwardly. "It wasn't like a visit, see. I mean, I knew you'd want us to stay." But out of the corner of his eye he glanced at Catherine savagely and she felt panicky.

"Please sit down," Mrs. Mumford said, and she smiled and nodded sympathetically, and it was terrible for both of them because she made them feel that she understood their embarrassment and only wanted to help them. So Catherine sat down by herself with her toes close together. After that one appraising glance, Mrs. Mumford turned away and tried to help Chris with the straps on the bag. His hands were pawing at the lock. His head was down and his ears were red as he fumbled with it. "If only you both had come for the evening we could have had such a lovely chat," Mrs. Mumford was saying. It seemed to Catherine, praying that Chris hurry, that the woman was mocking her. Beneath Mrs. Mumford's simple calmness she felt a vast assurance and aggressiveness that terrified her. If Mrs. Mumford had offered her suddenly to take a walk around the house, she felt she would get up meekly and do it. She began to long to find something within herself that Mrs. Mumford would see she could never touch.

Chris was still having trouble getting the edges of the bag together, and as he bent over the bag, muttering, Mrs. Mumford bent over, too, to help him. Their heads were close together. "What's the trouble?" she asked. "Let me try."

She jammed the edges together suddenly when Chris had his finger against the edge of the metal lock. "Ouch. Damn it, my finger!" he said.

"Why, it's your nail," she said. "Oh, dear. That's terrible. Let me see it." She took his hand and lifted it close to her face. "It's bleeding."

"It's nothing. It doesn't hurt at all," he said uneasily.

"It'll turn black. I'll get some ointment. Maybe I should put a piece of cloth around it." And suddenly she seemed to enfold him. Her face lit up with energetic warmth. She seemed to be ministering to someone she possessed. It was only a little thing, but Catherine stood up, frightened. It seemed to her that if she let Mrs. Mumford do one thing more for Chris he could never really belong to her.

"Why don't you leave him alone?" she whispered.

"Why, his finger's hurt," Mrs. Mumford said, startled.

"That isn't it," Catherine said breathlessly, as she took a step toward Mrs. Mumford.

"Catherine, please—" Chris begged her.

"It's just a little thing, I know," Catherine went on doggedly.

"What's the matter with her, Chris?" Mrs. Mumford asked.

"This is the matter," Catherine blurted out, white-faced. "Somebody's got to tell you. Why don't you leave him alone? Leave him alone. You don't own people. Stop trying to boss him around."

But the contempt she saw in Mrs. Mumford's eyes suddenly silenced her. She turned helplessly to Chris.

"I'm sorry," he was saying to Mrs. Mumford. "I didn't want this to happen."

"I understand, Chris," she said calmly.

But she kept looking at Catherine. Her long appraising look made Catherine feel she had to hurt her. "Come on, Chris," she said. "Come on, let's go. The lady doesn't think much of me."

Then her heart was pounding wildly and she didn't care what she did. And she swung her coat back and put her hand on her hip, showing the fine curve of her breast and her slimness and her young body. As she moved she swaggered a little, swaying her hips, her eyes mocking Mrs. Mumford and seeming to say, "Go on, take a look at me. You haven't got everything."

But Mrs. Mumford only turned to Chris, trying to get him to look at her. He was staring at Catherine, pain and surprise in his eyes. Then the shame and humiliation Catherine had been dreading ever since she came there flooded through her. She looked scared.

"Don't you think you made a mistake?" Mrs. Mumford said, turning to Chris.

"The mistake I made was in coming here," he shouted at her. And he swung away from her and grabbed the handle of the open bag and jerked it off the table. It flopped open and the suits spilled out on the floor. Then he and Mrs. Mumford looked down at the suits. "She's right," he said to her. "And you remember it."

Hoisting the empty bag under his arm he grabbed Catherine by the shoulder and pushed her toward the door, and he kept pulling her out and down the path of light from the opened door.

"I'm sorry, Chris. I'm sorry," she began to sob. "I acted like a cheap little chippie," she wept. "I didn't want to. I guess I had to."

"I told you to stay out and you didn't," he said. He was rushing her down the road and she could hardly keep up to him. "Maybe you should stay with her. Maybe she's right. You shouldn't be with me," she said. Her face kept turning to him, pleading, apologetic and ashamed. "That's it." Without stopping, he turned, stricken, as if scared she was going to deny him suddenly everything that had built his life up. His hand tightened on her arm. She felt a furtive leap of joy; they were going down the road faster, and he seemed to be holding her to him tighter than ever before.

THE HOMING PIGEON

When the fifth day passed and still his father, the doctor, didn't return to Frenchtown, Dick started out looking for him. He went over to Charlie's barbershop and sprawled in the chair. He was seventeen, big for his age, and he looked at the barber a long time with a serious, worried face before he spoke to him.

"How do you want it, same as usual — use the scissors at the sides?" Charlie asked, taking the scissors off the glass ledge.

"I don't want a haircut, I just want to ask you something."

"Go ahead, Dick."

"You know my old man hasn't shown up yet."

"That's bad, that's bad, that's getting worse."

"You know he stayed away before, and I figured you'd know where he was."

"Me?"

"Sure. You're the only one around here that knows he gets drunk."

As he took off his glasses and began wiping them with the hem of his white coat, the barber started to splutter, "I didn't think you'd be worrying much about the doctor, Dick. I mean the two of you don't get along very well — everybody knows that. There's things you've got to make allowances for. When a man's wife dies it upsets the swing of his life a little, don't you see?"

The doctor's son took an envelope from his pocket, showing it to the barber. On the back of the envelope there was a Twenty-eighth Street, New York address.

"Do you think he might be at this address?" he asked. "Have you been there with him?"

"Now, now, Dick. I wouldn't go there looking for him."

"Would he be there?"

"I'd let him look after himself if I were you, Dick. He'll come home when he's ready," the barber said.

The doctor's son went out and along the street to the garage where Williams' truck was waiting, and he yelled up to the driver. "Are you going right to New York, Bert?"

"That's right."

"Can I come?"

"Looking for your old man?"

Dick was a little ashamed and only said, "It's time I had a look at the big town, isn't it?"

But when he was sitting on the big high seat with Bert Williams, the round-faced, rosy-cheeked grocery boy who had grown up in the town with him, and the truck was swinging around the bends in the road in the late afternoon and swinging them close together, he found himself talking eagerly about his father.

It was true he and his old man had never got along very well — they just didn't seem to have any affection for each other, but there were times when he thought his father missed his affection; little things he said, ways he had of looking at him; and he himself was often puzzled and felt maybe their natures were just antipathetic. A few months ago, when his mother died, it got worse between them. Perhaps she had been all that held them together — held them with her soft gentle way and the little bits of encouragement she was always giving him to be friendly with the old man. She had made him feel that he simply had to like his father and that his love for her even was spoiled and no good unless he was willing to share it with his father. "There's just the two of us in the house now, and I got the idea today that's maybe one reason why he stays away. He's got an idea I've no use for him. What do you think? Maybe he'd like it if he saw I really wanted him back. We might start being good friends. What do you think?" he asked.

"It's very likely," Bert replied. "I always liked him."

"I figure my mother would certainly want me to dig him up no matter where he is," said Dick, and he lay back on the seat with his eyes half closed, watching the darkness creep over the low Jersey hills and thinking of the way his mother used to laugh. He had always felt that it was a secret between them that he knew she wanted most to be a gay, carefree, laughing woman, because she was always grave and polite when his father and other people were around the house.

Soon they were crossing the flatlands of Jersey, then crossing the great bridge and going through the tunnel, and as he looked at the lights of the city he felt an indescribable elation, a puzzled breathlessness, and exclaimed, "Gee, why do I feel like this?"

"What do you mean?"

"I don't know, it just seems pretty exciting to be going into the town," he said. "Maybe it's because I'm doing the right thing and I feel good about it."

"I thought you said you'd been here often."

"No, not at night, just a few times when I was a kid with my mother," he said.

He got off the truck at Seventh Avenue and Twenty-eighth Street and Bert yelled, "Here's hoping you find your old man, kid."

"I'll find him," replied Dick.

"Sure you got the address?"

"I know it by heart."

"Supposing you don't find him, or he don't want to see you?"

"I got a couple of bucks, Bert. Don't worry about me."

"Okay, lots of luck," yelled Bert, and the engine roared and he was gone and Dick was left there with his heart beating heavily as he looked up Seventh Avenue toward the rash of fire in the sky over Times Square.

There were four apartments in the house on Twenty-eighth Street, and when he stood in the dimly lit hall he was in a panic. He began to wish he hadn't come. The woman in the lower apartment said, "Dr. Harvey? No, I don't know no Dr. Harvey." On the second floor a man in his shirt-sleeves with his collar off, said, "You got the wrong number, son." He began to hope that he actually had the wrong number; he didn't want to find his father there. On the third floor a plump, red-faced, blond woman in a green dressing gown opened the door and said, "Dr. Harvey? Who wants him?"

"I do."

"What do you want?"

"I want to talk to him."

"Who are you?"

"I'm his son."

The woman hesitated, and half turning her head looked back into the room, and Dick knew his father was there. He was terribly disappointed. In Frenchtown everybody respected him and he was a good country doctor. But this soft, blowsy-looking woman with the mouth that was heavy and cruel in spite of the way she laughed so easily, half closed the door, and looking at him a long time, grinned and said, "He isn't here."

"I know he's here."

"Look," she said, tapping his arm as though he were a little kid. "You go home, and if I see him I'll tell him you were looking for him. See what I mean?" Her face was soft and smiling as she whispered, but her hard eyes were worried. He hated the way she was trying to tell him she knew what was good for him.

"I'm going to talk to him," he said, pushing her away.

"Hey, stopping pushing me!"

"Leave me alone, that's all," he said.

With one hand on her hip she stepped back and screwed up her eyes and made him feel young and unimportant by the way she sized him up. Unsmiling, she said, almost to herself, "I've heard about you." The knowing way she said it made him feel sure she not only knew all about him but about his family, his mother, the way they lived. His resentment against his father mounted as he strode past her into the apartment that smelled of beer, food and cheap perfume.

On a round table there were glasses and a trayful of cigarette butts. A bedroom door was open. He took a couple of steps toward the bedroom, and then stood still, suddenly afraid. The woman watched thoughtfully.

"Is he in there?"

"It's your party," she said, shrugging.

"Who's that, Tony, who's there?" his father called.

"A kid who says you're his old man," she called, and laughing in a soft, indolent, mocking way, she sat down lazily and linked her plump arms behind her head.

"This is going to be fun," she said.

There was the sound of the creaking of bedsprings, of feet hitting the floor, and Dr. Harvey came slowly into the room. He was a big, powerful man. His collar was undone, his short, tightly clipped, stiff gray hair was tousled and the big veins on the side of his head were blue and swollen against the ashen color of his face. He stumbled a little, then he stiffened when he saw his son, and his hand went out to the doorpost for support. He was still a little drunk, and when he saw Dick staring at him in a kind of desolate wonder, he shook his head and lurched toward him.

"What do you want?" he asked. "Where did you come from?"

"I've been worried. I wanted you to come home."

"Missing me, eh? Look, Tony, he missed me. You didn't think anybody would miss me."

"Yeah, I've been worrying," Dick said.

Rubbing his hands across his face, the doctor sat down, wanting to appear calm and reasonable. Then he turned to Tony and smiled cynically, "Why does he want to spy on me, Tony?"

Shrugging, she said, "Why don't you give the kid a break? Maybe he means what he said."

An idiotic laugh that made his face suddenly red came from the doctor, and then he couldn't stop laughing. His head just kept dropping down to the table as if his neck were too weak to support it, then he would jerk it back and the crazy laughter kept pouring out of him. Dick felt sick with shame. He had never before seen his father like this.

"Shut up, shut up," the big blond woman said. "Stop that crazy laughing or get out of here. Do you want all the neighbors in?"

"You've done this to him. Leave him alone," Dick said to her.

"I ought to throw the both of you out of here," she said. "What's the matter with me?"

"Wait a minute, wait a minute," the doctor said. "Why did he come here? He doesn't like me. He never did."

"I wasn't thinking of just you."

"You bet your life you weren't. There, didn't I tell you, Tony?"

"I was thinking of Mother."

"What about her?"

"How do you think she would feel if she saw you here like this?"

"What's the matter with it?"

"Here. With her," he said, nodding at Tony.

"He doesn't like me, George," she said, laughing. "Your wife wouldn't like me, he says."

"Come on and get dressed," Dick said, and he tried to take his father under the arm, but his father pushed him away heavily.

"Take your hands off me," he said. "You know what your mother would say? Nothing, absolutely nothing. What do you think of that? So don't lecture me. Leave me alone. I always left you alone, didn't I?"

"I don't care what you think about me," Dick said, and then he said desperately to Tony, "Why don't you help me to get him out?"

"I don't think he wants to get out," she said, and she grabbed the doctor by the shoulder, gave him a couple of stiff slaps on the forehead and shook him.

But the sight of his father, a respectable man, an educated man, a man who could walk down the street with great dignity on Sunday afternoons, letting himself be pushed around by a cheap, blowsy woman enraged Dick, and he cried out, "You ought to be ashamed! Why don't you get up and come home? Wherever she is now, she's ashamed of you and I am, too. "

"Ashamed of me?" the doctor shouted, and he jumped up and shoved Dick toward the door. "Neither she nor you have any right to be ashamed of me, so don't come around here insulting my friends."

"I'm ashamed because you're my father, that's all," Dick whispered.

"My God, listen to him," the father cried.

"That's the only reason," Dick said, refusing to budge.

"Is it, eh?" the doctor said savagely. "Beat it, beat it, do you hear? I'm not your father."

"What do you mean?"

"You heard me," the doctor said, glaring at him. Then the puzzled wonder in the boy's eyes made him turn away.

Like a bewildered child, Dick rubbed his hands over his face, and while they watched him and he tried to smile his eyes grew full of terror. He looked hopelessly at Tony,

wanting her to say something to him. When she didn't
speak he pleaded with her softly, "He doesn't know what
he's saying, does he?"

"He's crazy," she said. "He's been like that for days."
The doctor was walking up and down rubbing his forearms
as if they were cold and mumbling, "She's dead now. You
can't say I said anything while she was alive. It's better for
him to know. There never was any good feeling lost between
us." While he was walking up and down mumbling this jus-
tification to himself, Dick grabbed him by the arm and
cried, "You're crazy, you're a crazy fool," shouting in a
young wild voice. Then he looked around helplessly and
whispered to the doctor, who looked scared now.

"Would you mind telling me something?"

"I don't mind, Dick. You know I don't mind," the doctor said. "It just burst out, see? I didn't mean to say it. I
thought maybe you'd felt it for years. I didn't think it would
hit you like it did."

"Who's my father?"

"Don't keep at it. Don't keep at me."

"I've got to know."

"A man named Page."

"Where did he live?"

"Around here. I think he's dead now. Cut it out. Let it
rest, can't you?"

"Where was I born?"

"Around here. What's the use of getting into it?"

"He's right. Come on, son," the big blond woman said,
and she took Dick by the arm in a comforting way and led
him out to the hall. "You shouldn't pay no attention," she
said. "He talks a little crazier every day and most of the

time he takes it out on me. You just happened to be around."

But Dick was so bewildered he began to go down the stairs without answering; down, down slowly, as if there was nothing in the world for him but the terror of the sound of his own footfalls, and the feeling of descending into the dark, further and further away from his own life.

"Son, hey, son!" the woman was calling to him from the top of the stairs. She was leaning over the banister, worried, her dressing gown flopping open, and when he looked up, white-faced, she yelled down, "Go home and forget it. I'll send him home."

"I'm not going back there," he said simply.

"Where are you going?"

"I don't know," he said.

Outside, the wind struck his face and he began to feel alive again. He went slowly along the street and stood a while by the lamppost in the corner looking at the glow of the lights high over Times Square. Every time a man passed he stared at his face. He stared at each passing face as if searching for some sign of recognition, something that would pull him into place and time and life again. "My father and mother lived here. My mother used to be happy when she lived here with my father," he kept saying over and over. "And I was born here and maybe a part of such happiness."

He started to walk along the street, feeling that he would walk all night, that all the past, all the future was here for him, that he must let the sights, the sounds, the smell of the place seep into him, and maybe as he walked he would feel again that eagerness he had felt coming along the highway when he saw the sweep of the lights and felt as if he had been away for a long time and was coming home.

WE JUST HAD TO BE ALONE

---

*M*rs. Buhay had had two husbands, had worked in restaurants, hotel dining rooms and at racetracks, and at fifty-two she was the manager of a cafeteria. She had become stout and florid. Her hair was tinted a light brown, her neckline wrinkled, and she had very pale shrewd eyes. She used to say with a hearty laugh that she had had a very sporty life. But because she made people feel that she saw through them, she had no real friends and she lived alone in her apartment.

That summer she got a letter from a girlhood friend, Betty Holmes, who lived at a whistle stop about a hundred and fifty miles south west. Mrs. Holmes wrote that she was broke and dying of tuberculosis and that she wanted her eighteen-year-old daughter, Alca, to get on in the world better than she had herself, and she asked Mrs. Buhay if Alca, who was coming to the city, could live with her until she felt at home enough so she could look after herself.

Alca was a small-town girl with not much schooling but she was quick and intelligent, fond of music, had thick natural-blond hair with brown eyes and a lovely rounded figure. Mrs. Buhay liked her. She bought her a white linen suit and got her a job in a music store selling records. By September she realized that until Alca had come she had been unbearably lonely at night in the apartment.

Every evening she used to wait for Alca to come home so they could have a cup of coffee together before going to bed. Alca would get into her pyjamas and Mrs. Buhay would put on her gaudy blue dressing gown and they would sit in the kitchen joking with each other. Alca, who wasn't at all shy, liked listening to Mrs. Buhay's salty stories, and Mrs. Buhay, touched by her eagerness, her prettiness and her softness, often wanted to put her arms around her protectively.

She tried to teach her everything she knew. She told her about her own life in big hotels in many cities. She told her about clothes and how to handle customers in the store and she talked about men, too, with a coarse good-natured smiling contempt. Her plump elbows were on the table, her dressing gown flopped open and showed her great bosom and she nodded wisely at Alca.

"You're pretty, Alca, honey. You've got it. But even a blind shoeshine boy knows when a girl's got it and it makes her a mark. But the guy doesn't live who isn't an open book." Chuckling and winking she leaned across the table and patted Alca's shoulder, her own blue eyes suddenly hard and her mouth turning down at the corners.

"Look after No. 1, Alca," she said. "Never give anything away. This week I want you to open a bank account and no matter what happens it should be your secret love." Alca's respect for the big shrewd woman showed in her eyes and she knew there was nothing Mrs. Buhay wouldn't do for her. They were very different and they loved each other.

One night Alca told Mrs. Buhay about a young man named Tom Prince who had come into the music store to buy some classical records. She had never met anyone with such nice manners, she said. It was wonderful the way he had made her feel she was a very dignified person.

The glow in Alca's eyes and the pleasure in her voice worried Mrs. Buhay. "Look here, honey, don't let the first guy you meet knock you over," she said.

The next night Alca didn't come home till midnight. Tom Prince had taken her to dinner and then a movie and she had found out all about him. He had finished a course in commercial art and was taking a job in an advertising agency. Alca couldn't stop talking about him. Even after they had had their coffee she stood at her bedroom door remembering bright little jokes Tom had made and trying them out on Mrs. Buhay.

"Okay, a very entertaining guy," Mrs. Buhay said, putting her arm around her affectionately. "I remember the first guy who ever made a pass at me. I thought he looked wonderful because he wore shoes and pants. Let's see this guy up close." Alca laughed and said she would bring him home tomorrow night.

Mrs. Buhay was in her bedroom when she heard them at the door. When Alca called, "Mrs. Buhay," she followed them into the living room. They were both out of breath from running up the stairs and laughing and Alca had on her smart white linen suit. "Mrs. Buhay," she said softly, "this is Tom Prince."

"How are you, Tom?" Mrs. Buhay said heartily as she put out her hand. "I've heard all about you." She was surprised because he was good-looking, well-dressed, with an assured and cultivated manner and she wished she had dressed up a little more. With an easy smile he said he knew all about her too.

"I'll get some coffee and some biscuits," Alca said, and with her eyes she told Mrs. Buhay that she wanted to give her a chance to have a talk with Tom and get a good impression of him because she valued her judgement so very much.

"Sit down, Tom," Mrs. Buhay said, and she sat down and smoothed her dress. She soon got him talking amiably about his work. She had a lot of experience with men that had started when she was sixteen and working at the carnival lunch counter. In the beginning she had got the worst of it, but only in the beginning until she had learned to size a man up.

There were things about Tom that made her uneasy. Her blunt straightforward questions seemed to amuse him. He had a soft-voiced politeness and well-proportioned hands and he used very little slang. He wore grey slacks and a light-grey jacket with a blue check and as he leaned back on the sofa he was so much at home that he made her feel a bit clumsy and ill at ease. She began to take on an air of refinement and hated herself for doing it.

When Alca came in with the tray Mrs. Buhay sat back and listened to them and it seemed to her that Alca didn't even talk his language.

"I'll take those dishes into the kitchen," she said, so they could be alone together, and she put the cups and saucers on the tray and went out to the kitchen.

When she was washing the dishes Alca came into the kitchen and took her arm. "How do you like him?" she whispered.

"He's quite a guy," Mrs. Buhay admitted.

"He certainly is. Oh, I'm so glad you like him."

"Look, Alca," she said, one hand on her hip as she smiled wisely. "That fellow's a very intelligent young man."

"You bet he is, Mrs. Buhay."

"And well-educated, too."

"Yes, he went to college," she said proudly.

"Where does he live, Alca?"

"He's got a room of his own."

"And he'd like you to see it, I suppose?"

"He hasn't said anything about it."

"He will. And don't you go there, Alca. If I were in your place I'd watch that I wasn't alone with him too much."

"But I like being alone with him. Why shouldn't I?"

"Alca, Alca," Mrs. Buhay said indulgently. "What do you think that fellow's up to with you? Ask yourself that."

"He likes me. We like each other."

"Sure you do. But a guy like that, Alca, intelligent and educated, and with that look in his eyes. What's he up to with you, do you think?"

"I told you, he likes me," Alca said, and she was hurt because she trusted Mrs. Buhay's judgement. She blushed, feeling somehow belittled and she tried to hide it by turning away and picking up one of the dried cups and staring at the pink floral pattern on the rim. "Okay," she said, and she walked out of the kitchen.

Mrs. Buhay stayed there until she heard Tom going home and then she came out and tried to joke with Alca, who didn't laugh at all.

Alca kept bringing Tom to the house and one night Mrs. Buhay saw her glance at him with an uneasy question in her eyes, trying to see him as she had been told to. Whatever it was she saw, it made her look lonely and troubled, and Mrs. Buhay knew Alca was in love with him. Until then she hadn't known how much she herself loved Alca. "That smooth guy with his soft soap knows she's a soft touch for him," she thought, and was angry. Until Tom went home she couldn't sleep.

Each night it seemed to her that he stayed longer, and she took it as a sign he looked down on them. It outraged her. She used to look at the clock then get up and go to the bathroom noisily and call out warningly, "Alca, you know you have to get up in the morning." "All right, Mrs. Buhay," Alca answered and her tone, quick and placating, seemed to tell Mrs. Buhay what was going on between them, and her heart would ache for Alca.

One night a few minutes before twelve, she lay in bed listening and worrying, and when she couldn't hear them talking at all, she got out of bed and put on her dressing gown and went along the hall to the living room where they were sitting on the sofa close together. All her suspicious shrewdness was in her eyes as she stared at them. "I was going to get a glass of milk," she said, shuffling along in her slippers to the kitchen.

Tom looked at Mrs. Buhay and then at Alca, who flushed as if she knew he was getting a picture of her she didn't want him to have, and she was ashamed. When Mrs. Buhay came back from the kitchen Alca smiled self-consciously, but then she seemed to see herself mirrored in Mrs. Buhay's eyes, and she slumped back on the sofa.

Another night they hadn't come home and it was midnight. It had been raining hard, and Mrs. Buhay, lying in bed, worried about Alca not having a coat with her. She caught cold easily. Then she heard them come in. They closed the door quietly and she could feel them listening outside her room, and then they tiptoed along the hall.

After that she could hear nothing at all, and hating Tom Prince for making Alca furtive and sly, she got up cursing him, threw her dressing gown around her and strode out into the living room. They weren't there. The kitchen door though was closed. She went grimly to the door and pushed it open. "What's going on here?" she demanded.

Alca stood by the stove where the coffee pot was on, and Tom was at the end of the kitchen table with his coat off, and as she stared at him he stood up and Mrs. Buhay was sure they had heard her footsteps and were both acting now.

"Why are you in here with the door closed?" she said sharply to Tom.

"We are going to have a cup of coffee," he said, and he reddened and stared right back at her.

"You were asleep, Mrs. Buhay," Alca said. "We didn't want to wake you. We were just sitting here, really." Then angered by her own apology she put her hand on the coffee pot to show it was hot, and then had to jerk it away.

"Mrs. Buhay, do you object to me coming in for a cup of coffee? How about it?"

"I heard a noise," she said, hating him for his tone. "There was no one in the living room. Naturally I wondered why there was a light in the kitchen. Well, all right."

They were both stiff and tense, their eyes meeting as they waited for her to go, and when she got back to her bedroom and lay down she was sure she had been fooled somehow because Alca had looked so ashamed.

A faint streak of light from the window was on the ceiling and she watched it till she heard them come along the hall and say good night, and when finally she heard Alca go into her bedroom she relaxed and sighed, and turned over on her side and fell asleep.

A little sound woke her up suddenly, a little clicking noise like the latch on the door. Throwing the covers back she grabbed at her dressing gown, turned on the light, went out to the hall, then to Alca's bedroom. Alca wasn't there.

Hurrying out she forgot that she was a heavy woman and could easily trip in her slippers. She grabbed the stair banister and went running down. On the first landing she looked down the stairs that led to the apartment entrance and there was Alca sitting on the second step, her raincoat on, putting on her shoes.

"Alca, Alca," Mrs. Buhay called hoarsely, and she felt a little dizzy with relief. Holding her dressing gown in tight at the waist, she came heavily down the stairs and into the light while Alca backed away, staring at her.

"Alca, you little fool," she said, but she had to wait to catch her breath. "Where do you think you're going at this hour?"

"Out," Alca said sullenly.

"To be with that guy," and then she grabbed her by the arm. "Where was he taking you at this hour?"

"Just . . . just somewhere," and she jerked away from Mrs. Buhay.

"Where were you going? To his place?"

"I don't know."

"Answer me, Alca."

"I don't have to," she whispered defiantly.

"To his room," Mrs. Buhay said bitterly. "Where is he?" And she went to the big glass door and looked out. It was still raining, but just a little, and the pavement gleamed in the street light. Across the road was a cigar store and she could make out a figure half hidden in the entrance. "There he is. Come here, you little fool," she said, and took Alca's arm roughly and drew her to the door.

"Look at him, skulking around, waiting till I fell asleep. Like a dog when the moon is right, knowing you'll come running. Oh, dear," she said, sighing bitterly. "How nicely he played you. The boy with the elegant manner, the charm and the education. Slumming. Didn't I tell you you'd lose your head? Didn't I?" she asked furiously, and her fury frightened Alca, who still stood with her face pressed against the glass.

Then she turned to protest, but as she met Mrs. Buhay's knowing and scornful glance her own eyes were lonely and stricken. "Yes, it's wrong. I know it's wrong," she whispered. She ran up the stairs. Mrs. Buhay watched her legs in the light rounding the turn and then she sighed wearily. "Well, that's that," and gathering her dressing gown around her, one hand holding it in tight at the waist, she climbed the stairs slowly, breathing hard.

In the hall, she heard Alca crying and she thought grimly, "Maybe now she'll be wise to that guy," and she went back to her bedroom.

She lit a cigarette, sat on the edge of the bed and wished she had a drink, and then the sound of the heartbroken sobbing in the next room began to worry her; it tore at her affection for Alca. Slowly, she got up and went into Alca's bedroom and in the dark she could make out Alca huddled on the bed, her face buried in the pillow.

"Alca, be sensible," she said, kneeling on the bed, and as the spring sagged and rolled Alca toward her she reached out to touch her and was hurt when Alca drew away.

"Would you rather I hadn't stopped you, Alca?"

"No, I'm glad you did."

"Then why are you sore at me?"

"I'm not sore at you at all, Mrs. Buhay."

"Well, then," she said, puzzled. "If you're a little wiser now, it's all right. If you had gone to the guy's room and been easy for him then you're cheap stuff. Don't you see that?"

"I do see it."

"Well, then . . ."

"But you don't understand, Mrs. Buhay," she said half pleading as she sat up slowly. "When we came in tonight we didn't intend to go out, we didn't."

"As if you knew what was in his mind, Alca."

"It wasn't in his mind, Mrs. Buhay," and she shook her head with a desolate conviction. "Not in the beginning. We were just sitting in the kitchen with the door closed to be by ourselves. Then you came along; then it got that we had to be alone. I mean — it got different—"

"Wasn't I right about the guy?"

"No."

"Alca, Alca."

"You weren't right about him; you were right about me."

"How's that?"

"Well, you were sure I was no good."

"Alca, I never said you were no good."

"You didn't need to," she said, her voice breaking. "You said it every time you looked at me. You said it to Tom in the way you watched us, and tonight, well, I got mad and didn't care, and I said let's go somewhere else."

In the dark Mrs. Buhay pleaded, "Alca, your own mother would have taken the attitude I did."

"No, she wouldn't," Alca said quickly.

"She would."

"No, she would never make me feel that Tom was too good for me. But, of course, she's my mother, and maybe there's things she wouldn't see."

"Alca, you took it the wrong way," Mrs. Buhay whispered, shaken by Alca's lonely acceptance of her being no good and, bewildered at the failure of her own affection, she drew her dressing gown across her chest as if she were cold and rubbed her neck slowly with her right hand. As Alca, troubled and wondering, stared at her, she felt old and unknowing and glad of the darkness.

"Alca, I'm a fool."

"A fool about what?"

"Making you see things my way."

"I don't know what you mean."

"It's a fact, a fact," Mrs. Buhay said, then she shook her head and got up and shuffled out of the bedroom.

It was dark in the living room and she stood by the window looking down at the wet street. She couldn't see the cigar store where Tom had been waiting. As she watched to see if he would come along the street she thought of her own life and all who had passed through it and the two men who at one time had loved her, and how they had parted from her, and it seemed a very long time ago, and she felt lonely. And then she thought, "Oh Lord, if I wasn't like I am, Alca wouldn't be in there feeling cheap and common."

A shaft of light came suddenly from Alca's bedroom; she had turned on the light and was getting undressed. Mrs. Buhay went slowly toward the light. Alca was pulling her dress over her head. Mrs. Buhay stood behind her, hesitated, then helped her draw the dress over her head.

"Alca, listen to me," she said. "You were a good straightforward girl when you came here. A girl with good feelings." She groped for the right words, then went on urgently. "There's something I want you to do, Alca. Tomorrow I want you to go and get a room for yourself, you understand?"

"Leave here? Don't you want me here anymore?"

"That's not it, Alca."

"You've been kind to me, Mrs. Buhay. You've done everything for me. I know you like me."

"No, get a room for yourself tomorrow. I'll help you find one. Tomorrow, right, tomorrow. Take a chance with your own heart. It's good. You'll be all right." She fumbled the words because they were cutting her off from Alca, but all she knew was that she didn't want Alca's life to be like hers.

THE INSULT

*I*n the early evenings at the playground, Wilkins, the school
janitor, sat on the school steps wearing his wide suspenders and watched Miss James, the university girl, who
was the playground supervisor. She was only there for the
holidays and so she tried to be civil to Wilkins. But he had
been surly, hostile and malicious.

"You fancy girls who come around here are all the same,"
he said. "You don't know how to handle these kids and you
don't understand this neighbourhood. See that you keep the
kids out of the school and see that you lock up in time so I can
get away on time. That's all."

She wasn't responsible to him. He was only the janitor.
But he made her feel self-conscious.

She had no trouble controlling the little children who
were her charges; there was only a sand pile, a few quoit
games and three slides. But she was sure he was inviting the
whole drab neighbourhood of dilapidated rooming houses
with its swarm of children to share his resentment. He complained bitterly when school windows were broken and tried
to blame her, though the wilder kids broke the windows every
summer. It seemed to her that he encouraged older boys like
the big good-natured lout, Tom Daly, to sit on the fence and
offer her mocking advice. When she refused to take any non-

sense from an interfering, abusive mother who came to the schoolyard after her child had been sent home for bad behaviour, Wilkins had scowled and stood and circled around the two women, muttering, and she'd known he was mimicking her cultivated tone. He made her hate the whole drab neighbourhood.

One night, a tough little tramp named Annie Jones came into the yard. She pushed over one of the heavy slides. "Pick it up, Annie," Miss James said. "Try and make me," Annie said, bumping against Miss James. "I've a mind to beat you up good."

"Why, you vulgar . . ." Miss James said. Out of the corner of her eye she saw Wilkins, who had been sitting with his hands hanging between his knees, stand up expectantly. His malice so plain that it shocked her. She turned away from Annie and raised the slide herself.

Three times a week Wilkins' wife called for him just before the street lighting came on. She was a plump, solid, flat-faced woman who looked threateningly respectable.

Wilkins wanted to have the school closed up promptly so he could get away to a late movie, but sometimes at the closing hour a kid would run off with a quoit and toss it to a big fellow sitting on the fence, who made Miss James coax him to give it to her while he flirted with her. Wilkins would fume because his wife would be scolding him loudly: "So again we miss some of the picture because no one will show any respect for you."

One night, while Wilkins' wife was waiting, Miss James went to lock up and found that the lock had been taken from the school door.

"Mr. Wilkins, Mr. Wilkins," she called.

"What is it?" he grumbled, as he strode across the yard. "You're five minutes late already."

"Hurry, please, Mr. Wilkins. Those children are in the school. Can't you hear them?"

"I warned you. I warned you," he shouted angrily as he ran into the school to chase the squealing children, who fled from room to room, knocking over chairs and desks.

"You scamps!" he yelled, collaring them one by one. "No one to look after you. No one you have any respect for." He herded them to the door, drove them out and turned on Miss James. "I'm supposed to be through here and I have to go around cleaning up your mess with my wife waiting out there."

"Don't be silly," she said haughtily. "The lock was taken off the door with a screwdriver. Go and see for yourself."

"You don't know how to get the respect of those children."

"Don't you dare to talk to me in that fashion."

"No, I won't talk to you," he muttered. "I'll get you fired."

On the next day she got a call from Mr. Gatsby, the chief supervisor, asking her to come and see him during her lunch hour. As soon as she entered his office she asked, "Has that caretaker been around here complaining, Mr. Gatsby?"

"He has indeed, Miss James," Mr. Gatsby said, patiently. He was a mild, worried, good-hearted man with a high forehead and glasses, who had been doing his job for twenty years.

"You know yourself what that man is like," Miss James said bitterly. "Did he tell you the lock was taken off the door?"

"No, he didn't."

"You see, he lies. That ignorant, uncouth man hates all the girls who come around there. Are you going to believe him, Mr. Gatsby?"

"I know what he's like," the supervisor said soothingly. "I complained to his boss last year that he wouldn't cooperate. I complained the year before. He was on the carpet. Another complaint and they'll get rid of him and he'll lose his pension. I don't want that." Then he sighed. "You'd be doing me a great favour, Miss James," he said wearily, "if you could only indulge him."

"I see," she said, reflecting and realizing that she ought to be superior enough to Wilkins to indulge him for the rest of the summer.

All afternoon she spoke to Wilkins with great respect. It was almost comical. He didn't know how to cope with her. When she asked his opinion of the neighbourhood boys he couldn't resist giving an opinion, with a gruff condescension. One of the children threw a ball into a neighbouring yard; the woman wouldn't return it; Miss James asked Wilkins how to deal with the woman. He advised her not to quarrel but to report the incident to Mr. Gatsby.

As she flattered and soothed him he rubbed his thin hair and frowned. She asked him if he thought more sand was needed for the sandbox. Her tone was always gentle and considerate and deferential, and believing she accepted his authority he strutted around, making the playground his dominion, interfering with the children, yet making no real difficulty for her.

But when he stood with his hands on his hips watching her with those pale, troubled, washed-out blue eyes, she knew she would always be uneasy about him.

It had been unbearably hot one afternoon, then a puff of wind blew a cloud of cinder dust across the schoolyard. Suddenly it poured. All the children ran home and Miss James went into the schoolroom assigned to her for the keeping of her records. There she had to keep track of how many children played the quoit games, how many were at the sand pile. She sat at the desk with her legs crossed and her blonde hair falling across her cheek, until a noise at the door made her look up.

Wilkins was there. The heavy patches of hair on his bare arms caught her eye. He smiled; it startled her. He had never smiled at her. Coming closer, he put his hands on the desk.

"Busy?" he asked.

"Just catching up on my records."

"Can you let it go for awhile?"

"I suppose so. Why?"

"Come with me."

"Where?"

"Come on," he said, patting her hand awkwardly. "You'll see."

Maybe it was the lash of the rain against the window as his hand touched hers, and his soft tone, but she heard her heart beating and leaned back in the chair. "I've got to get this stuff finished," she said. Then he came around the desk, reached out and took her arm, and with a foolish smile gave her a playful jerk toward him and drew her out of the chair. His coaxing tone terrified her. "If you can wait a minute," she said, feeling her throat tightening. "I have to put in a call. It'll only take a minute."

"Sure," he said.

She tried to smile. He let her pass and go along the hall to the principal's office. Her hand trembled as she dialed Mr.

Gatsby's number. "Mr. Gatsby," she whispered. "I can't stay here. I'm going home. It's Wilkins. He's acting strangely, I'm afraid of him."

"I'll be right up," Mr. Gatsby said quickly.

Wilkins was there in the hall when she opened the door, and he smiled and she nodded, and didn't know why she nodded. "One moment more," she said, her voice husky. She hurried to her own room and grabbed her coat and darted along the hall and out the door.

It was still raining. She leaned against the door and trembled. She was ready to run as soon as she felt the door opening. In a little while, when she realized that he was not following her, she knew he had understood her fear of him and had remained back in the corridor, waiting.

She saw the supervisor's car draw up at the gate.. Mr. Gatsby came running, his feet splashing in the puddles.

"Is it all right, Miss James?" he called.

"I got out all right."

She told him exactly what had happened and he pondered and said it was a difficult situation. "We know what was in his mind, Miss James," he said. "But of course he'll deny it."

"All I know is I'm afraid of him, Mr. Gatsby. I won't stay in this school with him."

"This time he knows it'll mean his job," Mr. Gatsby said reluctantly. "But we can't have you afraid of him. Would you come in with me?"

"I don't want to go into that school, Mr. Gatsby."

"If you don't, he can say anything he wants to and try to make you seem hysterical."

"All right. Let him try," she said resolutely, but her face was burning.

Wilkins was pacing up and down the corridor and he turned and stared and went to raise his hand in a friendly silly gesture.

"Wilkins, would you come here?" Gatsby said.

"Sure," he said but he looked bewildered, not quite sure what was happening.

They went into her room and Gatsby sat down and she sat down beside him and Wilkins stood in front of the desk. It was hard for Gatsby to begin. Miss James twisted her fingers and looked out the window.

"Miss James has told me how you molested her and wanted to . . ."

"I wasn't molesting her," Wilkins said quickly.

"You certainly scared her, Wilkins."

"I know I did. I don't know why I scared her," he protested. "I've been walking up and down out there trying to figure out how I scared her."

"You know what it means, Wilkins, if Miss James is afraid to work around here."

"What are you getting at?"

"I wouldn't feel I had the right to send another girl here. It means I have to put in a complaint — and — well, Wilkins, this time it really means your job."

"I guess it does," Wilkins said slowly. In the long silence he stared at one spot on the wall as if seeing himself going home and telling his wife what had happened. The colour left his face. "Maybe if she'd think about it when she isn't feeling scared," he said weakly.

"I'm not scared now," she said grimly. "I'm not a baby. I know what goes on."

"But she doesn't know what was in my mind, Mr. Gatsby."

"All right, Wilkins, just what was in your mind?"

"Well, she's a nice girl. She's been kind to me."

"I dare say she has."

"No, I mean appreciative. And very kind in the way she spoke and acted."

"And you felt encouraged to make a pass at her."

"No. No," he protested. "I wanted to show I could appreciate it." He tried to smile but the smile didn't go well with his nervousness. "You see, Mr. Gatsby," he said, "the women teachers have a room all fixed up so they can rest and take their ease. I've never let any of the girls from the playgrounds see it. It's a nice comfortable room. I thought Miss James could use it on the rainy days. It's got a radio in it. I wanted to show it to her, that's all."

"What a joke," Miss James said. Her face was burning and she knew it and was angry. Her resentment of Wilkins flared up and was stronger than her embarrassment.

"It's hard to believe your story," Gatsby said. "You say you were worrying about Miss James' comfort! Well, it's just not like you, Wilkins."

"Why isn't it like me, Mr. Gatsby?"

"We've had experience with you. It's — well — it's not the kind of thing you do."

"How do you know what I can do? How do you know what I'm like?" he asked desperately. "I'm not supposed to be able to be kind and appreciative because you don't think I'm anything but what you see around here in the schoolyard — dressed like this. Well, I'm other things too."

"I don't follow you, Wilkins," Gatsby said.

"I mean," Wilkins began, groping to recall an aspect of himself that would convince them they didn't know him, "you can't see me making a friendly little gesture. Well, maybe there are lots of things you can't see me doing."

"Such as . . ."

"I don't know," he said, throwing up his hands. "Maybe — well — playing the piano — or — singing."

"True."

"Just the same, I sing."

"You're a singer?" Gatsby asked incredulously, and Miss James herself couldn't resist smiling coldly.

"See what I mean," he said eagerly. "That's not like me, either, is it?"

"It's not the issue, Wilkins," Gatsby said impatiently.

"Sure it is," Wilkins insisted. "I tell you something about me and you can't see me doing it. You're all wrong. I took lessons years ago. Opera. Listen." He started to hum "Celeste Aida," and when he saw their blank, wondering expressions he started to sing the aria in a tenor voice. But his voice broke, his eyes shifted from one to the other; he had a crazy pleading smile. Then he sang out again, and when his voice broke the second time tears came to his eyes and he turned his back on them and walked to the window.

Gatsby's astonishment had turned to laughter.

A tuft of greying hair stuck out over the back of Wilkins' collar and Miss James stared at it and was filled with embarrassment that an affront to her dignity had caused Wilkins to put on a ridiculous, desperate performance to try to save his job.

"You have a nice voice," she said, faltering as she stood up. "Hasn't he, Mr. Gatsby?"

"Why, yes, he has," Gatsby said, controlling himself.

"I didn't go on with it," Wilkins said, turning. "It costs money to work on a voice and well, I got married . . . too young, you know."

It was a relief to hear children running in the schoolyard. "It can't be raining now," Miss James said. "I should go out."

At the door she turned, troubled, for it struck her that even in her sympathy she was being superior.

"Mr. Wilkins, I'm sorry," she said and she put out her hand. "I apologize."

"It's all right," he said, taking her hand. "It was natural, Miss James, that you took it as you did, coming from me."

"Well, that's that," Gatsby said and he took Miss James' arm and walked her along the hall. "The point is," he said, "are you afraid to work here with Wilkins around?"

"Not at all," she said quickly.

On the school steps they both stood meditating for a moment, then Gatsby laughed. "You know, Miss James," he said, "he might have had a good voice at one time. Well, it certainly came in handy. So long, Miss James."

"So long," she said.

As she watched him crossing the yard to the street of dilapidated rooming houses where doors and windows were opening after the rain and the women were coming out on their stoops, it struck her with a shock that there had been something in her attitude from the beginning that had provoked not only Wilkins but had been an insult, too, to the whole neighbourhood.

THE FAITHFUL WIFE

*U*ntil a week before Christmas George worked in the station restaurant at the lunch counter. The last week was extraordinarily cold, then the sun shone strongly for a few days, though it was always cold again in the evenings. There were three other men working at the counter. For years they must have had a poor reputation. Women, unless they were careless and easygoing, never started a conversation with them when having a light lunch at noontime. The girls at the station always avoided the red-capped porters and the countermen.

George, who was working there till he got enough money to go back home for a week and then start late in the year at college, was a young fellow with fine hair retreating far back on his forehead and rather bad upper teeth, but he was very polite and generous. Steven, the plump Italian, with the waxed black moustaches, who had charge of the restaurant, was very fond of George.

Many people passed the restaurant window on the way to the platform and the trains. The four men, watching them frequently, got to know some of them. Girls, brightly dressed and highly powdered, loitered in front of the open door, smiling at George, who saw them so often he knew their first names. At noontime, other girls, with a few minutes to spare before going back to work, used to walk up and down the tiled tunnel to the waiting room, loafing the time away, but they never even glanced in at the countermen. It was cold outside, the streets were slippery, and it was warm in the station, that was all. George got to know most of these girls too, and talked about them with the other fellows.

George watched carefully one girl every day at noon hour. The other men had also noticed her, and two or three times she came in for a cup of coffee, but she was so gentle, and aloofly pleasant, and so unobtrusively beyond them, they were afraid to try and amuse her with easy cheerful talk. George wished earnestly that she had never seen him there in the restaurant behind the counter, even though he knew she had never noticed him at all. Her cheeks were usually rosy from the cold wind outside. When she went out the door to walk up and down for a few minutes, an agreeable expression on her face, she never once looked back at the restaurant. George, following her with his eye while pouring coffee slowly, did not expect her to look back. She was about twenty-eight, pretty, rather shy, and dressed plainly and poorly in a thin blue cloth coat without any fur on it. Most girls managed to have a piece of fur of some kind on their coats.

With little to do in the middle of the afternoon, George used to think of her because of seeing her every day and looking at her face in profile when she passed the window. Then, on the day she had on the light-fawn felt hat, she smiled politely at him, when having a cup of coffee, and as long as possible, he remained opposite her, cleaning the counter with a damp cloth.

The last night he worked at the station he went out at about half past eight in the evening, for he had an hour to himself, and then worked on till ten o'clock. In the morning he was going home, so he walked out of the station and down the side street to the docks, and was having only pleasant thoughts, passing the warehouses, looking out over the dark cold lake and liking the tang of the wind on his face. Christmas was only a week away. The snow was falling lazily and melting slowly when it hit the sidewalk. He was glad he was through with the job at the restaurant.

An hour later, back at the restaurant, Steve said, "A dame just phoned you, George, and left her number."

"Do you know who she was?"

"No, you got too many girls, George. Don't you know the number?"

"I never saw it before."

He called the number and did not recognize the voice that answered him. A woman was asking him pleasantly enough if he remembered her. He said he did not. She said she had had a cup of coffee that afternoon at noontime, and added that she had worn a blue coat and a tan-coloured felt hat, and even though she had not spoken to him, she thought he would remember her.

"Good Lord," he said.

She wanted to know if he would come and see her at half past ten that evening. Timidly he said he would, and hardly heard her giving the address. Steve and the other boys started to kid him brightly, but he was too astonished, wondering how she had found out his name, to bother with them. The boys, saying goodbye to him later, winked and elbowed him in the ribs, urging him to celebrate on his last night in the city. Steve, who was very fond of him, shook his head sadly and pulled the ends of his moustaches down into his lips.

The address the girl had given him was only eight blocks away, so he walked, holding his hands clenched tightly in his pockets, for he was cold from nervousness. He was watching the automobile headlights shining on slippery spots on the sidewalk. The house, opposite a public school ground on a side street, was a large old rooming house. A light was in a window on the second storey over the door. Ringing the bell he didn't really expect anyone to answer, and was surprised when the girl herself opened the door.

"Good evening," he said shyly.

"Oh, come upstairs," she said, smiling and practical.

In the front room he took off his overcoat and hat and sat down slowly, noticing, out of the corner of his eye, that she was even slimmer, and had nice fair hair and lovely eyes. But she was moving very nervously. He had intended to ask at once how she found out his name, but forgot about it as soon as she sat down opposite him on a camp bed and smiled shyly. She had on a red woollen sweater, fitting her tightly at the waist. Twice he shook his head, unable to get used to having her there opposite him, nervous and expectant. The trouble was she had always seemed so aloof.

"You're not very friendly," she said awkwardly.

"Oh yes I am. Indeed I am."

"Why don't you come over here and sit beside me?"

Slowly he sat down beside her on the camp bed, smiling stupidly. He was even slow to see that she was waiting for him to put his arms around her. Ashamed of himself, he finally kissed her eagerly and she held on to him tightly. Her heart was thumping underneath the red woollen sweater. She just kept on holding him, almost savagely, closing her eyes slowly and breathing deeply every time he kissed her. She was so delighted and satisfied to hold him in her arms that she did not bother talking at all. Finally he became very eager and she got up suddenly, walking up and down the room, looking occasionally at the cheap alarm clock on a bureau. The room was clean but poorly furnished.

"What's the matter?" he said irritably.

"My girlfriend, the one I room with, will be home in twenty minutes."

"Come here anyway."

"Please sit down, please do," she said.

Slowly she sat down beside him. When he kissed her she did not object, but her lips were dry, her shoulders were trembling, and she kept on watching the clock. Though she was holding his wrist so tightly her nails dug into the skin, he knew she would be glad when he had to go. He kissed her again and she drew her left hand slowly over her lips.

"You really must be out of here before Irene comes home," she said.

"But I've only kissed and hugged you and you're wonderful." He noticed the red ring mark on her finger. "Are you sure you're not waiting for your husband to come home?" he said a bit irritably.

Frowning, looking away vaguely, she said, "Why do you have to say that?"

"There's a ring mark on your finger."

"I can't help it," she said, and began to cry quietly. "Yes, oh yes, I'm waiting for my husband to come home. He'll be here at Christmas."

"It's too bad. Can't we do something about it?"

"I tell you I love my husband. I do, I really do, and I'm faithful to him too."

"Maybe I'd better go," he said uncomfortably, feeling ridiculous.

"Eh, what's that? My husband, he's at a sanitarium. He got his spine hurt in the war, then he got tuberculosis. He's pretty bad. They've got to carry him around. We want to love each other every time we meet, but we can't."

"That's tough, poor kid, and I suppose you've got to pay for him."

"Yes."

"Do you have many fellows?"

"No. I don't want to have any."

"Do they come here to see you?"

"No. No, I don't know what got into me. I liked you, and felt a little crazy."

"I'll slide along then. What's your first name?"

"Lola. You'd better go now."

"Couldn't I see you again?" he said suddenly.

"No, you're going away tomorrow," she said, smiling confidently.

"So you've got it all figured out. Supposing I don't go?"

"Please, you must."

Her arms were trembling when she held his overcoat. She wanted him to go before Irene came home. "You didn't give me much time," he said flatly.

"No. Irene comes in at this time. You're a lovely boy. Kiss me."

"You had that figured out too."

"Just kiss and hold me once more, George." She held on to him as if she did not expect to be embraced again for a long time, and he said, "I think I'll stay in the city awhile longer."

"It's too bad, but you've got to go. We can't see each other again."

In the poorly lighted hall she looked lovely. Her cheeks were flushed, and though still eager, she was quite satisfied with the whole affair. Everything had gone perfectly for her.

As he went out the door and down the walk to the street he remembered that he hadn't asked how she had found out his name. Snow was falling lightly and there were hardly any footprints on the sidewalk. All he could think of was that he ought to go back to the restaurant and ask Steve for his job again. Steve was fond of him. But he knew he could not spoil it for her. "She had it all figured out," he muttered, turning up his coat collar.

A Separation

W hen his mother went away Philip was ten years old and a little short for his age, though his legs were beginning to lengthen out and look skinny. As soon as his mother left the house he began to notice that even the small things from day to day were not the same. Night after night his father came home and sat alone with his own worried thoughts, usually in the big leather chair with his head thrown back and his eyes wide open.

Philip's father was a broad-shouldered man with thick black hair and a smile full of warmth when he was in good humour, but on these nights, just to look at him moving listlessly with such a solemn face made Philip feel lonely in the house. And he said to him one time, "What's the matter, Dad, don't you feel good?"

"I'm all right, Phil," his father answered, looking up with surprise and a sudden amused gentleness.

Philip tried to accept this answer, standing with his hands linked behind his back and a puckered smile on his face. He started to speak, hesitated gravely, then blurted out, "Maybe if Mother comes back everything will go on like it did before. Won't it?"

"Listen to me carefully," his father said. "I don't want you to mention your mother again. I don't want you to even think about her, do you hear?" he added sharply.

"I hear."

"And you'll remember, mind."

"All right, Dad," he answered timidly, turning his eyes away into a corner of the room. But he felt hurt. His face looked sullen and confused as he shuffled away uneasily. He began to feel vaguely resentful and then angry at his father. Sitting down in a chair, slouching, with his legs crossed at the ankles, and making absurd little noises with his lips, he let himself think of his mother, all kinds of wild hopeful thoughts, till he felt farther and farther away from his father and almost out of the room and in a fine exciting world.

Only a little while ago his father used to come home in the evenings and say, "What have you been doing today, young fellow, riding a white horse, or were you a pirate on the Spanish Main? Come here and tell me about it." With his blue eyes full of eagerness, Philip would tell of everything he had thought of doing on the way home from school. But on these days, with no one bothering much about him, his hair was always tousled, his shoes weren't cleaned as they used to be, his stockings were often twisted carelessly around his legs, and he wore the same green pullover sweater nearly every day. Also he had got into the habit of playing hooky from school with his friend Buddy Hawkins and going uptown to the big stores and hanging around all afternoon and then walking home and having fine talks about all kinds of things; or sometimes in the evenings, when his father had gone out, he would sneak out and meet Buddy on the street. Philip began to like being on the street in the evening almost better than anything. He and Buddy would go down to the corner by the drugstore where some of the big fellows in long pants were standing talking about the ball game, or girls, or fighters, and Philip would listen with his round face tilted up enthusiastically, ready to laugh loudly at any kind of a poor joke. He and Buddy would stay there till someone said, "For the love of Mike, chase those little kids out of here. Go home and tell your mother she wants you." Then Philip and Buddy would saunter away, sit down by themselves on the curb, and talk about getting long pants in a year or two and make bets about things they never expected really to happen.

Ever since the time when Philip had been warned not to mention his mother, or think about her, he had been shy with his father, but he was keeping out of his way mainly because he did not want to have to answer difficult questions about himself and school. One night, after dinner, his father, who was looking good-humoured and almost contented, said in a mild, coaxing voice, "Well, son, how's everything been going with you these days? How are you getting on?"

"All right, I guess." Philip said with a restless twist of his head.

"You don't talk like you used to. What's the matter, Phil?"

"Who, me? Nothing at all's the matter," Philip said. His face began to get hot. His father began to stare at him as if he had concern so deep that he was unable to express it, a fear that in a few months his boy had been drawn away from him, or even turned against him. "I don't want you to keep out of my sight, Phil," he said earnestly. "There's no reason for that, is there?"

"I'm always around the house," Philip said.

"Don't you like being just with me, son?"

"Sure I like it, Dad."

"We used to be great pals, you know, Phil."

Philip couldn't think of anything to say, so his father added, "You're feeling stubborn about something." He began to look disappointed, as though sure of hostility in his son. "This won't do at all," he said coldly. "And you'll have to get used to things."

Philip got up from the table and followed his father from one room to another, looking up eagerly and trying to get his eye so he would see how much he liked him, feeling too awkward to say anything. His father paid no attention to him.

The next time Philip stayed away from school, his father was told about it and he spoke to Philip; it was the night Mr. Moyer, an old friend, came to the house, but about half an hour before he came, "Come here, Philip," his father said, looking hard-eyed and brusque. "Where were you this afternoon?"

"At school," Philip said.

"You're a liar," his father said, grabbing hold of him roughly.

"I'm not lying, not really. Let go my arm. Oh, you're hurting."

"I want the truth, always the truth," his father said, slapping Philip and watching him cower away with his elbows up over his thin face. "If you think you're going to have your own way entirely around here, and do just as you please, you're mistaken. You've not been going to school. The Lord knows what you've been doing. And all the time around here, you're pouting and looking sullen as if you had no use for me." He slapped Philip again. "From now on you'll do what you're told and stop lying and being deceitful, do you hear?"

"I won't ever lie to you again, Dad."

"See that you don't. Stop crying now and go on out to the street for awhile. Mr. Moyer's coming here and he shouldn't see you like that."

Dragging his feet, Philip got his peak cap and went out to the street with his head down. From his coat pocket he pulled out a withered old horse chestnut with a cord through it and stared at it attentively while he swung it around his finger. Mr. Moyer would be coming along soon, he thought. He did not want anybody to see him while his eyes were still red from crying, so he walked along the street the length of the block to the corner. The street lights had just been lit. On the other side of the street, he saw Buddy Hawkins carrying a big paper bag, and he started to run, calling, "Wait a minute, Buddy." When he crossed the street he said to the other kid, "My dad found out about me staying away from school."

"Gee, maybe my father knows too," Buddy said. "My mother hasn't said anything yet. What did your father say, Phil?"

"He gave me a licking."

"I guess I won't go near your house for awhile."

"Come on and hang around awhile," Philip said, wanting company very much, but Buddy said, "I can't. My mother's waiting for these things. So long."

Whistling thinly, Philip leaned against the lamppost. At first his thoughts were jumbled, and he looked up and down the street, wondering where to go, then his thoughts became more vivid and he remembered that last time his mother had come to see him. It had been on a mild evening, clear and fine and not very late, and the kids he had been playing with had left him and he had sat down for awhile on the pavement before going into the house. His father, who had been out that evening, had made him promise to be in bed by ten o'clock. Sitting on the curb, in front of the house, he had looked up and seen her coming along the street, a tall woman dressed with elegance, with a fresh lovely face. He had jumped up and run toward her to take hold of her arm and had chattered away while leading her into the house. She had seemed to know his father would not be in at that hour, and sitting beside him, patting his head and laughing gaily, she had felt so happy she had begun to cry. He had said, "Why are you crying, Mother?" and she had said, "I'm just feeling happy, that's all." She had asked all about himself and had brought him two books of adventure stories. Then she had said, "Always make a little prayer for me at night, Philip, and I'll make one for you." Her lovely face had been smudged with tears as she hurried away.

Philip went on thinking about this very gravely. He began to wonder why it was, if his mother loved him and his father used to love him so much, that they did not always want to be together. He figured out that his mother had been glad to be in the house, and his father wasn't really happy when she was away. Why couldn't something be done, he wondered. Perhaps if they only understood how much he loved them both, they would want to be together. He had a sudden buoyant hope that his father might understand this clearly, if only he could go home now and do something to make his father very proud of him.

So with slow, conspicuous movements he entered the kitchen where his father and Mr. Moyer, the neighbour, were drinking a few bottles of beer. The two men were talking slowly, pausing from time to time to get the matter clear. As Philip, curling his cap in his hands, sat down, he didn't exactly want to be noticed, yet at the same time he would have liked them to speak to him. Mr. Moyer, a fat kindly man with thin reddish hair curling over a shiny pink scalp, had already taken off his coat for an evening's drinking. Philip twisted faintly the corner of his lip in a grin and Mr. Moyer gave him a sociable smile. Philip gave his father a broad, half-ashamed, good-natured smile, but his father, with a gloomy frown of despair on his face, didn't notice him and went on talking. "I suppose I ought to get used to the situation," he was saying.

"You're letting it go on worrying you too much, man."

"I can't help it."

"You make a mistake, John," Philip heard Mr. Moyer say. "It was a case of both of you working at cross purposes. Not just her. So you've got no right to hate her, you know."

"I don't hate her. You don't understand what I mean," Philip's father said, looking bewildered and indignant. "I don't hate anybody."

"I always liked Elsie myself. Of course I knew her well."

"You knew her, sure you did, and did you ever imagine she wasn't satisfied? I don't know what to believe now."

"Maybe she knows now she made a mistake, and if you got hold of her and talked straight . . ."

"No, that's out of the question. I couldn't rely on her again."

"Come on, John. Don't have such a tough spirit. It isn't like you at all."

"Supposing I did forgive her? Would it alter my own feeling?"

"I think candidly, since we know each other so well, that you might be generous enough to welcome her, if she hinted she wanted to try again."

"Am I not entitled to have any feeling at all about it?"

"Sure you are, and she's entitled to have some pride too. I say it would be a mighty generous gesture if you went to her yourself," Mr. Moyer said.

"Thank God I've got some pride myself. Oh, I know, you think I'm stubborn. Maybe I am, but . . ."

Philip noticed Mr. Moyer nodding toward him and saying, "Better drop the subject for a time, John." Philip had kept on lifting his head every time his father spoke. He knew they were talking about his mother, and every time his father spoke the disappointment within him grew heavier. But he liked Mr. Moyer for being so polite and agreeable about his mother. Mr. Moyer was saying, "He's a nice boy," and Philip ducked his head.

"He's growing up and getting wise like they all do. I had occasion to whip him tonight for not telling the truth."

"He's all right," Mr. Moyer said. "My wife often wishes we had a boy like him instead of all those girls of ours."

"You'll have less trouble with the girls. I don't know as I can rely on anything Philip says, and he gets stubborn and sullen, too. Look at him. Isn't he the dead image of his mother, sitting there? He's beginning to remind me of her every time I look at him. He's got all her little ways and does just what he wants, too."

Philip feeling ashamed, and wanting to run out of the room, tried to smile first at one, then at the other. And Mr. Moyer, forcing a laugh because he, too, was embarrassed, said, "You can't blame the kid for looking so like his mother, can you?"

"I suppose not," Philip heard his father say. "Only I don't expect much. I haven't much faith in him, that's all."

"Sh, sh, have some sense, John. You're making the kid feel bad."

Philip looked up once at his father who said, in a milder voice, "Better run along to bed, son."

In a single breath and with his head down, Philip said, "Good night, Dad, good night, Mr. Moyer," and he left the kitchen.

But he did not go to bed. Pulling his cap well down over his eyes, he went out, closing the door quietly. The way things were going he did not know what he could do. As he stood on the doorstep, with the night air cooling his flushed face, he had a sharp aching feeling of separation from everything he had ever liked. He clenched his fists stubbornly. He kept looking eagerly along the street. Then slowly he shuffled down to the sidewalk and began walking toward the corner. "I'll go away. When I'm big I'll come back and then things'll be different," he thought.

At the corner, in an aimless way he crossed the street, and then after standing still a few moments, he crossed back again, thinking steadily of strange places he could go till he grew older, thinking of places very far away till his imagination began to unravel many pictures in which he saw and heard himself speaking distinctly. But after awhile he thought fearfully. "If Mr. Moyer goes and Dad finds out I'm not in bed, there'll be trouble," so he started to hurry back to the house.

In the hall he brushed against Mr. Moyer, who was saying, "Good night, John." Both men looked very solemnly at Philip's scared face that kept twisting uneasily away from them. "Good night, John," Mr. Moyer repeated before he left.

Philip's father said to him when they were alone, "Where have you been, son? I thought you went to bed." He spoke in a mild coaxing voice and without waiting for an answer he walked away. He was frowning as if something was hurting him and he could not free himself. Twice he patted Philip on the shoulder when he passed him, with a faint, embarrassed smile on his face that quickly disappeared. At last he sat down beside the boy and began to speak with a mild diffidence, trying all the time without hurrying to find certain words which would explain that he was sorry. All he actually said was, "We'll be great friends again, boy," and he played awkwardly with Philip's arm, squeezing it hard, sometimes looking at him, and sometimes letting his own thoughts wander away.

Philip was still timid, but he began to like feeling his father's big hand patting him on the shoulder so steadily as if he were proud of him, and he could sort of feel them being drawn close together while his father was silent with such an eager expression on his face. He glanced up shyly. Then he said with sudden confidence, "I feel all right, Dad." His father, who had been watching him very humbly, took a deep breath and said, "That's fine, son. Everything will be all right. I'll do everything I can do. You understand?" Philip didn't know exactly what his father meant, and he hardly dared to let himself try and figure it out, so he just sat there feeling big with hope.

POSSESSION

*O*n the way along the street Dan looked up at the falling snow and the lights in the windows and it all began to shift away and then swing back before his eyes. He was scared of this sudden dizziness and he said, "It's nothing. That's just the way the snow slants across the lights. It makes my eyes tired, that's all."

As he went into his place he closed the door quietly and he went to go noiselessly up the stairs, but then he hesitated when he saw the little pile of letters on the table in the hall. He looked back at those letters and hope rose in him again. Three days ago he had written to an uncle he hardly knew in Detroit asking him for money, and now he tiptoed back to the table and flicked his thumb through the pile of letters while the wet snow melting on his hat trickled down and dripped on the floor, and he saw there wasn't a letter for him. And then, when he heard the click of a latch in the door at the end of the hall, he knew he had delayed too long. Mrs. Macillroy, who owned the building, hurried after him and caught him when he was only halfway up the stairs. She was a plump, quiet woman with grey hair who was smiling very softly tonight. "And how are you tonight, Mr. Lowery?" she called anxiously. By the solicitude and softness of her voice he knew what she really wanted to say, but he said, "I'm fine, thanks."

"Was there anything doing today?"

"No, nothing at all," he said, keeping the wide, false smile on his face.

"Is there anything in sight at all?"

"I thought there might have been a letter there for me," he said. "I wrote to Detroit for some money," he said.

It was a hopeless business trusting the tenants and letting the days go by but Mrs. Macillroy was a good-natured woman and she said in spite of her natural shrewdness, "All right. I hope something turns up soon for you," and she walked away soberly.

While he watched her shoulders and the little roll of grey hair at the back of her neck he wondered if he would ever be able to come in and get by the hall again.

As he sat on his bed waiting for the excitement that had risen in him so sharply to subside, it seemed he could not help remembering every job he had ever had. He began to think of all the money he had once wasted on foolish and lovely little things. He sat there with an intense longing in him to live over again the joyous moments when he had spent money freely, and in a little while he was so enchanted he could hardly move and more beautiful thoughts came just as easily and their loveliness was always heightened by the depth of his longing.

But when he heard someone rapping on the door there was such a leaping shock of excitement in him he could hardly stand it. Every little shock was the same these days. He took one shock after another and thought he was rolling away from them, but they left him light-headed and weaker and almost drunk. "Come in," he said.

Mrs. Macillroy's ten-year-old son was grinning brightly at him. "Mother says she forgot to give you a message," he said.

"A Miss Rowe phoned. She left her number and said you were to phone."

"Was that all?"

"That's all," the boy said.

An immense relief flooded through Dan and he wanted to hear Helen Rowe's voice, he wanted to hear her talking to him in her warm and friendly way so that bit by bit he might feel again that he had some dignity. He had met her just two months ago. She knew he was out of work but she saw him nearly every night. She worked in a broker's office. She was twenty-five. It was wonderful that she should spend so much time with him knowing he was without money and work and yet might want to marry her. And as one day followed another and all the days were the same for him she began to seem like something unbelievably bright and joyous in his life.

But when he went to the phone he began to worry and he thought, "Why is she calling me? She never called like this before," and then he waited and listened and heard her voice, and he closed his eyes and saw her face and she was saying, "Can you meet me early tonight, Dan, in about half an hour?"

"Sure I can," he said.

"Meet me at the corner, will you?"

"What's bothering you, Helen?"

"I've got to go home. My mother's very sick."

"Where have you got to go?"

"To New Hampshire."

"For how long?"

"About three weeks," she said.

"I'll be there in half an hour," he said. And while he sat there looking at the phone he grew more and more frightened that she was going away, for now it seemed that without her company and hope for him he could not live. As he put on his coat again and got ready to go out he began to think desperately, "I never really had a chance to be in love with her. I never got close enough to her. Where will I be in three weeks? I'll have to get out of here. I may go to Detroit. Something's got to happen. Something's got to break and then it's all gone and I've lost her. I may be dead by the time she comes back here if it goes on like this."

And his desperate anxiety so overwhelmed him as he walked along the street in the snow with his coat collar turned high that he knew he must try and possess her forever that night, he knew he must not let her go that night without taking her love forever, he knew he couldn't stand it if she went away and he had never had a chance to make love to her. "This'll be the only chance I'll have," he thought as his shoes swished through the wet snow and the flakes fell softy upon his face.

She was waiting at the corner of the avenue where the wet snow had quickly disappeared under so many passing feet. She was standing under the street light smiling at him. Then she hurried towards him, a girl almost as tall as he was, in a brown coat and a little brown hat. Her face was wet and shining in the light. "Hello, Dan," she said. "Isn't it terrible that I've got to go home?"

"Are you sure you've got to go, Helen? If you wait a little while maybe your mother'll be all right.

"I'm going in the morning," she said. And then when they began to walk along the street in step she asked the same question that she asked every night, "Anything doing today, Dan? Anything in sight?"

"No," he said. "Nothing today."

"Let's go into the Coffee Pot over there and have a cup of coffee and talk," she said. "We can't walk in the snow."

"What's the matter with the snow?"

"Nothing. I like the snow, but we'll get our feet wet," she said.

So they crossed the road to the restaurant and when they were sitting in a little booth by themselves and drinking their coffee with her watching him thoughtfully he became impatient. He knew she was thinking of him looking for work that day. He didn't want this kind of care and worry about him to be in her. He wanted to put out his hand and touch her, he wanted her eyes to grow soft in a different way, he wanted to see a flush and a shyness in her face; he tried to break the mood in her by saying, "We've only got a few hours before we go, Helen?"

But she did not seem to understand. She said, "Won't you have some kind of a big thick meat sandwich with your coffee, Dan?"

"Why do I want a sandwich at this hour?"

"Did you have your dinner?"

"You mean a big hearty dinner?"

"No, I mean something hot to eat."

"Sure I had something to eat," he said irritably. He wanted to forget himself and the monotonous days of his life and his clothes and his hunger and the tightness that grew in him day after day. He wanted to forget and lose himself in the warmth and loveliness of her. But she was saying again, "Please do eat a sandwich?"

"Will that end it if I do? Will you forget about it?"

"Yes," she said.

"All right. I'll have a hot roast beef sandwich," he said.

When they had brought the sandwich he said softly, "Gee, it's terrible to think you're going away."

"I wish I weren't going," she said. Almost to herself she said as she watched him eating the sandwich hungrily, "How many days go by that you hardly eat anything?"

"Not many, thank God."

"There must be very many when you're hungry like you are now. I've never realized it before. How do you eat, Dan?"

"Are you going to start talking about that again?"

"I want to talk about it. I'm going away and I'd like to know. I've never been able to find out much from you."

"I'll get along all right," he said. And then he began to feel that they would never share the same eager longing for each other while they sat there. It no longer mattered now whether he ate or worked, there was only one thing left in the world to do, he wanted to make love to her before it ended. And he said boldly, "Helen, will you come to my place for awhile so we can be alone?"

As his fear that she might refuse grew, he felt the softness of her eyes and he began to want her terribly. The hot coffee and the sandwich in him made him feel warm and eager. He took her by the arm and said, "Come on, Helen."

There was just one reluctant moment, and then she said simply, "All right, Dan."

On the way out she slipped the money for the food into his hand, and then she bought a package of cigarettes, and when he was buttoning his coat he found she had slipped the cigarettes into his pocket.

In her silence as they went along the street he thought maybe there was love and desire for him and this notion so exalted him that he felt more sharply aware of everything on the street that winter night than ever before. At his place she went up the stairs quietly, going ahead of him and never once looking back, and she waited with her head lowered timidly while he opened the door.

She looked around the room as if she had often wondered what it would be like, and then she sat down shyly on the bed.

"I'm glad you felt you could come here," he said nervously.

"I didn't mind coming tonight," she said. "I can't stay more than an hour, though."

He was pulling off his coat with his hands trembling erratically in his excitement, and then he began to take her coat off, too. Leaning forward, she looked at him and smiled and waited. As he put out his hand to touch her there was such a desperate eagerness in his face that she was startled. She began to feel as he put out his hand that he was touching everything he was missing in his life and all the love he could know.

And bit by bit he felt that she no longer pitied him and that warmth and desire instead was growing in her, and he kissed her and she clung to him, and it was so marvellous to have her close to him like that when he had never really been sure that she loved him that he said, "Helen, I love you. I want to have you like this so you can't be without me."

"I don't want to be without you," she said.

"This is what'll hold us together," he said.

And then the fear that she might go grew strong in him again, and he held her tighter, then he held her down and he began to cover her face and her neck with his kisses. He thought by the softness of her that she was willing and wouldn't resist him now. Then he noticed that her body had begun to tremble, and he noticed too, while he bent over her, that she had begun to cry. He was really disgusted and he thought, "Gees, so that's what she's like. You think she's willing and then she lets herself out by starting to cry," and he said in a flat, lifeless voice, "Don't bother crying. You don't need to be afraid of me. I thought you felt different, that's all."

"I'm sorry. I can't help it," she said.

"You don't need to cry. What are you crying about?"

"I was just thinking."

"Can't you ever stop thinking?"

"I just started and I couldn't stop."

"What were you thinking about?"

"I was thinking it was terrible for me to be going away for three weeks and spending all that money going up there with you needing it so bad here."

With her bright soft eyes she pleaded with him, and he knew then that it was now like it had been in the restaurant, that they were still thinking in different ways.

"You've got to go," he said.

"I know it," she said, "but look what you could do with that money, look how many meals it would buy."

They sat close beside each other, silent and feeling close together, and he could not bear to try and make love to her again.

"I'll have to go now," she said.

"I'll go down to the corner with you."

They put on their coats and they went quietly down the stairs and nobody heard them as they went out to the street. It was still snowing.

They hardly spoke at all on the way to the corner. They went down into the subway. When the train came he kissed her quickly and they parted and he stood there watching her running to get on the train and she hardly had a chance to look back.

When he went back along the street alone he felt again that desperate anguish of possessing nothing in the world. "I let her go. I was a fool to let her go like that," he thought. Everything began turning over and over in him rapidly and as he went along he grew confused. "I hold her forever and ever," he thought. The traffic passed, the city rumbled with noise and he seemed to roll away from it as the snow fell, and then he rolled into it again, and he kept growing more confused. He felt he held it all in him, he felt all the joy of full possession, and he could never be alone again.

Dates of Original Publication

Two Fishermen, *Canadian Accent: A Celebratin of Short Stories by Contemporary Canadian Writers*, ed. Ralph Gustafsson, Penguin, 1944

The Runaway, *Esquire*, September 1934

Silk Stockings, *The New Yorker*, April 1932

A Girl with Ambition, *This Quarter*, Paris, 1925-26

Rocking Chair, *The North American Review*, December 1932

A Wedding Dress, *This Quarter*, Spring 1927

Three Lovers, *Harper's Bazaar,* July 1934

The Cheat's Remorse, *Esquire*, October 1937

It Must Be Different, *Redbook*, February 1936

Poolroom, *Scribner's Magazine*, October 1932

The Bachelor's Dilemma, *Maclean's*, 1950

Getting On in the World, *American Mercury*, May 1939

The Novice, *The Canadian Magazine,* March 1930

The Two Brothers, *Esquire*, December 1930

Their Mother's Purse, *The New Yorker*, September 1936

Magic Hat, *Redbook*, December 1951

Younger Brother, *The New Yorker*, May 1931

This Man, My Father, *Maclean's*, March 1937

The Lucky Lady, *The Lost and Found Stories*, 1985

A Couple of Million Dollars, *The Lost and Found Stories*, 1985

The Blue Kimono, *Harper's Bazaar*, May 1935

With an Air of Dignity, *Maclean's*, January 1948

The Way It Ended, *Canadian Home Journal*, September 1953

Lady in a Green Dress, *Scribner's Magazine*, August 1930

A Pair of Long Pants, *Redbook*, October 1936

The Consuming Fire, *Harper's Bazaar,* August 1936

Father and Son, *Harper's Bazaar,* June 1934

It Had to Be Done, *Harper's Bazaar*, September 1938

The Homing Pigeon, *Harper's Bazaar*, June 1935
We Just Had to Be Alone, *Maclean's*, March 1955
The Insult, *Weekend Magazine,* 1955
The Faithful Wife, T*he New Yorker, December* 1929
A Separation, *Scribner's Magazine,* November 1933
Possession, *Esquire*, April 1935

Questions for Discussion and Essays

1. In her introduction to Volume Three, writer Anne Michaels points out that Morley Callaghan's body of work possesses a rare integrity. How does Callaghan achieve that sense of honesty and integrity in his writing and how does it impact on the way we read his stories?

2. How does Callaghan reveal motivation in his stories and how does he use descriptive detail to create the psychology of his characters?

3. Marriage and familial relationships play an important role in a number of Callaghan's stories. What is his view of marriage and family relationships and how does he use such relationships as the basis for creating dramatic narratives?

4. Callaghan's stories often leave a reader with the sense that objects are transformed into something more than themselves. Discuss his idea of "still life" objects and how he creates a sense of beauty and fascination for the reader while remaining a detached storyteller. What impact does Callaghan gain from refusing to editorialize about objects and their relationships to characters?

5. As a writer, how does Callaghan use honesty as both a theme and a stylistic compass in telling his stories?

Selected Related Reading

Allen, Walter Ernest. *The Short Story in English*. Oxford University Press, 1981. (Contains a chapter on Morley Callaghan.)

Anderson, Sherwood. *Winesburg, Ohio*. Introduced by Malcolm Cowley. New Edition. Milestone Editions, 1960.

Callaghan, Barry. *Barrelhouse Kings*. McArthur & Company, 1998.

Callaghan, Morley. *A Literary Life. Reflection and Reminiscences 1928–1990*. Exile Editions, 2008.

Conron, Brandon. *Morley Callaghan*. Twayne, 1966.

Dennis, Richard. *British Journal of Canadian Studies*, 1999. (Contains an essay by Richard Dennis: "Morley Callaghan and the Moral Geography of Toronto.")

Farrell, James T. *Studs Lonigan* (A Trilogy). Pete Hamill (editor). Library of America, 1998.

Flaubert, Gustave. *Madame Bovary*. Margaret Cohen (editor). Norton Critical Editions, 1998.

Hemingway, Ernest. *The Complete Short Stories*. Charles Scribner's Sons, 1998.

Joyce, James. *The Dubliners*. Penguin, 1999.

de Maupassant, Guy. *The Complete Short Stories of Guy de Maupassant*, 1955. Artine Artinian (editor). Penguin, 1995.

May, Charles Edward. *The Short Story: The Reality Of Artifice*. Twayne, 1995.

O'Connor, Frank. *The Lonely Voice: A Study of the Short Story*, with an introduction by Russell Banks. Melville House, 2011.

Snider, Norman. "Why Morley Callaghan Still Matters," *Globe and Mail*, 25 October, 2008.

Walsh, William. *A Manifold Voice: Studies in Commonwealth Literature*. Chatto & Windus, 1971.

White, Randall. *Too Good to Be True: Toronto in the 1920s*. Dundurn, 1993.

Wilson, Edmund. *O Canada: An American's Notes on Canadian Culture*. Farrar, Straus & Giroux, 1964.

Woodcock, George. "Callaghan's Toronto: The Persona of a City." *Journal of Canadian Studies* 7-2 (1972) 21-24.

Of Interest on the Web

www.MorleyCallaghan.ca
– The official site of the Morley Callaghan Estate

www.cbc.ca/rewind/sirius/2012/03/01/morley-callaghan/
Rewind With Michael Enright: An Hour With Morley Callaghan.
Thursday, March 1, 2012, CBC Radio One. This hour-long
broadcast features conversations with Morley Callaghan and a
splendid commentary.

www2.athabascau.ca/cll/writers/english/writers/mcallaghan.php
– Athabasca University site

www.editoreric.com/greatlit/authors/Callaghan.html
– The Greatest Authors of All Time site

www.cbc.ca/lifeandtimes/callaghan.htm
– Canadian Broadcasting Corporation (CBC) site

Exile Online Resource

www.ExileEditions.com has a section for the Exile Classics Series,
with further resources for all the books in the series.

Editor's Endnotes

Poets, starting with W.W.E. Ross in the 1930s, have always been interested in Morley Callaghan's short stories, intrigued by how — using a language almost devoid of metaphor — he achieved certain poetic effects. In 1960, Margaret Avison, the great poet, recipient of the Griffin Award, reviewed *Morley Callaghan's Stories* in *The Canadian Forum*.

CALLAGHAN REVISITED

Morley Callaghan's stories are the work of an artist with no axe to grind, who makes no concessions to the market's demands; a purity of artistic intention is everywhere unmistakable in him. Callaghan uses words to convey a whole impression from swift details, so skillfully that his contemporaries are unaware of art (or artifice). For artifice is there all right. If you imagine that the words of these stories are simply the spoken language of everyday life, think of the rapid change in idiom over the past four decades, and look at the stories again. Has any sentence "dated" — or lost its immediacy? The words *are* plain talk, but not a resonance is permitted, not an overtone that localizes the effect. Verbal play has no place. Subjective shading is not invited. The story's world, not the writer's response to it, establishes its language, and in this way it is projected into independent life.

Like all definite techniques this one imposes limits. People whose talk is not plain have little voice in these stories, for their terms would inevitably blur into the language of the writer's own thinking and confuse the writer's with his created world. When such people appear it is never in the foreground: the woman "who was interested in the new psychology" is not allowed to speak for herself. Overtones of sophistication are similarly avoided. In a bar a man spends an evening discussing American architecture — but in indirect discourse very far out of the limelight. Lawyers, advertising men, journalists, architects, even a student on a graduate fellowship may be characters in the stories but none of them is caught reading. One newspaperman who faked some exposés of Toronto bootlegging finally went west on a harvesters' train claiming that he "didn't want to be an author, just write one book something like *Anna Karenina*." Even that much of a literary allusion is rare.

Obviously this style sacrifices some of the powers of language. Monosyllables become obtrusive at times and there are so many people named Joe or Mary or Frank or George that all the characters tend to become memorably nameless. But these sacrifices are justified. "Very Special Shoes," for one, conveys in five and a half pages more than many full-length novels on the same theme — death, the desolation that follows, and its resolution. Life first: "Mrs. Johnson sat down, spread her legs, and sighed with pleasure and licked the ice cream softly and smiled with satisfaction and her mouth looked beautiful."

Then the death:

It was to be an operation for cancer, and the doctor said the operation was successful. But Mrs. Johnson died under the anaesthetic. The two older sisters and Mr. Johnson kept repeating dumbly to the doctor

"But she looked all right. She looked fine." Then they all went home. They seemed to huddle first in one room then in another. They took turns trying to console Mary but no one could console her.

A few paragraphs later the story is completed:

. . . as she stared at them, solemn-faced, she suddenly felt a strange kind of secret joy, a feeling of certainty that her mother had got the shoes so that she might understand at this time that she still had her special blessing and protection . . .Of course now that they were black they were not noticed by other children. But she was very careful with them. Every night she polished them up and looked at them and was touched again by that secret joy. She wanted them to last a long time.

A social attitude is implied by this choice of words, and their ability to project the stories does not explain it away. In at least six stories it is explicit. "I can see that I have been concerned with the problems of many kinds of people but I have neglected those of the very, very rich," the author says. Naturally there is poverty in those of the stories that evoke the Depression period. But what seems to me marked is not the "kinds of people" so much as the insistence on their common humanity . . . Callaghan the artist takes sides very seldom, but when he does in these stories it is in indignation at barriers set up by wealth or social confidence or learning. The stature and dignity of a human being is at stake. . . there is unrelieved desolation sometimes, tragedy, absurdity

— but every pattern leads out into a larger atmosphere of mercy and wonder . . . Many a writer in the last decade has forged his style in the same cause, but I can think of not one whose force of conviction brings it to such a burning focus.

Margaret Avison

THE EXILE CLASSICS SERIES

THAT SUMMER IN PARIS (No. 1) ~ MORLEY CALLAGHAN
Memoir 6x9 247 pages 978-1-55096-688-6 (tpb) $19.95
It was the fabulous summer of 1929 when the literary capital of North America had moved to the Left Bank of Paris. Ernest Hemingway, F. Scott Fitzgerald, James Joyce, Ford Madox Ford, Robert McAlmon and Morley Callaghan... amid these tangled relationships, friendships were forged, and lost... A tragic and sad and unforgettable story told in Callaghan's lucid, compassionate prose.

NIGHTS IN THE UNDERGROUND (No. 2) ~ MARIE-CLAIRE BLAIS
Fiction/Novel 6x9 190 pages 978-1-55096-015-0 (tpb) $19.95
With this novel, Marie-Claire Blais came to the forefront of feminism in Canada. This is a classic of lesbian literature that weaves a profound matrix of human isolation, with transcendence found in the healing power of love.

DEAF TO THE CITY (No. 3) ~ MARIE-CLAIRE BLAIS
Fiction/Novel 6x9 218 pages 978-1-55096-013-6 (tpb) $19.95
City life, where innocence, death, sexuality, and despair fight for survival. It is a book of passion and anguish, characteristic of our times, written in a prose of controlled self-assurance. A true urban classic.

THE GERMAN PRISONER (No. 4) ~ JAMES HANLEY
Fiction/Novella 6x9 55 pages 978-1-55096-075-4 (tpb) $13.95
In the weariness and exhaustion of WWI trench warfare, men are driven to extremes of behaviour.

THERE ARE NO ELDERS (No. 5) ~ AUSTIN CLARKE
Fiction/Stories 6x9 159 pages 978-1-55096-092-1 (tpb) $17.95
Austin Clarke is one of the significant writers of our times. These are compelling stories of life as it is lived among the displaced in big cities, marked by a singular richness of language true to the streets.

100 LOVE SONNETS (No. 6) ~ PABLO NERUDA
Poetry 6x9 225 pages 978-1-55096-108-9 (tpb) $24.95
As Gabriel García Márquez stated: "Pablo Neruda is the greatest poet of the twentieth century – in any language." And, this is the finest translation available, anywhere!

THE SELECTED GWENDOLYN MACEWEN (No. 7)
GWENDOLYN MACEWEN
Poetry/Fiction/Drama/Art/Archival 6x9 352 pages
978-1-55096-111-9 (tpb) $32.95

"This book represents a signal event in Canadian culture." —*Globe and Mail*
The only edition to chronologically follow the astonishing trajectory of MacEwen's career as a poet, storyteller, translator and dramatist, in a substantial selection from each genre.

THE WOLF (No. 8) ~ MARIE-CLAIRE BLAIS
Fiction/Novel 6x9 158 pages 978-1-55096-105-8 (tpb) $19.95
A human wolf moves outside the bounds of love and conventional morality as he stalks willing prey in this spellbinding masterpiece and classic of gay literature.

A SEASON IN THE LIFE OF EMMANUEL (No. 9) ~ MARIE-CLAIRE BLAIS
Fiction/Novel 6x9 175 pages 978-1-55096-118-8 (tpb) $19.95
Widely considered by critics and readers alike to be her masterpiece, this is truly a work of genius comparable to Faulkner, Kafka, or Dostoyevsky. Includes 16 Ink Drawings by Mary Meigs.

IN THIS CITY (No. 10) ~ AUSTIN CLARKE
Fiction/Stories 6x9 221 pages 978-1-55096-106-5 (tpb) $21.95
Clarke has caught the sorrowful and sometimes sweet longing for a home in the heart that torments the dislocated in any city. Eight masterful stories showcase the elegance of Clarke's prose and the innate sympathy of his eye.

THE NEW YORKER STORIES (No. 11) ~ MORLEY CALLAGHAN
Fiction/Stories 6x9 158 pages 978-1-55096-110-2 (tpb) $19.95
Callaghan's great achievement as a young writer is marked by his breaking out with stories such as these in this collection... "If there is a better storyteller in the world, we don't know where he is." —*New York Times*

REFUS GLOBAL (No. 12) ~ THE MONTRÉAL AUTOMATISTS
Manifesto 6x9 142 pages 978-1-55096-107-2 (tpb) $21.95
The single most important social document in Quebec history, and the most important aesthetic statement a group of Canadian artists has ever made. This is basic reading for anyone interested in Canadian history or the arts in Canada.

TROJAN WOMEN (No. 13) ~ GWENDOLYN MACEWEN
Drama 6x9 142 pages 978-1-55096-123-2 (tpb) $19.95
A trio of timeless works featuring the great ancient theatre piece by Euripedes in a new version by MacEwen, and the translations of two long poems by the contemporary Greek poet Yannis Ritsos.

ANNA'S WORLD (No. 14) ~ MARIE-CLAIRE BLAIS
Fiction 5.5x8.5 166 pages ISBN: 978-1-55096-130-0 $19.95
An exploration of contemporary life, and the penetrating energy of youth, as Blais looks at teenagers by creating Anna, an introspective, alienated teenager without hope. Anna has experienced what life today has to offer and rejected its premise. There is really no point in going on. We are all going to die, if we are not already dead, is Anna's philosophy.

THE MANUSCRIPTS OF PAULINE ARCHANGE (No. 15)
MARIE-CLAIRE BLAIS
Fiction 5.5x8.5 324 pages ISBN: 978-1-55096-131-7 $23.95
For the first time, the three novelettes that constitute the complete text are brought together: the story of Pauline and her world, a world in which people turn to violence or sink into quiet despair, a world as damned as that of Baudelaire or Jean Genet.

A DREAM LIKE MINE (No. 16) ~ M.T. KELLY
Fiction 5.5x8.5 174 pages ISBN: 978-1-55096-132-4 $19.95
A Dream Like Mine is a journey into the contemporary issue of radical and violent solutions to stop the destruction of the environment. It is also a journey into the unconscious, and into the nightmare of history, beauty and terror that are the awesome landscape of the Native American spirit world.

THE LOVED AND THE LOST (No. 17) ~ MORLEY CALLAGHAN
Fiction 5.5x8.5 302 pages ISBN: 978-1-55096-151-5 (tpb) $21.95
With the story set in Montreal, young Peggy Sanderson has become socially unacceptable because of her association with black musicians in nightclubs. The black men think she must be involved sexually, the black women fear or loathe her, yet her direct, almost spiritual manner is at variance with her reputation.

NOT FOR EVERY EYE (No. 18) ~ GÉRARD BESSETTE
Fiction 5.5x8.5 126 pages ISBN: 978-1-55096-149-2 (tpb) $17.95
A novel of great tact and sly humour that deals with ennui in Quebec and the intellectual alienation of a disenchanted hero, and one of the absolute classics of modern revolutionary and comic Quebec literature. Chosen by the Grand Jury des Lettres of Montreal as one of the ten best novels of post-war contemporary Quebec.

STRANGE FUGITIVE (No. 19) ~ MORLEY CALLAGHAN
Fiction 5.5x8.5 242 pages ISBN: 978-1-55096-155-3 (tpb) $19.95
Callaghan's first novel – originally published in New York in 1928 – announced the coming of the urban novel in Canada, and we can now see it as a prototype for the "gangster" novel in America. The story is set in Toronto in the era of the speakeasy and underworld vendettas.

IT'S NEVER OVER (No. 20) ~ MORLEY CALLAGHAN
Fiction 5.5x8.5 190 pages ISBN: 978-1-55096-157-7 (tpb) $19.95
1930 was an electrifying time for writing. Callaghan's second novel, completed while he was living in Paris – imbibing and boxing with Joyce and Hemingway (see his memoir, Classics No. 1, *That Summer in Paris*) – has violence at its core; but first and foremost it is a story of love, a love haunted by a hanging. Dostoyevskian in its depiction of the morbid progress of possession moving like a virus, the novel is sustained insight of a very high order.

AFTER EXILE (No. 21) ~ RAYMOND KNISTER
Poetry/Prose 5.5x8.5 240 pages ISBN: 978-1-55096-159-1 (tpb) $19.95
This book collects for the first time Knister's poetry. The title *After Exile* is plucked from Knister's long poem written after he returned from Chicago and decided to become the unthinkable: a modernist Canadian writer. Knister, writing in the 20s and 30s, could barely get his poems published in Canada, but magazines like *This Quarter* (Paris), *Poetry* (Chicago), *Voices* (Boston), and *The Dial* (New York City), eagerly printed what he sent, and always asked for more – and all of it is in this book.

THE COMPLETE STORIES OF MORLEY CALLAGHAN (NO. 21–25)
Fiction 5.5x8.5 (tpb) $19.95
ISBN 978-1-55096-304-5 (v. 1) 328 pages
ISBN 978-1-55096-305-2 (v. 2) 320 pages
ISBN 978-1-55096-306-9 (v. 3) 344 pages
ISBN 978-1-55096-307-6 (v. 4) 334 pages

Attractively produced in four volumes, the complete short fiction of Morley Callaghan appears as he comes into full recognition as one of the singular story-tellers of our time. Introductions by Alistair MacLeod, André Alexis, Anne Michaels and Margaret Atwood.

CONTRASTS: IN THE WARD. A BOOK OF POETRY AND PAINTINGS
Poetry 7x7 168 pages ISBN: 978-1-55096-308-3 (tpb) $24.95

In 1922, while the Group of Seven was emerging as a national phenomenon, Lawren Harris published his only book of poems – *Contrasts* – the first modernist exploration of Canadian urban space in verse. Harris also wandered the streets of Toronto, sketching and creating a powerful set of city paintings. *Lawren Harris ~ Contrasts: In the Ward* brings together for the first time Harris' original book of poems, and sixteen colour images of the artist's early urban paintings in this compact, beautiful-to-hold-and-read, genre-crossing collection. Edited and introduced by Gregory Betts.